Waterlilies Over My Grave

Waterlilies Over My Grave

Patricia A. Guthrie

Fresh Ink Group
Guntersville

Waterlilies Over My Grave

Copyright © 2022
by Patricia A. Guthrie

Fresh Ink Group
An Imprint of:
The Fresh Ink Group, LLC
1021 Blount Avenue #931
Guntersville, AL 35976
Email: info@FreshInkGroup.com
FreshInkGroup.com

Edition 1.0   2008
Edition 2.0   2022

Cover design by Stephen Geez / FIG
Cover art by Anik / FIG
Book design by Amit Dey / FIG
Associate publisher Lauren A. Smith / FIG

Cataloging-in-Publication Recommendations:
FIC030000 / FICTION / Thrillers / Suspense
FIC031080 / FICTION / Thrillers / Psychological
FIC025000 / FICTION / Psychological

Library of Congress Control Number: 2022909771

ISBN-13: 978-1-947893-52-8 Papercover
ISBN-13: 978-1-947893-53-5 Hardcover
ISBN-13: 978-1-947893-54-2 Ebooks

Waterlilies Over My Grave is dedicated to those women living in life-threatening relationships, who must leave the ones they love by disappearing and revamping their lives.

Acknowledgments

Many thanks and appreciations go to:

Fresh Ink Group: Gary "Stephen Geez" (publisher, 2nd edition), Beem Weeks (editor, 2nd edition), and Lauren A. Smith (associate publisher).

My dearest friend, the late Bruce Berg who wouldn't let me give up and kept telling me, "A man wouldn't say that." Bruce was always there for me.

Linda Daly, Micki Peluso, Joannie Lemonte, Margaret Kelly who told me to keep going—no matter what.

Table of Contents

Prologue

etrayal. Sentence—death. A judge and jury of one. "No mother, no! Oh God no!"

The movie *Psycho* muffled the noise coming from the New York City streets that ran in front of Dr. Duncan Byrne's private study. The large cherry hutch that encased the television stood against heavy dark maroon curtains, blocking all illumination from the window. A corner desk lamp and the doctor's laptop screen provided the only light he needed.

A "to-do" list lay by his laptop, scrawled in a handwriting virtually unreadable by anyone but himself. No matter. He'd shred it anyway. No sense condemning himself with the evidence.

She would die.

Her divorce papers lay in a picture-perfect neat stack next to his legal pad. D-I-V-O-R-C-E. Nobody got rid of Duncan Byrne unless he wanted to be gotten rid of, and he wasn't quite through with Annabelle Lee just yet.

He grabbed a bottle half-full of Johnny Walker Red, poured the amber liquid into a crystal whiskey glass. He took a sip and let the liquid swirl around on his palate before letting it slide down his throat.

What method shall I choose next?

He eased into his office chair, his hands behind his head. Thinking. The ideal set-up should have had Annabelle standing precariously close to the edge of the over-crowded Lexington Avenue Subway platform. An express barreling its way through the station. One firm push.

But it hadn't worked. Someone grabbed her as she pitched forward.

No. This new method had to be foolproof. He'd been wrong to think a public accident would kill her. He needed a more fitting and private death.

The face of his beautiful Annabelle Lee perched in a sterling frame on the corner of his desk. The broken glass from when he'd smashed it formed a mound at its base. He stared at the photo. A beautiful woman—a modern day Helen of Troy. A contemporary Jezebel. He eyed his gun cabinet and frowned. To pierce her beautiful voluptuous body would be sacrilege.

He sipped his whiskey and stared into that ethereal face, with those perceptive eyes and the long, silky hair that even Helen of Troy would envy. So innocent when he'd married her, so diabolical when she'd divorced him. So much like—

An image of her falling down the stairs last month drummed up a song in his mind:

She flew through the air with the greatest of ease, The daring young girl on the flying trapeze.

He gulped. The whiskey burned his throat. After coughing for a few seconds, he sipped it slower.

Annabelle had flown through air all right. She'd struggled to keep her balance, bounced off the stairs, swirled like a top and crashed onto the hardwood floor below.

The scream he'd heard sounded more like a child than a woman. It must have come from that she-devil she carried inside her. He shuddered and took another sip.

So much like his mother. Sooner or later they'd all betray him.

Bitches, all.

As far as he could tell, Annabelle had no cognitive recall of the incident. She'd woken in the hospital with Dissociative Amnesia. She couldn't remember the push down the stairs. But, her subconscious knew, and it would surface, sooner or later. The police had ruled the whole unfortunate affair an "accident."

Gulping down the last remnants of his whiskey, he pondered killing methods that would not pierce the skin, yet would provide glorious, exquisite agony. He'd like there to be bubbles. Bubbles and bubbles and bubbles. Just like in his bathtub as a child.

First the paralyzing fear of being held under, then the struggles and frantic splashing of water as the body, hungry for air, starved. Duncan shuddered. There'd been a time when he was paralyzed with fear. When he'd been the one desperately splashing. When his body had been the one starved for air. And there'd been laughing in the background.

This would be no joke.

Something caught in his gut. The visualization was no longer Annabelle Lee. It was his mother.

The phone interrupted daydreams of terror. *Damn.* He'd been enjoying this. "Morning."

The woman on the other end was pleasant, almost bubbly. He hated bubbly.

"Good morning. Is this Dr. Duncan Byrne?"

"Yes, Dr. Byrne speaking, can I help you?"

"Dr. Byrne. This is Dr. Julia Driscoll from the Lake Nager Medical Center in upper Wisconsin. We received an application from one of your students. I believe she recently received her PhD?"

His eyes rolled up. *Another one?* "Yes?"

"She's applied for a position at our medical center here in Lake Nager, Wisconsin."

"Her name?"

"Dr. Annabelle O'Brien."

Well, well, well. He still might have control over her destiny. He hadn't been sure where she was going. Whether or not she'd even stay in New York. Now, apparently, she was planning to move—far. And he'd know exactly where she went.

Dr. Byrne cleared his throat. "I can't recommend Dr. O'Brien highly enough. In fact, she was my best student. Has a great deal of insight and is excellent with patients. Yes, I'd be happy to recommend her."

"Thank you, Dr. Byrne. May we have a letter of . . ."

"Of course. I'll send one out to you on our official stationery, if you'll just give your address to my secretary?"

He transferred the call and sat back to think.

I know where you're going, my darling Annabelle Lee. I'll follow you to the ends of the earth 'til you come back to me'.

Chapter 1

> "It was many and many a year ago,
> In a kingdom by the sea,
> That a maiden there lived whom you may know
> By the name of Annabel Lee . . ."

Dr. Annabelle O'Brien stared at her cell phone. "I think you have the wrong . . ."

"And this maiden she lived with no other thought than to love and be loved by me."

My God. What th . . . ?

The tone set the back of her hair on end. She recognized the voice, yet she didn't. A sing-songy, almost child-like tone had replaced the beautiful baritone that had been Duncan's. A horrid taste of bile rose in her throat, her palms moistened, and the phone slipped from one hand into the other then fell onto her oak veneer desk with a thump. She had a hard time picking it up again.

Annie's throat turned to sandpaper, but she managed to squeak out, "Duncan. What do you want?"

The man on the other end cleared his throat as though he were exercising the greatest of patience to an elementary school student. "Do you remember, my dearest Annabelle, 'Til death do us part'?"

Air lodged in her throat. She forced herself to breathe. In-out, in-out, until her intake came in steady shallow streams, gradually lengthening to deeper breaths. Slow. Relaxing. She was finally able to speak. "How did you get this number?"

The caller laughed. The laugh turned to a whisper. "Doesn't matter how I got your number, love. No matter where you run, where you go, where you hide, you cannot get away from me."

No! He couldn't be threatening her now.

Her usually cool nerves betrayed her as her stomach pitched like it had plunged straight downhill doing sixty miles an hour on a roller coaster.

Annie concentrated on an oil painting, the focal point of burgundy and gray walls. Waterlilies her mother had painted for her when she was a child. It went everywhere with her. Made her feel at home and at peace no matter how hard life got. She wished she could walk into that scene right now. Her eyes shifted to the stack of client folders on her desk and back to reality.

She forced tensing muscles to relax. "Duncan, knock it off." Drumming her fingers against the desktop, fear rapidly turned to resentment. "Look, I'm no longer in New York. I've moved away." Apparently, not far enough.

"I know exactly where you are." His tone held a stony edge.

Annie's jaw stiffened. *He's fishing.* "How?"

"My dear girl. I know that you are sitting in your new office in a hospital in upper Wisconsin."

Annie gasped. He knew where she was. Could see into her office? Her gaze swept out through the large picture window and across the parking lot. Besides a drizzly day, she didn't see anything out of the ordinary. No movement of cars or people. Surreal. As quiet as a black, white, and gray painting.

Until the voice broke the silence. "Then, how could I know that you're wearing that gray suit with the mini-skirt that shows off your lovely legs? How do I know that your hair is tied up in a knot that reveals a neck as delicate as a swan?"

A moment's frozen silence settled upon the room, until what he'd said registered. Then her elbow knocked into a plastic vase of tiger lilies. The water spilled over the edge of the desk, flooding the carpet.

Chuckle. "Don't you think you ought to wipe that up before it gets all over your client's charts?"

Her muscles tightened and, in spite of herself, her voice shook. "How did you know that?"

"Lucky guess."

"You heard the noise through the phone." Time for some bravado. "Look, I'm not afraid of you."

Again, that chuckle. She couldn't put a finger on the sound he was making. Some hybrid of humor?

"Oh, but you should be afraid my dear. Very afraid. You'll never be rid of me. And you'll never know where I am, or when I'll turn up. I could be behind the next corner, in the shadows, in a dark alley."

"Duncan . . ."

"Or on the banks of Lake Nager." Another clearing of the throat. "Oh, and one more thing. If you try another restraining order, there's no law enforcement that will honor one against me. Just try."

Now, Annie was getting just plain mad. "What do you mean the law won't arrest you for violating a court order? Who do you think you are, God?"

Click. Silence.

She stared down, her brain slow to comprehend the significance of that conversation. A long-exhaled breath came in one long quick whoosh.

Maybe he did think he was God. But that didn't escape the fact she was shaking from the top of her head to the bottom of her soles. And it wasn't like Duncan to try and scare her like that. He'd given her the divorce graciously. He'd offered her anything she'd wanted. Everyone had thought she was nuts to give him up. But maybe he was finally starting to exhibit certain signs she'd seen coming for years—and yet had never quite believed.

Duncan was slowly going insane.

She couldn't put a diagnosis on it yet, but he needed help, and she didn't think he'd get it.

She looked at the mess on the floor. Oh bother. Look what the idiot made me do. Giving herself something else to think about, she picked up the vase, grabbed a handful of tissues and dried the water that still dripped from her desk onto the gray carpet.

Then, in a sort of fog, she closed the vertical blinds and shut out the outside world.

Insanity—such a broad term. And she was supposed to understand it, help treat it. Yet here she was, a psychologist, and didn't feel she knew the first thing about it. She wondered if anyone did.

Annie was alone in a strange town where she knew nobody, and some psycho . . . no, not some psycho—her psycho ex-husband had just threatened her. But threatened her with what? Word games? What did he want? Could he really be here in Lake Nager? Not possible. He was in New York City attending a psychiatry convention.

She dwelt, only briefly, that he'd described what she wore.

Accurately.

She forced her muscles to loosen, to relax. First day on the job. Trying to make a good impression. The phone call from hell. What else could go wrong?

Chapter 2

"Excuse me? Are you Dr. O'Brien?"

Annie looked up from her client list. Two men stood at the open threshold of her office.

Her first client—coming on the heels of this. *Regroup, Annie.*

All she had to do was reach the bathroom and dab cold water on her face before they figured out anything was wrong with the one person who was supposed to make things right.

Taking a deep breath, Annie mustered a half smile and rose. "Hi, excuse me for a minute." She hurried into the small bathroom in her office, closed the door, steamed a washcloth, then held it to her face, forcing herself to recover. She looked at herself in the full-length mirror, straightened her suit, pushed back a stray strand of hair, decided she looked as good as she was going to get and walked back in.

Annie forced herself into a "business as usual" attitude and started in their direction. She forced the biggest smile she had as she glanced from one to the other. "Hello. I'm—"

"*That's* the shrink?" The man attached to the voice had his arms folded and his legs crossed. He rested with his back against the open door.

His tone stopped Annie in her tracks. Well, well, well. Hostility alert. The day was getting better and better.

"I'm Dr. O'Brien," she said, her gaze glued to his. "And I'm a psychologist, if that's what you're asking."

The man turned to his colleague. "You want me to see a woman about *this?*"

Oh Lord. Isn't that wonderful. First, I get a call from my ex-husband who's a psychopath, and now I get a client who has issues with women.

The other man bumped past Mr. Hostility and shook her hand. "Dr. O'Brien, I'm Paul Reinert."

"Chief of Police." Annie smiled, trying to combat a shaky first impression. "We've spoken on the phone. It's nice to meet you."

Chief Reinert glared toward the doorway and then back to Annie. He cleared his throat. "Nice to finally meet you too, Dr. O'Brien." He turned toward the other man. "That example of friendliness and charm is Detective Mark Driscoll."

Yes. She'd remembered the conversation. The detective who'd killed a man in the line of duty.

Mark Driscoll said nothing. He didn't have to. His eyes filled with vulnerability and highlighted by deep circles said it for him. He probably hadn't slept in days. But he still dared her to hold his gaze. This technique might have worked, except her focus was already on his jeans and T-shirt that looked like they'd been slept in for days. She thought she'd like to throw him into a hot shower, clothing and all.

"Mark, Dr. O'Brien's the new psychologist from New York." He placed his emphasis on New York, like the city stood as the epitome of the intellectual elite. Chief Reinert's enthusiasm seemed to deepen the growing resentment spreading over her would-be client's face, and Mark Driscoll glared at the older man, opening his mouth as though to say something.

The chief cut him off. "Dr. O'Brien, Detective Driscoll is one of the best detectives I've ever worked with. But right now, he has a few issues."

Mark looked down and shook his head, before bringing it up to meet her gaze, until she felt *she* was the one about to be analyzed. "There's no issue I have, that I can't handle myself, Dr. O'Brien. Sorry to have wasted your time."

Annie stood and stared at him for a few moments, until she was certain he had to be uncomfortable. "Detective Driscoll." She softened her tone. "The criminal world is a dark and dangerous place. You police have a hell of a job ridding the community of the people who make walking the streets a living nightmare for the rest of us. My job is to help clear your mind when the streets become too hard to handle."

He didn't blink. "My mind doesn't need clearing up. I'm just fine." He spoke between clenched teeth. His expression read, "and I don't need you".

His chief stared at his shoes. His face was turning red and puffed out, like looking like he might blow a gasket.

Okay. So, maybe a sociable approach might work better. "Mark, why don't you call me Annie?" She went around her desk and sat, then motioned him toward a chair on the other side. He didn't move.

"Detective Driscoll will do just fine, Dr. O'Brien."

Chief Reinert stiffened even more if that were possible.

"Mark. Doctor O'Brien is good at what she does."

Driscoll's face darkened. "Perhaps. And, again I apologize, Dr. O'Brien. You probably do know what you're doing. But you don't know me. And I don't want to know you. If I come off rude, I'm sorry."

Annie felt the blood rush to her face in anger and embarrassment.

What had she ever done to *him*?

The chief approached her desk and leaned over. "Did you read his file?"

Annie nodded and tapped the desk, where several folders were stacked.

"Okay then, I think I'll leave you two alone." He turned to go. "I'll be outside, I need a cigarette."

Mark took a step inside the room. "Wait a minute. You've got my *file?*" His eyes flashed with indignation. "You have no right."

He swung around and glared at his chief.

The older man took off his hat, ran his fingers through steel-gray hair and put it back on his head. "Mark. This is non-negotiable."

Annie looked at the two. They could have almost been father and son. Mark was taller. Late twenties, maybe early thirties. Lean, with well-muscled arms, tight stomach muscles hidden under that wretched too-tight T-shirt. A body that was kept fit.

Annie estimated Paul to be in his fifties. A man who probably sat behind a desk doing administrative work, enjoying his coffee and donuts.

Mark stopped and turned back. "Look Paul, this is ridiculous." The chief nodded. "Yeah, maybe. But I'll still put you on two-week suspension until the review board sorts out all the details."

Mark grew larger than life and huffed. "You *are* the review board. Besides, it was your ass I was saving."

Paul Reinert nodded to Annie and stepped past Mark, forcing him to move back. "I know you did," he said. "Dr. O'Brien, I'll just be sitting in the lobby giving myself a nice case of lung cancer, if you need me." He nodded toward Mark. "Be nice. It's either her or a two-week furlough." He turned and disappeared from the room.

Annie had a tough time deciding whether to explain just how bad lung cancer was or break out laughing. Instead, she focused on Mark. Judging by Mark's expression, Annie thought the worst thing Paul could do was to take him off duty. But it also might be the thing he needed most.

Annie emptied any animosity she had for anyone and put on her professional smile. "Come on Mark. Why don't you sit down and talk to me?" When he didn't oblige, she practiced the golden rule. She did unto him as he'd done unto her. It was eye-to-eye combat.

Mark didn't sit, but he didn't leave. He put both hands on the cushiony back of the chair and leaned toward her. "Look Doc," he said. "Have you ever killed a man?"

Annie thought of the numerous times she'd have liked to strangle the daylights out of someone. Like him. But she shook her head. "No."

"So how can you possibly know what I've been going through?"

How indeed? "I can listen. I'm pretty good at that. Maybe help you sort things out?" Trying to keep her cool, she folded her hands on top of the desk, looked him in the eye and waited.

Silence filled the room. The man shifted his weight, balled up his fists and glared.

Annie stared back.

The intensity in Mark's face, the strength around his jaw, dark insolent eyes only added to the stark determination in his face. She thought he was trying a little too hard to look mean.

Mark sighed, dropped his hands and shook his head. Then, he moved around the chair and sat. "Ma'am. Two weeks ago, I killed a seventeen-year-old kid. He went down in a pool of blood. I held him as terror spread across his face when he knew it was over. I felt the last beat of his heart and saw the whites of his eyes filling with blood. What can you possibly tell me that will make that okay?"

Annie couldn't help the intake of air that escaped as he said "seventeen-year-old kid." She remembered the case file. A drug pusher, a young murderer. It was his life or Paul's. What could Mark have done differently?

The rush of adrenaline forced her heart to beat faster. *The push down the stairs. The pain. The blood. Another young life—gone.* She shook herself away from the past.

His mouth turned down and he shook his head. "I didn't think so." He pushed himself into a standing position. "There's nobody that can help me with what I'm going through. Sorry I wasted your . . ."

"Wait." She motioned for him to sit again. "Please."

Mark gave her an impatient shrug. "So, here's where you say it will all get better? Time heals all wounds."

Annie's thoughts raced to find the right words. She shook her head, looking at the desk rather than him. "No. I wasn't going to say that. It isn't going to get better. Not really." No, she thought. It would never get all better.

He leaned forward. "Oh, that makes me feel good. Thank you for pointing that out."

Annie raised her hands in desperation. "Please. I meant, you'll hurt from the memory. But look, you'll also remember you saved a man's life. And, detective, this is your job. A job you must hold in high esteem, otherwise, you'd never be able to do it."

"Well, thanks for telling me my job, Dr. O'Brien. This is going nowhere. So, let's make this short and sweet, shall we? I killed a kid. You think I hated destroying his life?"

As Mark placed both hands on the desktop and rose to a half-standing position, Annie rolled back her chair.

Mark leaned in further. "I loved shooting him. I hated seeing him die. But I relished seeing the bullet pierce through *a seventeen-year- old boy,* Dr. O'Brien. Now, you know what kind of person I am."

He turned and left, ignoring her plea to return.

Annie gulped several breaths before she came down to normal. Well, that went well, she thought. *Now, who else can I help?*

Chapter 3

Restraining order my ass.

Duncan, now calling himself Edgar Allenton, turned up his air-conditioning and re-focused his binoculars. She'd closed her blinds, but not before knocking over that vase. He'd scared her. Served her right. She'd worn that suit with the mini skirt *he'd* bought. How *dare* she wear *anything* he'd bought her?

All he'd done for her. Him—the elite of the psychiatric community. He'd made her. He could break her. She'd never be rid of him. Never. The ridiculous little giggle he'd been repressing came out again.

He peered into his rear-view mirror. He'd done an excellent job with his disguise if he did say so himself. Thanks to contact lenses, his gray-blue eyes were brown. The shaggy steel-gray professor hair that had turned on so many of his young female graduate students was gone; now cut short and dyed blonde, making him look ten years younger than his forty-plus. Hell, he'd lost weight and was physically fit. An athlete, he decided. A salesman on a quest for a good time mingling business with pleasure alongside the Fourth of July vacationers at Lake Nager, home of the best fireworks in the state of Wisconsin.

A prickly sensation crept down his neck. The sweet smell of water lilies filled the air. Even though no flowers lay in his SUV and he was miles from the lily pond at the far edge of Lake Nager. His imagination? Or sensory premonition.

Duncan shook off a shudder and scanned the employee's parking lot. Many cars. No people. Middle of the afternoon shift, he guessed. He picked up the stolen cell phone he'd used to call Annabelle, opened the door and slid out.

Suddenly, something made him turn around. *What the . . .* He could have sworn eyes were on *him.* He walked toward the pine trees at the far side of the lot, trying not to be seen. But no matter what he did, he couldn't get rid of the feeling. Somebody was watching him.

He shivered. Could his illness be turning into paranoid schizophrenia? Granted, he was smelling flowers that weren't there, but he *knew* he didn't hear voices. No, he *wasn't* schizophrenic. Maybe a bit psychotic. Erotomanic would have been his own diagnosis of himself. But paranoid. Never.

Under the pines, the ground was soggy from all the rain. Digging a hole in the ground and burying the phone wasn't hard. The owner might try tracing it, but unless it had a tracking device installed, they'd never find it.

A rumble of thunder came from the west. The dayshift would let out soon.

The perpetual hollowness deep in the pit of his stomach attacked him again. He got back into his vehicle and popped an antacid pill. The damned woman had given him an ulcer.

He checked his mirror to find holes in his disguise. None.

Checked to see if anyone sat in nearby vehicles. No one. Checked to see . . . ridiculous. He'd never put flowers in his SUV.

Duncan pressed the tape of city sounds in his CD player. He picked up his own cell phone and called the Hyatt in New York City.

"Good afternoon. This is the Hyatt."

"Dr. Duncan Byrne. Haven't had a chance to check my messages. Anything for me?"

"One moment, sir."

The sounds of horns blasted from his CD player.

"No sir. No messages. I hope you're enjoying the convention, sir?"

"Yes. Doing my best to get lost in the crowds for a change. I'll be sight-seeing this afternoon. Funny how few people who live here actually appreciate the greatness the city has to offer."

"Yes, sir." The man sounded bored.

"I'll be putting a 'do not disturb' sign on my door when I get in. Please make sure I'm not disturbed."

"Nobody will disturb you, sir."

"Thank you."

He clicked off the call and redialed. "Hello?"

Duncan turned into Mr. Congeniality. "Kurt, enjoying the convention?"

"Yes sir. I taped the workshops like you asked. Haven't recognized anyone yet. Everything is going well."

"I'm glad you're having an enjoyable time. And remember: You must maintain the utmost secrecy. If anyone found out about your… past, they wouldn't let you back into the university. You understand that don't you?"

Silence.

The boy had been caught hacking term papers from some of the grad student's. Lucky, Duncan had been the one to catch him. But, not only that, Duncan also thought with glee, he'd found out more. Kurt Adder had been a virtual drug addict in his undergrad days. He'd helped the kid through a private detox program. *Never let it be said, I didn't do anything for the human race.*

Duncan acknowledged he'd used the kid as a virtual slave ever since. *After all, we all have to pay for our sins.*

"Yes sir. I appreciate what you're doing for me."

"Good. Any more workshops today?"

"No sir."

"Take the rest of the day and go to see the sights. Empire State Building, Statue of Liberty. Use my credit card. Have dinner somewhere expensive."

"Yes, sir."

"When you get back to the Hyatt, put on the 'do not disturb sign'. Any messages, I'll pick up later. Night."

Click.

Hope he throws himself off the Empire State Building.

No, he supposed that would never do. He had to keep up this front until he and his Annabelle were together for eternity.

Before that though, tonight he'd give her the scare of her life.

Chapter 4

Annie followed the afternoon shift through the double doors and into the back parking lot. Thunder clouds laced with horizontal streaks of lightning rolled overhead. Humid, claustrophobic air pressure and heavy scents of forest and lake pressed down on her like weights. Drizzle fell in beautiful Northern Nowhere, where it seemed to rain at five sharp every day. The sky looked ready to let loose again.

Well, she hoped it would provide relief. She rubbed the sweat from the back of her neck and imagined soaking off this rotten day in a scented lily-of-the-valley bubble bath. Two shadows had already formed on her newly found happiness. The chauvinist detective and that ridiculous and frightening phone call.

"Dr. O'Brien."

Annie jumped out of her thoughts as Chief Paul Reinert fell in step. He looked at the sky. "Another blasted thunderstorm coming through. I hope this damnable weather doesn't screw up the Fourth of July celebrations. You parked close?"

Annie pointed toward a green Impala on the other side of the lot. "Good. I'll walk you to your car. I'd hoped to catch you before you left."

Annie smiled. "Chief Reinert—"

"Paul."

"And I'm Annie. I'm surprised to see you're still here."

"Kid and his motorcycle had a falling out on the service road leading down to the lake."

"Service road?"

"Couple of miles out of town where the highway cuts through the forest. A dirt road runs downhill until it stops at the lily pond. Ought to go boating one day and stop there. Word of warning, you don't want to attempt driving that road unless you have a four- wheeler." Paul spoke with a quiet emphasis. A gentle but authoritative tone. She liked him. It was really nice to have a Chief of Police in her corner.

"I'll keep that in mind."

He shifted his gaze toward her for a brief second before looking away. "So, how was your first day?"

Annie's smile deteriorated into a frown. She didn't want to relive her afternoon disaster. "Well . . ."

Paul smiled. "Okay, so your first client didn't go so well," he said, taking her arm and sidestepping away from parking lot traffic.

"I'd say hostility ran rampant," she said. "In fact, I'd say your detective hated my guts."

"Probably not that extreme, but I'd say he's not too thrilled with either one of us at the moment."

Thunder blended with a cough directly behind her. Mark Driscoll passed by and glared. Frost suddenly seemed to replace the hot, oppressive atmosphere.

"Speaking of the devil," she whispered. Determined not to let him see he'd gotten to her, she flashed him a smile.

He wavered for a second. "If it isn't the two co-conspirators. Planning something else that will screw up my life?" He shrugged dismissively before Annie had a chance to respond, then he disappeared around the corner of the brick building taking the icicles with him.

"So, what is he still doing here?" she asked.

"He probably went to talk to his mother. She's a doctor here. Have you met her yet?"

"No," she said, blinking off droplets of water. "Should I have?"

"Maybe not. But Dr. Driscoll was on the panel who hired you.

One of the best docs around." "What's her specialty?"

"Internal medicine and OB/GYN. But our docs wear many hats."

Dr. Driscoll. Annie's stomach lurched hearing her name. *Oh bother. On the panel who hired her. Son she'd managed to get suspended. Good going Annie.* "I'll probably get fired my first day."

Paul looked at her. "Why? Because Julia's son acted like a jerk? She doesn't work that way. Besides, she knows what he's been going through. She'll probably give you an award for bravery and invite you to dinner."

Small town environment. Everybody probably knew everybody else.

"You came highly recommended by the head of your department. I hear Dr. Byrne's one of the top psychiatrists in the country. Julia would have done anything to get you after the glowing report he gave."

Annie was so surprised, she stopped. "Duncan Byrne recommended me?"

"Yep. Said you'd make an outstanding psychologist. That you had all the right instincts and that you worked well with people. Just by looking at how you handled Mark today, I'd say he was right."

"Thank you for the vote of confidence." Annie laughed, although an inner nag kept asking why Duncan, after she'd divorced him, would give her a glowing commendation. Didn't figure. How had he known about the job offer? She hadn't listed him in her references.

A sudden painful ache hit her abdomen. When the attacks came, they hurt like hell. The only solution? Pain killers. Well, they didn't hit her frequently enough to warrant mind-altering drugs.

She stumbled into a pothole filled with water and nearly went down.

Paul caught her arm, helped her regain her balance then his eyes searched her face. "You okay?"

Hmm. The man was perceptive. Annie swallowed the fear that prompted the attack. She smiled.

They started walking again. "Annie. Be careful about those potholes. I keep telling the medical center to fix them, but the administration insists they're the town's responsibility. The town says they're the medical center's. I might come and fill in the damned things myself. Or better yet, have Mark do it since he has time off."

Annie laughed.

"I just want you to know, you were right to recommend Mark take a vacation."

"Thank you."

Paul stopped and faced her. "Look, we have a small police force here. We all work together, despite our official positions. Mark worked two, sometimes three, shifts to help get a couple of drug dealers who decided they wanted to turn our tourists into customers.

One night Mark and another officer cornered them and called for backup. One nearly put a hole in me, but Mark got him first. He saved my life. Now, it's my turn to save his."

Annie considered that. Then she asked, "But, why does he hate women so much?"

"What?" Paul looked puzzled. "Oh, that. No, not women. He hates psychiatrists and psychologists of all kinds."

Her voice rose in surprise. "Why?"

Paul gazed somewhere into space. "Dr. O'Brien—Annie. Look, it's important for you to know this. Mark's father was a cop. He had a few problems. He talked to the resident psychologist who was here at the time. Something happened in that session—even I don't know what it was. But he went out on a call shortly after and was killed. Mark blamed the psychologist. He can tell you more if you can get him to open up. Usually, he walks away."

Annie nodded. "I'm sorry," was all she could say.

The afternoon shift was leaving as the evening shift replaced them. The rain fell in a steady stream.

"Were all those drug dealers caught?" Annie asked in afterthought. "Because if not, and you have any serious trouble . . . well, in the condition he's in, his life could be in danger."

Paul grunted in agreement. "I think so. At least the ones who were there. But you never know who else . . ."

His cell phone went off. "What? Okay, where?" He sighed and shrugged. "Duty calls. Listen if you're not busy later, why you don't stop at 'The Hole'? It's a local hang-out across from the police station. I'll introduce you to some people."

Annie nodded. "Sounds like a plan. I could use the diversion." "Then, see you later." And he was gone.

Annie walked between two cars when a SUV lurched toward her. She scrambled out of its path and fell up against a van, mud and water splattering everywhere.

"What the . . . ?" *Stupid driver.* She looked for the license number as the vehicle drove out of the lot, but it was too splattered with mud to be recognizable.

Annie brushed herself off and managed to smear the mud deeper into her raincoat.

"Great, just great," she mumbled. "The idiot."

Annie pressed the button on her remote and the car door clicked open. She slid into the front seat. From somewhere in the bowels of her purse, her cell phone rang. "Oh bother." Digging deep inside, she threw out two pens, her wallet and her makeup purse, before almost cutting her finger on nail clippers.

Damn. "Hello?"

"Annabelle Lee . . ." That voice again. Its tone echoed the rumble of thunder. Lightning flashed above.

Annie went stone cold. "I beg your pardon?"

"Neither the angels in heaven above, Nor the demons down under the sea, can ever dissever my soul from the soul of the beautiful Annabelle Lee."

The hair on the back of Annie's neck stood on end. "Duncan, I'm warning you."

"Duncan? Is that my name? I thought it was *Nemesis*." The laughter was cold. "I am glad I didn't run over that beautiful body, Annabelle Lee."

Nemesis? *"Nemesis?"* She repeated aloud. Annie forced herself into a deep breathing mode and kept her voice steady and cool. "Leave me alone," she said. "I mean it."

"Leave you alone? No, I don't think so. You see, you're mine. Either dead or alive. I don't care which." The caller clicked off.

A bolt of lightning shot out somewhere from the north. Across the lake. A crack of thunder followed.

The phone rang again. This time she turned it off and pulled out of the parking lot.

Chapter 5

A sign flashed 'The Watering Hole' over the bottles of liquor reflected in a floor-to-ceiling smoked mirror. Customers pressed in, crunching on peanut shells strewn over wood plank floors. They reached over each other, grabbed chilled beer steins and mixed drinks, and plopped money onto the polished oak bar. Most of the patrons were locals spending a few hours to wind down at their favorite watering "hole" before they went home. Some were vacationers who'd stumbled into the place. The owners didn't spend much effort in recruiting the tourists. They didn't have to. Everyone found their way to 'The Hole' eventually.

Paul planted himself at Mark's booth and signaled the waiter for two more bottles of Bud, before Mark could tell him to go away. Then he sat back with an *I-know-you're-pissed-at-me* look.

Mark grudgingly acknowledged his presence. He didn't want to talk to his boss—his *friend* just now. He drank up the last dredges of his beer and put down the bottle.

"I see you cleaned up," Paul said.

"I did." Mark conceded. "So what?"

"And you're taking my advice."

Mark grimaced. "Do I have a choice?"

"No." Paul grinned. "What you need is some R and R. A good drink, some fishing, maybe take that dog of yours along. Go out. Date. When was the last time you had a girlfriend?"

"A relationship is the last thing I need." He looked around the crowded bar for familiar faces. He'd gone out with almost all the women in the place at one time or another and half of them weren't speaking to him.

But the anger smoldering inside since he'd gunned down that kid blocked that out. He couldn't sleep. Couldn't eat. Strangely enough, he'd always known it might happen. He'd just never figured on his own reaction when it did.

He could, however, drink. The waiter brought two chilled beer bottles and a basket of peanuts. Paul paid and saluted when the day dispatcher walked by. She waved and kept walking.

"Even she won't stop and say hello," Mark said, his gaze following her until she was out of sight.

"Didn't you date her?" Paul asked. "It seems to me that women don't talk to you not because of what you do at work, it's what you do to them after work."

"I don't date women from work."

"You've been working far too hard—double, triple shifts. When was the last time you had a decent night's sleep?"

"I can't remember." Mark put down the bottle, sat back and ran his fingers through his hair. "Not for a while. I'm not cut out for killing people."

Paul slammed the bottle on the table.

Froth spilled down the sides and caught Mark on the cheek.

Mark wiped it off with his sleeve. "Shit," he said.

Several people at nearby tables stared before going back to what they were doing. Paul leaned forward and lowered his voice. "Damn it. Look, if you hadn't done what you did, I'd be in the cemetery right now. Doesn't that count for anything?"

"Of course, but . . ."

"I don't need a physical and mental wreck on my team, Mark. Why didn't you let Dr . . . ?"

"Look. I don't need this doctor—what's her name—examining my 'feelings' to tell me I feel like shit." Mark glared into the older man's eyes. The blue had turned gray in the dim light.

Paul stopped in the middle of a sip and put down the bottle. "Dr. Annabelle O'Brien."

"Huh?"

"Couldn't you at least hear her out?"

"I could have." He shook his head and continued, his irritation rising. "But damn it, I don't want this blonde bimbo telling you I need to be off the streets."

"You do need to be off the streets, and Annie's not a bimbo." Mark leaned forward. "Oh, it's Annie now?"

Paul ignored him. "And you didn't give her a chance to tell you anything. Look. Those creeps are in jail, because of you."

"For a while." Mark conceded.

"So, stop putting yourself down. Let it go. Remember we *talked* about this, Mark. Remember? Way back when you made detective. The pressure in doing the duties that aren't pleasant?"

Mark retained a sullen silence. His eyes cut down to his beer.

Paul was right, of course. But he still wasn't handling it well.

Paul's mouth turned upward into a grin. "If it's of any consolation, you've been labeled a hero by the mayor."

Fleeting fame. Shit. Mark gulped his beer and ran his hand across his mouth, beer residue spreading across his knuckles. "Hero, huh?"

"Yep."

Mark shrugged. "I don't want to be a …"

But his sentence trailed off when a shadow covered their table, and a faint scent of lily-of-the-valley joined the aroma of beer.

Dr. Annabelle O'Brien. Gone was the tight knot at the back of her head. Her hair hung loose and flowed halfway down her back. Instead of the skirt that slid up her thigh when she sat, she wore black slacks and a white cotton blouse unbuttoned so he could just make out a silver cross and the shadow of her cleavage. For a second, he grudgingly admitted to himself that she was pretty. Very pretty. Then he hardened himself to the charms of an unwanted shrink.

"Chief Reinert," she said. She ignored Mark and focused her attention on his boss. Nodding toward Mark, she said, "Sorry, didn't realize you had company." She turned to walk away.

Paul half stood and scooted across the bench to make room. "Annie, stay and have a drink with us. I promise Detective Driscoll will behave himself."

How could Paul be so sure about that? Maybe he didn't want to behave himself. Maybe he wanted to get drunk.

Annie, who'd been standing by his side, took the two extra steps away from him and headed for the seat next to Paul. She slipped on scattered peanut shells and almost went down. Mark bolted up to steady her before Paul could react. The flush on her face was worth the effort. She pulled away from Mark's grasp and sat next to Paul.

Well, shit. So, she didn't like him. The feeling was mutual. "Dr. O'Brien," Mark said. He took a swig of beer. "Better watch those peanuts. They could be lethal. Wouldn't want to go into work in a cast, would you?"

With a slight upward curve of a smile, her attention focused on Mark's face, making him exceedingly uncomfortable. "My name's Annie."

"Whatever," he said, waiting for something—anything.

But Annie's gaze suddenly jerked toward the bar, like she'd seen someone? Her face drained of color. What the . . .?

Mark studied her. She was thin and pale. Ethereal with just a hint of flush on her cheeks. Then there was the color and texture of her hair.

He seldom noticed things like that. He was more of a breast and leg man. But she was different. Her hair was like silk. And what the hell was that color? He thought of landscapes. What was that scene? Of course, the wheat fields at the edge of the forest. Annie flicked back a strand of hair that dangled in front of her eye when she'd jerked her head around. It stuck to her hand.

Kind of floating into the air with some kind of a kinetic energy. Annie turned back. Color had returned to her cheeks, and she'd put on a smile. Put on was the word. The smile was brittle. She was putting on a good front. Why? This woman was troubled. And he'd be damned if he knew why it bothered him.

Chapter 6

The entrance/exit sign glowed like a beacon to a stranded wanderer. Annie hadn't even been there for fifteen minutes, and already she wanted to run away. And there it was. Her eternal wish to run away from any personal confrontations. Her wish to be left in peace. But she wasn't finding that here. She wasn't finding that anywhere.

She glanced around. A human throng packed the bar. Not an empty seat in the place and everyone seemed to be enjoying the company of others. Why did she think her ex-husband was here? He wasn't. Period.

She racked her brains about that phone call. It sounded like Duncan's voice. But he was in New York, wasn't he? If it weren't him, who else could it be? Someone who knew her ex-husband was obsessed with Edgar Allan Poe? Someone who knew he called her Annabelle Lee. Someone, maybe, who hated *him?*

A cold sweat swept over her. She thought she knew how to manage Duncan, but the fear of an unknown persecutor . . .

And speaking of persecution . . .

Mark Driscoll. The hostile idiot who sat across the table, wearing jeans too tight for his own good, a blue T-shirt and a leather jacket in eighty-degree humid weather. Granted, it was a little chilly in here— but why did he feel the need to wear a leather jacket in July?

Annie summed Mark up in about two seconds. Mid to late twenties, yes, but aged due to the stress of his job and maybe relationships that hadn't worked. Or he didn't want to work. He wasn't married. That much she'd gotten from his file. Maybe he was a man who shied away from commitments and was handsome and wild enough to have every woman in town after him. He'd probably had more affairs than she'd had psychology courses.

He was popping peanuts and washing them down with beer when he wasn't staring at her. She shuddered and wondered if it was because she despised him, he hated her, or because she was finding him sexy. Those dark eyes penetrated.

She was about to make some inane comment when her skin prickled on the back of her neck. She jerked her head back toward the bar. This time the movement pinched a nerved, and she cried out. Realizing she was making a spectacle of herself; she shut her mouth and embraced the pain until it dulled and finally went away.

"What's the matter?" Paul turned and looked, then rested his gaze back on her. "Annie, what's wrong? You're tense as hell."

"No kidding," said the grump across the table.

The patrons were engrossed in conversation. Nobody was watching her. But someone's presence seemed to hover . . . suffocating her.

This time Mark scrutinized the people at the bar. "See someone you know?"

She fought off the butterflies that were now floating around in her stomach. She lowered her eyes and shook her head.

"I thought so, but no. I'm new here. I wouldn't know anybody." She smiled. A college-age waiter with "Brighton University" on his T-shirt appeared with a pad.

"Hi, gorgeous," he said, grinning from ear to ear. "Can I get you something? Coffee, tea—me?" he added hopefully.

What a dumb pick-up line.

He was about to speak again when Mark cut him off.

"Yes, she is gorgeous," he said. "But she's here with us." He pushed his jacket back to flash his badge and his *gun*.

The kid backed up a step, holding his hands in the air. "Sorry," he said.

Mark didn't take his eyes off the waiter. "What do you want, Annie?"

Annie's eyes grew wide in surprise. Chivalry was the last thing she expected from him.

She glanced at their bottles. "What they're having will be fine. Just put mine in a frosty mug."

The waiter backed up a step. "Okay." And he was gone—poof . . . disappeared.

Mark rubbed his hands together, looking pleased with himself. "That's one way of getting rid of someone."

Annie wasn't sure whether to be annoyed at Mark's presumptive attitude or flattered that a young college student had been flirting with her. The waiter blended into the crowd as Annie studied the people, the atmosphere, the gossip, the friendship and desperation. Every human emotion. Voices overly animated. Women trying too hard to impress. Men trying too hard to score.

So, this was the proverbial "Meet Market." Or was it "Meat Market?" She assumed a little of both. This sports bar that seemed to double as a pick-up joint had thirty-two-inch TV's enhanced with subtitles mounted in each corner. The Milwaukee Brewers were playing on each TV . . . and losing. Many were engrossed in the game, cheering and booing when the occasion called for their input.

"Dr. O'Brien?"

Annie barely heard her name.

"Yo . . . Annie?" Mark put a hand on hers and gave it a gentle shake.

She focused back on her two companions, but still only half of her seemed to respond.

"Yes?"

Mark's attention suddenly shifted. "Bloody hell."

A woman with long dark, curly hair tied back in a ponytail and wearing a peach, lace-trimmed tank top and white capri's, flashed him a smile. Painted toenails of "notice me" shocking pink peeked out from under hi-heel sandals. "Hi, Mark." She didn't stop but pushed a note next to his beer and kept on going.

Mark's hand shot off Annie's, and he stared, like every man in the vicinity, until the woman drowned into the pool of humanity.

"Someone you know?" Annie asked.

"Yeah," Mark said, picking up the note and not reading it. He stuffed it into his jacket pocket. "You could say that."

Paul's eyes narrowed. "Laura Campbell." Then he smiled at Annie. "Nager's a small community. It's hard not to make your share of friends and enemies."

"And she's one of the enemies?" Annie asked. "Sort of," Mark mumbled. He stared into his beer.

A group of baseball enthusiasts cheered a home run by the Brewers.

Mark leaned forward. "So, Annie, what made you want to give up the bustling life of Manhattan and throw yourself into Lake Nager?"

She'd been practicing her "why-she-came-here speech," but the way he'd phrased it made her laugh.

"I lived in the city, but I'm really from a small village on Long Island. I wanted to get back into a small-town environment." She lied.

"And you decided to move all the way out to Wisconsin to seek the country?" Mark asked. "They don't have country in New York somewhere?"

Annie found herself defensive. "I just needed a change." She willed him to leave it alone.

Paul changed the subject. "And you're not married."

Another waiter, a girl this time, brought her a frosty mug and a beer and placed it in front of her. "Everyone all right for now?"

They nodded. Paul paid then persisted. "So, Annie?"

"No. I'm not married." She sucked in the air as she contemplated the next phrase. "I'm divorced." She sipped the froth off the beer.

Mark sat back and folded his arms. "Oh?"

A lump caught in Annie's throat. Why was he so sarcastic? "Detective Driscoll," she said. "Marriages don't always have a 'happily, ever after'."

His lips twisted into a cynical grin. "I know. That's why I'm not, nor have any intention of getting married."

So, why was he making that declaration to her? "Why?" she asked. "Just because people don't always find the right person the first time around, doesn't mean it can't happen."

"In our profession, Dr. O'Brien."

"Oh bother," Annie said, irritated and unable to hide it anymore. "Huh?"

"We're having a beer together in a bloody bar. Can't you get informal just for tonight? My name is Annie."

She watched Mark study her, then clear his throat. "Yeah right. Annie. Look, we put ourselves in danger every day. That puts our families in danger." He looked over at Paul, and Paul's expression went vacant.

"Did you lose someone because of your job?" Annie asked Paul. Paul nodded, slowly. "Yeah," he said, in a toneless voice. "I put this guy on death row when I worked in Chicago years back. Someone got even. Killed my wife while she was standing on the front stoop of our house. I left. Couldn't stay there anymore. Came back here." When he looked up, his eyes glistened.

Oh Lord. Annie glanced back and forth between the two men. She'd never realized what the police went through. "I'm so sorry," she said. "Did you . . . I mean, do you have children?"

He shook his head. "No. We'd decided to wait. I wish... well..."

"But yet you remained a detective." She said it more to herself than to them.

Mark said to Annie, "See, Princess Shrink, not every problem can be 'worked out'."

"What?" she asked. Princess Shrink? How stupid and glib could he get? She chose to ignore the remark. "I never said they could," Annie replied, her tone soft, but on edge.

"Do you have children, Annie?" Paul asked. It would have been a great segue if it hadn't slammed the hurt even deeper.

"No. I don't have a child." She thought she'd said it in a conversational manner, but Mark gave her a strange look.

Nobody said anything in reply. She drank her beer.

"Another?" Paul asked, raising his hand and looking for the waiter.

"Sure," Annie said, determined to hold her own.

A shadow of annoyance crossed Mark's face. "But even in little Nager, it seems big city crime haunts our humble streets. It sometimes floats in with the tourist trade," Mark said, his face expressionless. "Seems to me, *Dr. O'Brien*, you're running from the city only brought you back to where you came from—same crimes, only with a lake and trees." He took a sip of beer. "You might reconsider going back to New York where you belong."

Ouch. That was a stinger. Where she belonged? She sat up taller and narrowed her eyes at him. "And how can you tell where I belong? Is it written on my forehead?"

"Look around you. You look like one of the tourists."

Paul huffed. "Like hell she does. Stop ragging on her. You've already made her first day hell."

"Yeah, well sorry, but I don't talk to bimbo witch doctors."

Paul's face blanched.

Annie stood, fury almost choking her. "Well, I can rid you of my presence. I'm sorry you don't like me, Mark. I've done nothing to deserve this. As far as I'm concerned you can go straight to hell."

Several women sitting at a nearby table clapped. Mark turned away. Then Annie's cell phone rang. The sound made her jump.

Mark sat back, arms folded. "Some hotshot society boyfriend no doubt wondering when you'll come back."

"Mark, shut up," Paul said, his eyes narrowing.

The prickles on the back of Annie's neck returned. She let the phone ring.

"Going to answer that?" Mark asked. Annie bit her lip and dug out the phone.

"Annabelle Lee." The voice began.

No.

"The stars never rise but I see the bright eyes of the beautiful Annabel Lee."

Annie first felt the heart palpitations and the rush of blood going to her head, then the thousand needle pricks running up and down her arms. She took a deep breath and kept a hard grip on her phone. "Hello?"

No answer.

"Where are you?" Panicked, she looked around. Nobody was paying attention, except the two men at her table who'd gone from a normal complexion to a kind of ashen.

"I am so close I can almost breathe on your neck."

"*What?*" Annie's throat went dry. She could hardly squeak out the question.

"You really are coming down in company, darling. From society to scum. Tsk tsk. And to wear such tight pants and a blouse down to your naval? That could give someone the wrong . . . or should I say the right idea?"

Indignant she said, "I am *not* wearing a blouse down to my naval." A knee-jerk reaction. She'd have to act smoother than that. "Okay, so you can breathe down my neck. So, what?" She looked around. Everyone around her was engrossed in conversations. Not a cell phone to an ear. "Which would be hard because nobody around here is even on a cell phone. So, first off, *who* are you? And second, *where* the hell are you?"

"Oh, my Annabelle Lee." The caller laughed and clicked off.

Annie barely heard Paul or Mark's voice. She shook Paul's hand away from her arm. She thought about leaving . . . running away . . . never stopping.

Then the pain in her abdomen that had plagued Annie on and off for the past year, leapt from Annie's side to her brain in a split second. She was hard pressed to find breath and when she did, the pain intensified. Why did it always come at these inopportune moments? She took in shallow breaths, which usually lessened the agony. She made a mental note to carry her painkillers with her next time, and not drink alcohol. Maybe if she took them as prescribed, the pain wouldn't be so intense.

But the scrutiny from the two men at the table caused her to forget the pain and focus on another kind of discomfort. They were staring. Damn. Couldn't she have even one painful moment in private?

"You okay?" Paul's hand was on her shoulder.

The ache was lessening. She started to breathe again. "Yes, I'm . . . I'm fine. Sorry about that."

"No need to be sorry. Who was that on the phone?" Paul asked. "I'm not sure. Somebody who seems to know me and thinks I should know him too. He didn't give his name."

"Really?" Mark rubbed the back of his ear. "Do you have a lot of admirers like that?"

Another dig. It was becoming a constant companion. But his dislike was the last of her problems. She regarded these two cops. Dedicated, both of them. She should tell them. *Tell them now, Annie.* Then Annie thought of the divorce, and the events that precipitated it. If they looked into her background, they'd drag that up all over again. Think she was delusional, and that the medical center had hired a nutcase. They'd make sure she was put on the first plane back to New York. Paul's cell phone rang.

"Yeah? Uh huh? Shit. Be right down."

"What's wrong? You need help or something?" Mark asked, a smirk crossing his face.

"Don't worry about it." Paul laid his parka over his arm, set for the rain that was long gone. "Gotta go. A disturbance at a 7-11. It's on my way home, anyway."

Paul turned to Annie and looked serious. "I want to know more about that phone call." He cleared his throat. "Look, if you need my help, here's my card." He scribbled another number on it. "Don't be afraid to call me at work or at home." He laid it in front of her and followed a group out of the bar.

Annie was about to say she had to go too when the sensation of being watched hit her again.

"Annie?" Mark was staring. "You all right?" Stupid question. No, she wasn't. "Yes, just fine."

Mark whispered across the table, "Do you want me to see you home?"

She was tempted. She didn't want to go home alone. Mark, as obnoxious as he could be, was her ticket out of here. But he'd get the wrong idea, and she didn't need complications.

"No, thank you, Mark. I don't think that would be a good idea. We don't seem to get along. You don't like me, and I certainly do not like you. I don't want to be seduced by you, and I won't be a notch on anyone's bedpost." She stopped and put her hands to her mouth. She couldn't believe she'd just said that to a Lake Nager detective. One who'd *almost* been her client.

Mark put both hands on the table as though to rise. "Who the hell's trying to seduce *you?* You're not worth the trouble."

They stared at each other through a ringing silence. Her eyes narrowed at him. His eyes never left hers.

Annie finally shook it off. "Have a nice life."

Chapter 7

Annie stepped through the double doors and onto a vast porch that went from one end of the building to the other. She skirted around a group of men in business suits crowding through the doorway then walked down two steps onto the wet pavement.

Friday night in downtown Lake Nager. The Hole was a local sports bar where locals and tourists mingled. Here, unless you knew better, you couldn't tell the rich from poor, or who came from the upper echelon of Lake Nager and who came from the ram shackled section of Brighton.

A group of boys dressed in jeans with holes in the knees, their bodies hovering over teeny bopper girls wearing cut offs and midriff tanks, grouped around a GT3 Porsche. They were shuffling through ID cards. Annie chuckled. Probably trying to find the ones that were legal. Not that those kids even remotely looked like they were twenty-one.

As Annie passed the group, the boys whistled. She winked and walked just a little bit taller. No. Maybe strutting was a better word. At twenty-seven, that she could still be cat-called by teen-age boys was pretty cool. Her ego felt much better now that she'd left the presence of the jerk who thought she ought to go back to where she came from.

But now she had to deal with other issues. The parking lot was full. It would be hard to tell if anyone might be her anonymous caller. Except for appreciative glances from some guys, no one especially lingered around her. Certainly, nobody who looked like Duncan

Byrne. If she did see him, she'd give him a piece of her mind and sic the law on him. Restraining orders had to count for something. Even ones issued out-of-state. She would not allow *anyone* to intimidate her. Never again.

She took in a whiff of after-the-rain breezes. Ducks quacked in a flight plan, headed back to the lake from wherever they'd been. Off to the side, an orangey-blue body of water peeked out from behind the trees. A warm, lovely evening.

She got into her car and started the engine. She backed up.

Thump, thump, thump.

Her tire. *Oh no. Please, not here. Not now.*

When she got out, she looked down and froze. All four tires had been slashed. All four sat on their rims.

The shock momentarily sent her into a dizzy spell. She had to balance with both hands on the hood. "Oh God, no." Forcing herself to get a grip, she looked to the sky—to a group of geese, honking and flapping toward the lake.

Maybe it had been some kind of horrific hallucination. She peered down again.

No such luck.

She stamped her foot in frustration. Screaming would have been her first choice, but that wouldn't have done her any good. Help. She needed help. However, everyone, including the teeny boppers had suddenly disappeared.

Now, she *was* desperate. She could think of only one person at hand who could help her, and she'd just told him to have a nice life.

Chapter 8

Duncan Byrne sat near the end of the bar hidden from the rest of the room behind an unfinished pine post with genuine knotholes. He could pretty much observe everything when he moved his head a certain way around a group of waiters singing "Happy Birthday to you" clap-clap, as a birthday boy was handed a gratis drink.

Outside of that, he kept his eyes on his whiskey glass or the female bartender dressed in a short black skirt and a tight white T-shirt with 'The Watering Hole' embossed on the front, showing her boobs off to their best advantage. His type of place. He'd occasionally talk to girls on either side, but his concentration lay across the room and the drama that was playing out.

She was walking out the door, but she'd be back. Of that he was absolutely certain.

He regarded the detective, now sitting alone, popping those damned peanuts. Tall, rugged and he supposed handsome to the female species.

Annabelle was as beautiful as he'd ever seen her and that pissed him off. She was supposed to be pining for him, instead she dressed like a cheap slut looking for a quick pick-up. Maybe the detective was one of them. His Annabelle. Untouched when he'd married her. Unsullied. About to commit the sin of adultery. Never mind those divorce papers. Once married. Always married.

He sipped his Johnny Walker Red. *'Til death do us part.'*

He should never have agreed to this divorce. This was his fault. For this he'd be reprimanded. And the reason his Annabelle Lee had to be punished.

That detective . . . the man had better leave her alone, otherwise more than one—no, make that two lives would be taken this week.

By the looks of it, the detective seemed to be the local Casanova. Familiar to the women here; probably in the biblical sense. It was time to talk to the local ladies.

The woman to the right of him had short red hair. She seemed to be popular with the locals, but she'd had her eye on him ever since she'd sat on the bar stool.

"Hi," he said. "Can I buy you a refill on that whiskey sour?"

She smiled and showed him a brilliant Julia Roberts type smile. "Yes, thank you."

The bartender stopped in front of them. "Whiskey sour," the woman said.

"Another shot of Johnny Walker Red for me." "Right away." The bartender hustled to the bottles.

"I'm Candy," the woman said. "I haven't seen you here before. Are you new? One of the vacationers?"

"Yes, I am. My very first time. Maybe you can tell me something about the town and the people here?"

"Well," she said. "If you want to know about the people in this town, you've come to the right place. Everyone in Nager knows everyone else."

"You know everyone in town?"

"Just about."

The bartender brought their drinks. Duncan paid.

Then he turned back to Candy and listened as she told him everything he wanted to know about the town and the detective sitting across the room.

Chapter 9

Mark felt like a bastard. He hadn't meant to hurt Annie's feelings by suggesting she go back to where she came from. He'd been feeling vile since Paul suspended him that afternoon. He blamed her.

It hadn't helped when Laura Campbell walked by. She'd given him the smile that invariably made him take his hand off any woman he was with. He looked around to see if she was still here. She was, but sitting at the bar, her attention focusing on a tourist sitting next to her. Maybe he had money and she'd latch on to him and leave town, again. Thank God. He pulled out the scrap of paper she'd left with him. Just a phone number and a smiley face. "Call me," it read. He ripped it into shreds and stuffed it into an empty beer bottle.

A few women who'd witnessed Annie's exit smirked, but quickly went back to their conversation when Mark stared at them.

He'd deserved it, and he knew it. He'd treated them badly, he guessed. He'd gotten a well-deserved reputation.

Still, he had no room in his life for a relationship. He'd nearly gone down the road of matrimony with Laura. The fact she'd stood him up two days before his wedding had proved a good thing in the long run. A blessing in disguise, his mother had said. But then, she hadn't liked Laura. He supposed she'd seen right through her.

He sighed and studied a peanut shell, trying to forget what a jerk he'd been. Annie O'Brien. He'd never lashed out at anyone the way he had at her. He'd probably made an enemy for life.

That was why he was surprised to see her standing at his booth again.

"Back again?" he asked, his tone surprised in spite of his efforts to keep emotion out of it. "Changed your mind?"

Mark took one look at her and shut his mouth.

Annie's face was as gray as the cigarette ashes left in a ceramic ashtray at the next table. Her eye's held a stony anger, and her expression grim, full of desperation. Annie said, "I'm in trouble. I need a ride." Her voice sounded raspy, as though she had a problem getting out the words.

He started, his brain not quickly grasping the seriousness of the unexpected. "What happened?"

"Somebody slashed my tires," she whispered.

Mark banged his knee into the booth trying to get out. "Oh shit, are you sure?"

She rolled her eyes.

"Yeah, I guess you wouldn't be telling me this unless you were. Come on."

By the time they'd gotten outside, a crowd had started to gather around the vehicle. Mark checked her tires. They'd been slashed all right. He gave up the notion maybe she'd run over a nail or glass or something. This was a deliberate attack.

Nobody had seen *anything*. According to witnesses, no one had approached her car, loitered by her car, anything by the car. There'd been potential witnesses, but nobody had seen anything. Of course, as one pointed out, he hadn't been really paying attention.

"When I came in a half hour ago a fight was breaking out," a man said. "They had a tough time breaking it up. The guys hung on to each other like pit bulls."

"Did you see how it started?"

The man shook his head. "Nope. I stay away from fights."

"Anybody called the cops?" Mark asked.

"Cops? You're all in there." The man motioned toward the bar. "Besides, the fights around here usually stop by themselves."

"Oh? And did this one stop by itself?"

The man opened his mouth to say something, then apparently changed his mind." He coughed. "Nobody got killed, did they?"

"So, you didn't notice anyone around my car?" Annie asked.

The man looked at her like she had three heads then walked away.

Mark was about to offer a suggestion, when Annie turned on him, angry and challenging. "Look. You didn't do this, did you?"

"Huh?" His eyes widened in surprise. "In some perverse way of getting even?"

"Christ, Annie. I've been in the bar, in your presence since you walked in. And . . ."

"You could have gotten one of your friends to do it."

Mark touched her arm, and she shook it off. "If you did Mark, you really are a sick . . ."

"Annie. I didn't do this to you. I might be an insensitive jerk sometimes, but I'd never destroy anything . . ." Or anybody, he'd been about to say. But that didn't quite come out.

Annie walked around her car, peered down and stood up. Tears now bordered the rims of her eyes.

He blocked her from making another turn. "Look, I swear it wasn't me, or any of my friends. But I have a mechanic who can replace your tires and check out the rest of your car."

Annie's mouth flew open. "You mean you think they did something else to it?"

Mark shook his head. "I doubt it, but I'll have them check just in case. Meanwhile, I'll take you home."

She squared her shoulders, ready for a fight, he thought. He diffused by smiling. "I promise I'll be on my best behavior."

Annie relaxed. Her face softened. "Okay. If it's not too far out of your way. Otherwise, I could call."

"Where do you live?"

"In an apartment complex . . ." Annie looked around as though studying the terrain.

"By the medical center?"

She nodded. "But how did you know that?"

"Because it's the only apartment complex in town. I have an apartment there. So, it won't be out of my way."

"We live in the same complex?" Annie folded her arms over her chest and frowned, indicating it wasn't quite okay he was living within the same state let alone the same complex.

Mark's mouth took on an unpleasant twist. "That okay with you?" His voice oozed with a sarcasm he couldn't help. *Don't worry, Miss Princess Shrink. I won't be breaking down your door anytime soon.*

She tilted her head in a nod, her face expressionless.

Mark got down to business. "Anything you need from your car before we go?"

She glanced inside and shook her head. "No."

Mark held the door to his blue police-issued Dodge Charger to let her in. As he buckled his seat belt he asked, "This was a random act, wasn't it? You don't know anyone around here who's harboring a grudge against you."

She knitted her brow and scratched her forehead then looked sweetly into his eyes. "Besides you? Not a soul."

Bloody hell. Mark almost cracked a smile. Almost. But his instincts wouldn't let him buy her act. He was certain she'd been looking for someone in the bar. Then there'd been the conversation on her cell phone. Someone had frightened her to death.

Mark pulled out of the parking lot and stopped at the intersection of Main Street and Forest Avenue, a long winding street that dead- ended at the pier on the north side and the apartment complex at the southern end. These units had been a signature of the modern development slowly inching into the quaint lakeside resort town. Anyone who didn't own or rent a house in Nager, mostly the single population, lived there.

He felt the need to get Annie's mind off her slashed tires, so he found himself telling her all about Lake Nager, whether she wanted to hear it or not.

"Nobody could say that Lake Nager didn't go all out for the Fourth of July. The brunt of the town's tourist business comes from this week alone," he said. "Main Street houses most of the local businesses and as you can see, flags hang from every light post."

Annie's shoulder's slumped slightly and he sensed that she was beginning to settle. She seemed interested in what he was saying, so he continued.

"See that inn over there? The one that backs up against the pier? Well, that's Nager's famous Campbell Inn."

"Oh. I've wanted to see that inn," Annie said. She glanced out her side window to see souvenir shops, boat rentals and concession stands selling hot dogs, ice cream and cotton candy. Across the street from the inn stood the Village Green, where the town's main attraction, the Clock Tower, stood. She'd remembered reading about it. The Clock Tower reportedly dated back from the eighteenth century. During the week of the Fourth of July between the clock tower and the oldest oak tree in Nager hung a massive banner. *Happy Fourth of July. Welcome to Lake Nager.*

Mark turned right and stopped at the light at the corner of Main and Forest. Across from The Hole stood a big red brick building that housed the police station and the village hall. An American flag hung from the center of the entrance. A statue of Nathan Hale getting ready to be hanged stood on the lawn under a tree.

"See that statue, Annie?"

"You mean the one draped in a red, white and blue sash? Very patriotic."

"Yep. Every day of the year. At Christmas time Nathan wears a red, white and blue Santa Claus hat."

Annie smiled. "You're kidding."

Mark glanced sideways at her. Sophisticated, probably spoiled city girl. Someone who thought she had all the answers. Could someone else besides him resent her being here? He'd been upset when she asked if he'd slashed her tires. Could she have rubbed someone else the wrong way? Maybe a disgruntled client from New York who had followed her? In fact, maybe *that* was why she'd moved here. Stalkers could be hard to track, they could be malicious—even deadly.

A horn blasted at his side.

"Mark!" Annie braced against the dashboard.

"Sorry," he muttered. He concentrated on his driving.

Chapter 10

The apartment complex stood in a carved-out alcove of the forest at the end of the street. The three-story apartment buildings, a club house and swimming pool were only a few blocks from the medical center. Despite its close proximity, the forest provided a natural sound barrier to the drama that played out there every day. The dwellers resided in relative privacy and isolation. Each apartment had its own balcony, and the complex formed a horseshoe around a duck pond. For the holidays, the balconies were strung with red, white and blue lights.

Annie had never lived alone before and cherished her new-found privacy. She loved her apartment with a stone fireplace, and a balcony where she could watch the ducks play in the pond and see Lake Nager peeking through the trees. An ideal place for a single person. So, why was her stomach suddenly in knots?

They drove around the back where tenants had their own parking spots. Annie pointed to hers under a grove of trees. As much as she wanted to get out of Mark's company, still the incidents with the tires and the phone call made him suddenly important to her safety. She wanted him with her.

"Look Mark. I don't want you to get the wrong idea … I . . ."

"Want me to come up?" Mark turned and looked at her. He was no longer the seductive jerk who'd been making snide comments all night. Now, Mark's expression displayed nothing but absolute professionalism.

Annie nodded and to her dismay, her voice broke. "Yes . . . please." Gone was the self-assured lady from New York City. Her palms were sweaty, and she was on guard. She had a bad feeling about this.

An unexpected warmth crossed over his face. "Okay. But, before we go up, is there anything you want to tell me?"

Puzzled, she looked at him, her eyebrows raised. "Like what Mark? I live alone, except for a cat. His name is Nemesis."

Mark grinned. "He always gets his mouse?"

Annie cocked her head and smiled. "Always. He's a brat, but I love him. Duncan brought him home from the Anti-Cruelty Society as a present."

That was when she and Duncan had a close relationship. She'd always loved Nemesis, but since the divorce, he'd become an even more valued friend.

They walked toward the east complex headed for the elevators inside the lobby next to the mailboxes. "So, where's your apartment?" Annie asked mainly to shut out her nervousness.

"West side of the complex. I'm not anywhere close to you."

"Oh, I didn't mean . . ."

"Sure, you did."

The elevator dinged and the door opened. Mark pressed his hand along her back and ushered her inside. When he brushed across her to press the button, the hairs on her arms stood at attention. What was *that?* So, the guy was good looking. So were a lot of men, and she didn't have that reaction to *them.* She didn't even *like* this guy.

The floors of the hallway were carpeted and usually immaculate. This particular day they must have forgotten to vacuum because mud stains led to the elevator.

"They're going the wrong way," she said, pointing down.

"The mud stains. They should be going toward the apartments, not away."

"Another budding young detective. Yeah, I'd think so too." Well, bless his heart. He'd actually agreed with her.

When they got to her door, she fiddled with her keys and couldn't seem to get the right one in the lock. She lost her grip, it flipped up and out of her fingers, falling into Mark's waiting hand. He managed to put the right key into the lock, and Annie felt stupid.

Mark grinned. Broadly. She wished he wouldn't stand so close.

He was starting to really annoy her.

He tried to open the door, but the bottom seemed to be stuck on something. Mark pushed again and the sound of metal grinded against the door. One more push and the door lurched open.

Annie stepped inside and stopped-dead. She couldn't move, her feet cemented to carpeted floor.

Mark was right behind and almost fell over her. He quipped, "You sure don't know how to clean . . ." His words faltered into, "Shit."

Annie leaned back and fell against him.

"No!" she whispered. "This can't be happening."

Annie's desktop computer lay at her feet. Its monitor looked like someone had taken a hammer and smashed its screen. Her hard-copy dissertation, the result of years of cumulative research was torn to shreds and scattered all over the floor. Books were out of the bookcase, their insides torn out. Dishes smashed to smithereens. Goblets, precious to her mother, thrown against the wall and shattered into splinters.

Her clothes were cut into ribbons, and the pieces of material were mixed in with the broken glass. Her jewelry box had been forced open and emptied.

But the worst sight was the writing on the wall. Paint? Blood? "Whores die" and "What is given can be taken away".

Then she heard the screaming. In front of her, in back of her, inside her. And something warm was holding her so she wouldn't keel over. Her eyes burned from the tears running down her face. Sobs congregated in her throat and for a moment, she couldn't breathe at all.

"Annie." The voice seemed far away but was hovering above her. "Annie. Easy. Easy." The voice crooned, soothed what could not be comforted.

She was being led. Then lowered into a chair. "Sit over here. Don't touch anything."

But, almost fascinated, Annie got up again and walked toward the wall. She reached out to touch the words.

Hands pulled her back. Mark's voice whispered, "Get away from there. The wall is covered with blood."

"Blood? But there's . . . Nemesis! Where's Nemesis?" Annie looked around. Her cat was not there. "Where's my cat?"

Mark looked under the sofa then went into the bedroom. Annie heard the outcry. A cry of anger and pain mingled into one short sound.

Annie bolted off the sofa.

"Don't come in here."

But it was too late. Annie was over the threshold. Her cat lay on the bed. It's neck broken, it's body slashed. Blood soaked into the bedspread.

Annie went numb. She shook. She wasn't sure whether she was screaming or whether the sounds came from the inside of her head. She grabbed for her cat.

Mark grabbed her hands. "Don't touch, Annie." He walked her into the living room, but Annie couldn't take her eyes off her pet and walked backward, her teeth chattering, until they were well around the corner.

"Don't touch anything. There could be fingerprints." "Fingerprints?" she whispered numbly. "Yes—fingerprints. Finger ..." Everything seemed to mold into everything else. Once again, the room swirled, and this time her vision grew dim. She fainted.

When she regained consciousness, she was in Mark's arms, and somehow, comforted.

"Are you all right?" He handed her a glass of water. "Drink this."

Without any will of her own, she took the glass and drank, then automatically handed it back.

She looked around at the room. Her life—her things were strewn around, broken, like so much garbage. All she had in the world.

But Mark wouldn't let her dwell on a broken past. "What is this, Annie? This is no routine burglary. Who'd want to hurt you like this?"

She forced herself to talk, to remember her name. "I'm Annie O'Brien," she whispered. "That's my name. Annie."

"Annie?"

She flipped back into reality.

"Duncan did this," she said without even thinking.

"Duncan?" Mark asked. "Duncan who?"

Annie stopped thinking. It poured out. "My ex-husband. That message, that which he gives he can take away. He gave me Nemesis. Saved him from a shelter. Now, he's taking him away, as he's been taking away my entire life—little by little."

Her cell phone rang. She pulled it out of her purse and stared at the number.

Mark raised his eyebrows—questioning.

Her voice shook. "It's a New Jersey area code. I don't know anybody in New Jersey."

"Here, give it to me."

Annie gave him the phone and listened with him.

"I told you my name was *Nemesis*." The voice didn't sound quite human.

"My God, Duncan. You killed my cat. You took a *life*!" The laughter that emerged was beyond human. Maniacal. "Duncan, you need help!"

Click.

"Son of a bitch," Mark said. He looked at her and snapped the phone shut. "The bastard hung up."

Chapter 11

It was many and many a year ago,
In a kingdom by the sea,
That a maiden there lived whom you may know
By the name of Annabelle Lee;
And this maiden she lived with no other thought,
Than to love and be loved by me.

Duncan put down the poem and his flashlight and sipped his Johnny Walker Red from a sterling silver flask. The shadows of the moving trees in the parking lot in the back of Annie's apartment building played tricks on his imagination. Dancing figures of specters—apparitions—ghosts.

Well, well, well. So, the nice detective had given the damsel in distress a ride home.

Cruel, brutal anger tensed his body. Was Annabelle now sobbing on the shoulder of the willing detective? A man with no scruples. A man with a reputation. He'd learned all he needed to know about Mark Driscoll from a spurned lover.

A mixture of repulsion and adoration burrowed deep into his heart. The love-hate muddle of obsession, insanity, damnation. His soul would soon be free of this torment.

He reached into his glove compartment and took out a tracking device, crept into the shadows and scooted under Mark's police car. Done. Now, there wasn't anywhere that man could go undetected.

Duncan snuck back into his SUV and resumed watch.

Sadly, he fixated on earlier, happier times. His beautiful Annabelle Lee. Who'd lived for nothing more than to love and be loved by him. The woman who'd cared for him more than anyone in the world.

Damn her. He'd made her. Now he'd break her.

Sweat broke out on his forehead. What had the detective been planning? To seduce her?

Annabelle was naïve—a rare beauty whom he'd rescued when her last living relative died. He'd taken her in. Married her, loved her body and soul, supported her, given her a child.

Another sip of whiskey. The child. She'd loved that unborn baby more than him. She talked about *it* more than she talked about *him*.

Visions of his Annabelle Lee, who soon would take his hand and float—side by side—in their private kingdom by the sea. There was no sea, but there was a lake. A lake much like the one where he'd pushed his mother from the boat and smacked her with the oar. The perfect spot.

He shook with anger. Whiskey spilled on his shirt.

"Damn it." He reached for the towel that eternally lay on the passenger seat. Couldn't allow anything to spill. Especially onto the car seat. Couldn't do that or mother would beat him.

But there was no mother to beat him. He could spill the whole flask onto the seats if he wanted. But maybe she'd come back and put him into that closet again. She couldn't do that either. He'd killed her. Held her head under water, the same way she'd done to him when he'd been naughty. Well, she'd been naughty and when he held her under, *she* didn't come up—alive.

Sirens were the first indication that they'd called for backup.

Patriotic flashing red, white and blue lights weren't far behind.

Duncan pulled out of the back exit of the lot as the police pulled into the front.

The irony of the good guy pulling out as the bad guys pulled in.

Duncan chuckled.

The detective had undoubtedly gone up to Annie's apartment with the idea of a one-night stand with *his* beautiful woman. What they'd found instead would be a nightmare.

Well, good night Mark Driscoll. Good night Annabelle Lee.

Now, begins the terror.

Chapter 12

The inner sanctum used for interrogation, employee interviews and lunch had seen better days. An industrial clock ticked loudly on the wall, a ceiling fan squeaked above them and an oscillating fan cranked from side to side. Paul sat at a long rectangular table that had undergone at least two coats of chipping paint. Cigarettes and a full ashtray lay in front of him, along with police report forms.

Annie sat on a wooden chair at this table, pale, tense and shaking. Red rims surrounded her eyes and perspiration ran from her forehead down her cheek. In one day, her life had gone from eager young psychologist, to homeless and hunted prey.

Mark paced the floor behind her. She was about to screech out "stop it" when he came to an abrupt halt. "Annie, what's happening here?" He had his hands on the back of her chair and leaned over her shoulder.

Annie turned on him, crashing her forehead into his nose.

Mark leapt back. "Damn, Annie." He turned his back on her then moved two seats down. He checked under his nose. Annie supposed—for blood.

Mark had been supportive on the way back to the station. He'd held her close on the elevator and helped her into his car. But the moment they entered the interrogation room he seemed to change. He went back to playing hard-nosed detective. Now, he didn't seem to want to believe her at all.

She snapped at him. "Isn't it obvious enough? I'm being stalked, harassed and threatened." She paused and thought about her next statement. "And somebody is trying to erase me from the face of the earth."

Paul had been sitting with his elbows on the table, his hands pressed against his mouth in prayer position. He pressed the bridge of his nose into his fingers and rubbed his eyes. "Annie," he said softly. "Have you had death threats?"

She had to think fast. Either she could give them her history with Duncan and risk not being believed or she could stick to present events. She chose the latter. "Actual death threats . . . I think the blood on the wall spoke for itself, don't you?"

"What do you think?" Mark asked.

Annie analyzed him. Unlike this morning, his eyes were sharp—assessing. He'd gone from a lost, exhausted wreck that stood in her office this morning, to a massive self-confident presence in the room. If she felt intimidated as a victim, she could only imagine how an actual suspect felt.

"'Whore's die' and 'What is given can be taken away' both sound like threats to me."

Mark asked, "What did 'Whores die' refer to?"

"Damn it! I don't know. I hope you're not taking that literally," she said.

Paul cleared his throat. "Have you had anything happen before this? Something that might have happened in New York. Maybe some incident you'd never associate with a threat?"

Oh boy. "A couple of months ago—when I was still in New York, I . . ." The memory temporarily paralyzed her. It had been a frightening situation. A packed underground subway . . . A train screeching into the station, grinding to a halt. The people hovering on the edge waiting for the doors to open. "I was standing at the subway platform, in the front of the rush-hour crowd waiting for the train, when a wave of movement came from behind me, and the swell pushed me. I nearly fell onto the tracks."

The clock ticked out the silence in the room. Annie's gaze went down to the table avoiding the stares. She bit her lower lip and looked up. "Somebody pulled me back before I went under."

"Good God," Paul said.

"Do you think it was deliberate?" Mark asked.

"As I say, I don't know. It probably wasn't. Those subways are accidents waiting to happen. But the timing seemed deliberate."

"How?" Mark asked.

Annie fumbled with her hands. "It came a week after my divorce was final."

Mark rubbed the back of his ear. "And you think your ex-husband is responsible. This Duncan . . . ?"

"Byrne."

"Who exactly *is* this Duncan Byrne?"

Paul said, "A prominent psychiatrist in New York. Dean of the school of psychiatry at NYU."

Mark made a clicking noise with his tongue. "Should have known. Psychiatrists are crazier than their patients."

Annie narrowed her eyes at Mark. "Duncan is far from stupid. The man's brilliant. It would be dangerous to underestimate him."

"Okay," Paul said. "But even so, this doesn't make sense. He gave you a great reference when you applied at the mental health center. Why would he have done that if he hated you."

"Why else?" Annie replied, on the edge of her seat. "So, he can keep track of where I am."

"How much animosity was there between you when you divorced?" Paul asked.

"A lot," Annie replied. "He didn't want a divorce."

"So, you initiated the divorce proceedings?" Mark asked. "If you don't mind me asking, why did you divorce him? A brilliant and prominent psychiatrist. You obviously had a lot in common."

"I had to get away from him."

"Why?"

Good question. Why had she wanted to get away from the man who'd swept her off her feet, gave her a home, when she was about to be evicted, and taught her almost everything she knew. How much of the truth should she tell? Looking at Mark's skeptical expression, she doubted he'd believe her. Even the NYPD who'd been on the scene hadn't believed her. Better she kept quiet.

"Duncan became very controlling," she said. "He tried to monitor my every movement. He insisted I only work on my projects with him—no one else. Then I found out he was using my research and claiming it as his own. When I started working with a group of other grad students, he accused me of having an affair. It got ugly. I . . ."

Annie shifted in her seat to meet Mark's intimidating stare. She couldn't go on with this. Why she divorced Duncan was none of their business. "Oh, bother!" Annie abruptly rose, her hands leaning on the table. "Look, I'm the victim here. Remember? Stop staring at me as if I'd just killed someone."

Mark threw up his hands and stood. "Look, Annie."

Paul gave Mark an almost imperceptible shake of the head.

Mark paced the floor until he came to the end of the room, where he leaned against the wall, arms folded. "We're just trying to get some background," he said, a bit gentler than before. "Look, I know you were looking around the bar for someone. Did you think he might be there?"

She nodded. "It was a possibility."

"Okay," Paul said. "That was before you knew about your tires or apartment. How long have the phone calls been going on?"

"The phone call I got in the bar was the second—no, third. The first came just before you came for your session, Mark."

"Damn," Mark said, almost under his breath. He got up and walked to the window.

"You handled yourself very well, under the circumstances," Paul said, glaring at Mark.

Mark said nothing. He hunched his shoulders and crossed one foot over the other.

Paul nodded to Annie. "Go on."

"After you left me in the parking lot, an SUV almost ran me down."

Mark made some kind of growl, but Annie couldn't make out anything intelligible. "Did you get the license plate number?" he asked.

Annie shook her head. "Couldn't, it was splattered with mud."

"Get a look at the driver? Anything?"

"No. The SUV was black. I've seen a lot of them around here. I believe the windows were tinted, but I was so busy getting out of the *way*, I forgot to look at his *face*." Like she'd had time to get a detailed description of the guy. Right.

"You said third phone call," Paul said. "When was the second?"

When I got into my car. He said he was glad he hadn't run me over. He also said he intended to have me dead or alive. He didn't care which. So, to answer your previous question, that does sound like a death threat."

"Annie," Paul said. "Have you seen anyone who looks like Duncan around here?"

"No. I haven't spotted him." But I've felt his presence, she thought. *Yes, I've felt him.* "One thing you have to understand, Duncan is a master of disguise. He played leading roles in his college's theater productions. He had his own psychodrama workshops. He can play any part he wants. If he's here, he'd look like a tourist. He wouldn't come dressed as Duncan Byrne." She took a deep breath before she continued. "I might not even recognize him. He was that good."

Mark shook his head. Oh bother! He obviously didn't believe her. Annie closed her eyes to get his skepticism from her view. When she opened them again, she avoided his eyes.

"Mark," she said, flat—toneless. "You don't have to believe me, but if you don't, Duncan will be twice as hard to catch.

"Annie," Paul said. "Besides the vandalism, was anything stolen?"

"My jewelry is missing. There wasn't much, but what I had is gone." A sudden acute sensation of loss hit her. All of those memories lost, slashed or broken to bits on the floor.

Paul took out a small pad from his shirt pocket and a small yellow pencil. "What exactly was stolen?"

She thought of the engagement presents that Duncan had given her. The pearl earrings, a diamond pennant, her engagement and wedding rings. Her eyes started to burn. She wiped the tears off her cheeks with her sleeve and told them.

Paul pushed over a box of tissues. "So, this was a robbery."

Mark shook his head. "With so much destruction? Robbers get in and get out. They might throw things around a bit to find stuff they can sell, but this just doesn't feel right." He walked back and sat next to Annie again. "Tell me about this research. Could somebody be after that?"

"Doubtful. A copy of my research is with a friend in New York. And besides, the paper was already published. It was my dissertation for my doctorate. There's also a copy of it on my laptop in my office."

"What was the subject?" Mark rested his hands on his chin and gazed at her.

"I'd written a paper on types of psychotic mental disorders. That's what got published. But I hadn't stopped there. I was expanding my research into obsessive personalities, especially stalkers. How they get that way, how the condition progresses, and the destructive effects on both the obsessed and his target."

"You think this fits the profile?"

"Maybe—maybe not. They will make harassing phone calls, show up at your house, follow you around. Usually, take something . . ."

"He did." Mark pointed out.

"Yes, but he wouldn't destroy everything."

Paul leaned back. "Did you recognize his voice?"

Annie shrugged. "Yes . . . No. He had an eerie tone. Kind of sing songy—like the inflection of a child."

Mark threw up his hands. "So, you're not sure it was Duncan. It could have been someone else?"

Annie bristled from Mark's continued disbelief. "No. He knew too much about me. Who else could it have been?"

Mark shook his head. "Why the hell are we even having this conversation? This psychotic personality on the phone doesn't sound to me like a prominent psychiatrist. You haven't seen him here. It's more like a robbery staged to look like vandalism or retribution."

Mark's almost-brutal accusation stung. "Do you know what a prominent psychiatrist sounds like? Look, it's been a long, rotten day. Probably ranks among the worst I've ever had. For you to sit here and be so hostile . . ." The sheer force of the hurt forced a groan and a flood of tears. *Keep control. Don't lose it.*

Annie grabbed a hand full of tissues and dabbed her eyes. With all the patience she could muster, she said, "Because, Mark, Duncan was the only person that called me Annabelle Lee."

"Your name is Annabelle."

"First of all, everyone who knows me calls me Annie. Second, my name is Annabelle not Annabelle Lee. Duncan loved the Edgar Alan Poe poem so much, he'd call me that all the time. Third, why would a thief slash my tires and kill my cat?" She bit her lip refraining from calling him an idiot.

Mark's face clouded over. He conceded. "I can see how you'd come to that conclusion."

Paul slapped his hands on the table. "Well, we'll need to continue this tomorrow. There's a lot more I want to know about your relationship with this man."

"Me too," Mark said.

"But first, let me see your cell phone."

"My cell phone?"

"Yeah. I want to check those incoming call numbers."

Annie dug down into her purse and pulled it up, handing it over.

She came around behind him and watched him click on the call log to received calls. The last few numbers had a New Jersey area code.

"Does that number mean anything to you?" Paul asked.

Annie shook her head. "No. That doesn't look familiar at all. I don't even know anybody in New Jersey."

Paul wrote down several numbers and handed the phone back. "Look, I think you should keep this off for a while."

"Okay."

"And since it's a crime scene, you won't be able to go home. You'll need a place to stay."

Annie shivered at the thought. "I could never go back to that apartment. I'd never feel safe in there again. Maybe a motel?"

"No motels," Paul said. "I want you somewhere where you'll be protected." He looked at Mark, and a slow grin came over his face. "And I know the perfect place. Mark, I've just put you back on the job."

Mark blinked and looked wary. "Oh yeah? Doing what?"

"You'll be Annie's bodyguard for the duration of the two weeks you're off the street."

Mark looked like he was going to choke. "Not a chance. I'm not going to spend the next two weeks babysitting."

You supercilious bastard, Annie thought, but kept her mouth shut.

"I don't think you have a choice." Paul snapped, frowning at him. "This is an assignment, not a damned date." He looked back at Annie and nodded. "And I know exactly where you'll go."

"Where?" Annie and Mark asked, almost at the same time.

"To your house, Mark."

Annie's jaw clenched. "I don't think so," she said. "I'm sure Mark has far too many women there as it is."

Mark looked at her through cold dark eyes.

But Paul was shaking his head. "No, only one. You'll go to his mother's house not his apartment. Julia Driscoll . . ."

Mark glared, then sighed.

Overall, this had been a day from hell.

Chapter 13

A two-lane highway wound out of town, leaving the houses and streetlights behind. Mark zipped past darkening fields and finally entered the Two-Lakes State Forest, which deepened on both sides as they drove through. The moon had already risen. Glaring headlights illuminated the wet pavement and occasionally blinded him, as they flew by on the other side of the road.

He glanced at the figure huddled against the edge of the passenger seat, her face plastered against the window.

He'd hurt her. He'd made sure she felt unwelcome and tried to make her feel incompetent. In that, he wasn't sure he'd succeeded. But, overall, he'd made sure she didn't trust him. And now, she needed him, because she had no one else besides himself and Paul to turn to.

Annie shifted her body within the confines of her seatbelt and turned toward him. Without her uttering a word, he knew what she was going to ask. His mind raced with possible answers.

"Why do you dislike me so much?" Her voice was so soft, he could barely hear her. She sounded defeated, like she was at the end of her rope and hadn't a clue how she got there.

"I don't . . ." He started to lie, but she cut him off.

"Yes, you do. From the first minute you saw me, you've done nothing but make snide comments and put me down. Especially, the cute one about why didn't I go back to where I came from. Do you normally try to make perfect strangers feel like idiots? Does that come from being a detective? Or is it just aimed at me?"

Now he needed a satisfactory answer, and the truth was, he didn't have one. "Okay. I'm sorry. I was hot, discouraged and damned mad. Look, Dr. O'Brien, I have to deal with my conscience for killing that kid. I don't feel I need to talk it out with a stranger."

Annie's stare pierced through Mark's temple, giving him a headache. His focus might have been on the road, but the corner of his eye rested on her.

"With all due respect," Annie said. "It was my job. Paul needed to know if you were competent enough to be out on the street. You weren't. It didn't take a PhD to understand that. You should have known that yourself."

"Okay, so Miss Princess Shrink, I'm tired and burned-out. Maybe I should just damned quit." His gaze landed on her for a brief second, as a truck flew past.

"Excuse me?" Her eyes narrowed. "Miss who?"

Exasperated, he remained silent.

"Damn it Mark, can't you just admit you have limitations? I'm not even sure why I'm letting you drive me. In your state, you could get us killed."

"In my state? Letting me?" He was raising his voice. It was becoming increasingly hard to control it. "Look lady, you don't have a choice. I drive or you walk." His voice came out sharper than intended.

"Okay. If you feel like that, why don't you just give me directions and I'll walk there. Stop the car. Now."

Mark came to a screeching halt by the side of the road. His stomach hit the seat belt instead of the steering wheel. Annie was thrown forward, then back. She'd grabbed hold of the ceiling handle and now was unbuckling her seat belt.

Mark grabbed her arm. Annie cringed, wide-eyed, then pulled away from him. "Get your hands off me." Her voice bristled in anger. She opened the car door and stumbled out.

Damn, how had it gotten to this? He got out after her. "Annie, come back here." He stood looking at her doe eyes in the headlights. Angry as hell, but frightened and ready for a fight. A conditioned response? Why?

Well, hell. Somebody has been making harassing phone calls and destroyed everything she had in the world. Wouldn't anybody be frightened as well as angry under the same circumstances?

She was breathing heavily, bent over, hands on her knees. Then up. Ready to run.

He softened his tone into an apology. "Annie, I'm sorry. I didn't mean to frighten you. Please get back into the car. It's ten miles to my mother's. There's nothing but wilderness out here. No houses for miles. If anything happens to you, there won't be anyone to help. Please get in."

Annie stood motionless. Her face was white against the backdrop of the black forest.

Mark's voice came out soft with underlying intensity. "I can be a bit overbearing at times."

She still didn't move.

"Please, get back into the car. I won't touch you again. I promise."

In his years on the force, he'd seen women cringe, pull away, get angry and fight for their lives, then suddenly withdraw into themselves. These women had been crime victims. Had Annie been one of those women? He didn't get a chance to think about it. Annie pulled herself up, walked back to the passenger side and got in.

"Thanks," he whispered. He buckled his seat belt and glanced over. It was dark. He could barely make out her features from the dashboard lights. "Buckle up, Annie, okay? We've got a way to go yet."

When he didn't hear her buckle click, he reached over to do it for her. What he saw made him draw in a sharp breath of air. Her eyes were closed, but tears spilled down her cheeks, and she hugged herself. This girl wasn't only emotionally drained, she was in physical pain.

"Are you all right?"

Annie didn't look at him, but slowly nodded. "Yes," she whispered.

No, she wasn't, but Mark didn't contradict her. He pulled out onto the highway again.

"Look, maybe I was a bit too harsh on you, but damn it, isn't there anything you love so much you'd die for it?"

She started for a second but recovered. It was too late. He'd seen it.

Quietly, Annie turned the question around. "Are you trying to tell me you're obsessed with your job, Mark?"

"God, I hate people who answer questions with a question."

"Are you?"

"Okay, yes. I'm committed to my job. If that's an obsession, so be it."

"Only if that job becomes so engulfing, you can't think about anything else . . ."

"Annie," he said. "You might as well have cut off my right arm."

Annie shook her head. "I doubt that."

"Damn it. How can you tell me what I'm feeling?" He bit down on his lower lip in anger, only it hurt. "Okay, maybe that was a slight exaggeration. But I wasn't talking about me. I was talking about *you*. Something *you've* loved and lost."

He heard the sharp intake of breath and saw her flinch from the corner of his eye.

She sighed. "Right at the moment, I'm obsessed with having control over my life." She spoke matter-of-factly, like she'd rehearsed a speech. "You know, to be free of—"

"So, we're both committed to being single and free. It's refreshing to see a woman who hasn't made it her mission in life to domesticate every single male that comes along." He wasn't sure he really believed that, nor did he believe she was buying it. But another episode of her trying to flee from him in the middle of nowhere was not something he needed.

"No," Annie said. "I'm not about to domesticate anybody. Either a man wants a relationship, or he doesn't. And, I admit, I do cherish my privacy. I've never been absolutely on my own before.

"But I'm also not committed to being single. Just free. You can have a good relationship and still have your own identity. You don't have to feel like you have to own your partner."

Her hair fell into her face as she turned away.

"You think men feel like they own their wives?" he asked.

"Some definitely do. For me, I just want to be free to make a difference in my own little piece of the world."

He gave her a brief nod. "I guess that's a little like me. But the difference is I take the bad guys off the street. You take good guys off the street, make snap judgments and play mind games that make a cop lose focus and get themselves killed." There he'd said it. He'd wanted to say that to a shrink for a very long time.

"My God Mark," Annie said. "Who hurt you so badly? Did you have a bad experience with a psychiatrist?"

Mark hit the brakes and forced the car to the side of the road.

Annie's seatbelt jerked her back. "Stop it!" she yelled.

He changed his mind. One pullover was enough. "Hell Dr. O'Brien, I don't need you to psychoanalyze my life. Let's just say yes. Some shrink hurt someone I loved, and it had drastic consequences. I don't want to talk about it."

"But—"

"Annie," Mark said. "Just be quiet."

His eyes were following the path of the broken yellow lines on the middle of the pavement. Broken like the paths of his life. But the verbal punch he'd struck at her came back like a boomerang and belted him right in the stomach.

Fortunately, he didn't have much time to think about it. They were pulling into the driveway. And through the darkness, his mother's house shone like a beacon of warmth and welcome.

Chapter 14

The breeze over the lake shot through her Annie's light cotton blouse. She rubbed her arms to relieve the shivering and goose bumps that seemed to pierce her skin like an ice pick.

She looked around and discovered that the chilly night air wasn't the only ingredient that made up this rugged land. The main difference between New York City and upper Wisconsin country at night was the country's sense of peace. The stars shone with a brightened intensity that the city couldn't provide with its streetlights, buildings and pollution. In New York, the city never really shut down. Horns honked and the traffic never stopped. Here, the lake shimmered in the darkness. Its only disturbance, a plop, a splash and then silence. Yet, in some ways, the stillness was louder than the city streets.

Mark stood in the front of the car. "Coming?"

Bother. If his mother was anything like him, Duncan's craziness might be a pleasant relief. She shivered now more from nervousness than from chill.

The porch lights came on and a figure stood at the top of the stairs. Annie walked behind Mark, who gave a woman with red, shoulder-length, curly hair and large gold hoop earrings a kiss on the cheek. She wore jeans, wedged sandals and a yellow sweater over a shirt.

"Hi Mom," he said. "This is Dr. Annabelle O'Brien, the woman I called you about."

Annie offered the woman her hand. "Hi, please call me Annie."

The woman looked her up and down, Annie thought possibly appraising her. She nodded and Annie blew an inward sigh of relief like she'd just past some unknown test.

"Annie. I'm glad to finally meet you. By the way, I have a name. It's not mom. It's Julia Driscoll. You can call me Julia." When she laughed, Annie's whole body relaxed. She felt immediately at ease.

A gust of wind blew in through the trees, causing the return of chills and goose bumps. She rubbed her arms through her cotton sleeves, trying to get warm. It didn't work. "It gets cold up here." Julia put her arm around Annie's shoulders. "You're freezing, honey. Let's get you inside." She turned to her son. "Didn't you have the sense to tell her to bring a jacket?"

Annie said, "It wasn't Mark's fault, Dr . . ."

"Julia."

"Julia. My jacket—my clothes were all . . ."

For a minute, the woman's eyes widened, and then she nodded. "Yes," she said quietly. "I'm sorry. Mark should have stopped at his apartment and brought one for you."

Mark sighed and leaped up the stairs onto the porch.

"I don't mean to be a bother. But I don't think Mark likes me much," Annie said softly.

A dog's bark came from the inside of the house.

"Well, my son doesn't like a lot of people right off the bat," Julia said, as they approached the steps. "And a lot of people don't like him right away either. He's an acquired taste."

"Hah," Mark said, on the top step.

A tri-color collie nudged its nose through the screen door, padded out and immediately leapt off its haunches in anticipation. Mark bent down and the dog lowered its paws onto his shoulders.

Mark ruffled the top of the dog's head. "Hey Lady, how're you doing girl?"

Lady licked his cheeks, then his nose then her focus shifted to Annie. She left Mark in a whirlwind of tail and bounded down the steps, nearly knocking Annie over in her excitement.

"Oh, a *collie*. Hi honey." Annie put out the back of her hand for the dog to sniff and knelt to her level. "You're a lovely, lady, do you know that?"

Julia laughed. "Yes, I'm afraid she does. She's rather spoiled."

Lady barked, circled three times then bounced back up the porch steps, stopping to look back at them.

Julia took Annie by the arm and ushered her through a wicker-furnished screened porch, into the house. The aroma of brewing coffee filled the air.

Julia turned to Annie. "When was the last time you ate?"

To be honest, she hadn't any idea. Sometime before she left for The Hole. "I think I grabbed a cheeseburger and a milkshake, but I don't remember what time."

"We'll have sandwiches and coffee in the dining room. Mark." His mother turned to Mark who'd started for the stairs. "You can help, too."

Mark stopped and turned back, his gaze meeting Annie's. She quickly looked away. Mark's scornful attitude obliterated the one decent thing he'd done for her. Like given her shelter. She swallowed the last of her pride and sat at the dining room table.

Julia settled a plate of sandwiches in front of her while Mark poured coffee. Annie took a bite of turkey sandwich.

A collie nose settled on her lap, tail wagging. The dog sniffed and focused her full attention on Annie's plate.

Julia looked up apologetically. "Lady down."

The dog took one more hopeful look at Annie, barked once and with a soft "woof" lay down under the table. Annie thought more than just crumbs would fall into her mouth.

"Lady would have you believe she'd die of starvation if you don't offer her at least half of what's on your plate." Mark said.

"Uh huh," his mother replied, passing potato salad to Annie. "And, I wonder, who trained her to do that?"

Julia now turned her full focus on Annie. "I know a little about what happened tonight. Just very little. I want to know the whole story. I want to know what we may be facing here."

Annie took a sip of coffee and settled down to explain.

When Annie had finished, Julia leaned forward, her expression clouded in anger. "That is abominable. If that is your ex-husband, Annie, they'd better catch him. God knows what he's liable to do next."

Mark coughed. "If it is her husband. Annie couldn't identify the voice."

"If her gut feeling tells her it was him. It was him."

Mark squared his shoulders. "Woman's intuition again."

"Yes, damn straight. Something men should develop."

When Julia faced Annie, she talked through gritted teeth. "Nobody has the right to hurt or intimidate anybody. Period." She put down her fork. "I want you to know something about this house. Since Mark's father died, and Mark moved to his apartment in town, I've used it as a kind of unofficial sanctuary for women in trouble. Abusive relationships, pregnancies, runaways. The police secretly bring them here until we can find resolutions to their problems. We don't have a name. We're not registered—so few people know about us. In the beginning, we had quite a few women, mainly from the Brighton area. Lately, not so many. I haven't had anyone come stay here in over six-months.

"I have a direct line into the police station and whenever I have a guest, usually a volunteer helps guard the place. Paul told me Mark will be your guardian angel."

"No," Mark said, sipping his coffee. "I'm going back to work tomorrow morning."

Julia raised her head. "I don't think so," she said.

"No, you don't," Annie said. "You're on a two-week furlough, and your boss ordered you to protect me. I'm your assignment."

"Thanks to you." Mark spoke between clenched teeth. He didn't look up from his coffee.

"Mark." His mother raised her eyebrows and half stood. "I will not have you talking to my guests that way. Now settle down."

Mark leaned back in his seat and stared at the two women. Julia stared back.

Mother and son. Annie could see the resemblance, despite his mother's copper hair and Mark's dark brown. But where Mark was belligerent and hostile, Julia was gracious and—what? Strong. Yes, Julia was a strong woman. She didn't think Mark would outstare his mother. She was right.

Mark shrugged. "My boss doesn't order me to do anything. He *suggested* I take a two-week furlough. He can try to bully me, but if I were determined, I could have been on the street the next day."

"Oh, so you admit I was right?" Annie said. "I mean, about needing some time . . ."

Mark's mouth was open, ready to speak, but Julia got to her first. "Of course, you were, Annie. Mark is a mess. Now Mark, don't you protest. You know it's true. Protecting this lady is a great assignment. She's an essential asset to Nager. And it will give you some badly needed time away from your job. Besides, this is Independence-Day week. You haven't had the Fourth of July off for years."

"Look, I brought Dr. O'Brien here because I knew she'd be safe.

They're going to need me on the streets this week . . ."

Julia's chin jutted straight out with belligerence. "Bull, Mark. You're not on street patrol. How will she be safe if she has an ex-husband with a screw loose threatening her unless there's someone who can handle him?"

Mark shrugged. "We're not even sure it was her ex-husband. He's supposed to be in New York. Besides, Annie's terrific in dealing with people. She's already got all the answers."

Oh Lord. This was going from bad to worse. Annie put down the cup a little harder than necessary. "I don't know how to handle a gun, nor fight a madman. If this is my ex-husband, and I'm saying if, because I don't know for sure, he'd be an ergo-maniac. A psychotic psychiatrist. A very dangerous man, especially since he knows how to get into your mind and play games.

"I'm not sure Mark's bringing me here has done you or anyone around you any favors. I really should find somewhere else to go. This isn't right to put you into the middle of this."

Before anyone could protest, Annie stood and moved to the back of her chair. Putting her hands on the back railing, she said, "I appreciate your taking me in like this. Tomorrow, if my tires have been replaced, maybe I could find more suitable arrangements. Somewhere that won't put anyone else in danger."

She wasn't looking at them. Didn't want to see their reactions. Just as she didn't want to look into a future of running scared.

Julia cleared her throat. "Oh yeah? Where?"

Stunned by the ferocity of her tone, Annie looked up.

"First of all, the garage is closed for the next couple of days. They go on a family outing near Sturgeon's Bay. So, you can't pick up your car until after the Fourth, anyway."

Annie sat again.

"Look, Annie, I don't know what Mark's issue is with you, but I'll tell you right now, I don't have a problem. You're honest enough to tell me you might be bringing danger here. You've stood up to my son, pretty well. Not everyone can do that."

Annie couldn't help but smile, but she couldn't quite look at either of them. She swallowed and regained her composure.

"Julia, I believe it was my ex-husband, Duncan—"

Julia interrupted. "Duncan. Did you say your husband's name was Duncan?"

Annie nodded. "Dr. Duncan Byrne. I was Dr. Annabelle Byrne. O'Brien is my maiden name."

Julia narrowed her brow, looking confused. "But I thought . . ." She scratched her head. "I thought Duncan Byrne was the one from NYU who gave you your recommendation."

Annie tried to smile but gave up. "He did. I didn't ask him to. He wasn't on my list of references, but someone called the university to check my references and apparently, they got him."

Julia nodded. "Yes, I remember. We called the university. He wasn't there, so his secretary gave us his home number. Something, I'm sure she wasn't supposed to do."

"It was nice of him to give me one, considering all we'd been through. But now, I'm wondering about his motivation."

"So, what makes you think it was him, then?"

"The message on the wall said, what he gave, he could take away. That's no idle threat. I believe that he's convinced that he gave me my life back when he took me in after my aunt died. He'd mentored me, so he took away my dissertation by taking credit for the research, then destroying the manuscript. He brought home a cat for me then destroyed him."

Annie started to tremble.

Mark left the room and came back with an afghan that he placed over her shoulders.

Annie hadn't seen him coming and started. She hadn't expected— "Thank you," she whispered. "I . . . well, thank you." She fingered the heavy wool stitching. This obviously had been hand-made by a loving member of the family. She looked to Julia for confirmation.

"That was made by my grandmother. We have two or three around. Every distaff member of the family had to make one. My mother's is on Mark's bed, the one I made is on my bed, my great- grandmothers— well, let's just say Lady made it hers when she was a pup. She chewed and swallowed so much of the wool, she needed surgery. Lucky, we have a good vet."

Annie chuckled. "Poor Lady. It's really not funny, but . . ."

"Not to worry. It's a great war story. If she'd died, it would have been awful. But that she survived that—and more—says a lot about this dog. So, you may laugh. We all do. Needless to say, she doesn't eat afghans anymore."

Mark was feeding Lady a piece of turkey under the table. "Mark! I'm telling you you're going to spoil—"

Mark grinned. "Going to? I think it's way too late for that."

This time Annie burst out laughing, got a fit of the giggles. When she stopped, Julia started up and that started Annie up again.

Mark raised his eyebrows, folded his arms and sat back, grinning from ear to ear.

So, Mark did have a sense of humor. And he really was good-looking when he smiled—the smile seemed to start from his eyes and work its way down to his mouth. Somewhere, under all that frustration, anger and hurt, Mark was a decent human being.

Julia was the first one to stop.

"Annie, I'm sorry to change the subject back to Duncan, but—tell me more about what you meant about him thinking he has the right to take whatever he wants from you."

Ouch. Her mood sobered. It was kind of like going from a class in Humor 101 directly to Criminal Psych 200.

Annie sighed. "Okay, if you really want me too. Anything, if it will help." She looked down at her plate and suddenly lost her appetite. "I'm positive Duncan could easily think he has the right to take away everything I have."

The baby. He'd given her a baby, and he'd essentially murdered it before it even had a chance to live. But that was something she wouldn't reveal to anyone.

Nobody said anything. A cheerful little yellow bird popped out of a cuckoo clock. Annie started.

Julia was frowning. "Jesus, honey, you're shaking through that blanket." She stood and faced her son. "Mark, be a dear and clean these up, will you?"

She didn't give him a chance to answer but straightened her sweater and moved toward the French doors. "Annie, come on upstairs. I've gotten a spare bedroom ready for you, and I have an assortment of clothes, including nightgowns you can wear. We'll sort all this out tomorrow.

"The stores will be open in the morning. We'll go shopping.

"I have a study and a bedroom downstairs where I sleep, so I won't wake you if I have an emergency and have to go into work."

Julia started for the stairs. "I work at all hours. This month I'm on night shift. Some weekends I don't come home at all."

"What about Lady?"

"She usually follows Mark around, or a neighbor looks after her. There's never lack of support in this town. You should know that. Nager is a tightly knit community."

The second time she'd heard that today.

Still—Annie opened her mouth to protest.

Julia said, "Look. You'll be safe here with us until we can either find somewhere safer, or until Mark catches this bastard." She started upstairs.

Annie started to follow but saw Mark staring at her. He had his hands on his hips, his expression unreadable. Why she cared about what this man thought about her, she wasn't quite sure. But his ambivalence hurt. She turned to follow Julia up the stairs and stopped.

Julia stood at the top of the stairs and turned toward them with both hands on the railing. Covered in shadow, Annie wasn't sure whether she was frowning or smirking.

<h1 style="text-align:center">Chapter 15</h1>

Mark slammed the dishes into the dishwasher and crammed the leftovers into the refrigerator. The footsteps overhead and accompanying laughter only made things worse.

He looked for his dog. "Come on Lady." She pricked up her ears, grunted and went back to sleep.

"Oh hell." Mark headed out the porch door and walked down the gravel path toward the lake, grabbing a handful of stones. He turned back once to see Annie and his mother's image in the upstairs window before the shade came down and only their shadows appeared.

What was it about Dr. Annabelle O'Brien that upset him? That she'd effectively put his career on hold for a half a month? Or was it because she was the first woman, he'd met who couldn't stomach him?

Mark felt a shiver pass through him. The image of that fragile doe-like creature caught in his headlights haunted him. Those light blue eyes mirrored her fear and vulnerability, but there was something else. He stepped onto the dock and nearly slipped on the wet surface. When he regained his balance, he leaned on a post. An image came to him. Lady, many years ago. The dog had given birth to a litter of still-born puppies. He'd never known animals could express such grief as when he'd taken those dead pups away. And now, he'd seen it again this evening in Annie's eyes. His heart rate increased. The similarity was unmistakable.

And something else. Annie had been in physical pain. She wouldn't admit to it, but something was wrong. Something more than slashed tires and a destroyed apartment.

He stood on the dock and threw a stone into the water. The moon had started to peek out from behind the clouds and reflected an accordion like ripple over the surface. Probably for the first time in his life, he actually felt like a heel.

Why the antagonism toward that woman? That he didn't like her, but just figured out he wanted to kiss her silly? That she had an independent spirit? He didn't hate independence in a woman. He admired it. He loved a woman he could have an intelligent conversation with. It wasn't that at all. Then what the hell was it?

Because she was a psychologist. What was it about the profession that created monsters? Shrinks that had kitchen timers and cut off their sessions, sometimes in the middle of a sentence when their patients were their most vulnerable. So, that some poor bastard could go out and get killed.

He looked across the water toward the Campbell Inn. Laura. Back, wanting him to call her. Crap. She'd left him at the altar once, he was damned if he'd get shit on again. Now, all he wanted was easy. No complications. No strings.

He picked up a heavier rock and threw hard, nearly throwing out his elbow. The splash caused a minor tsunami onto the shore.

What kind of man was he?

The answer stung him in his gut. Made him feel like he was an emotional cripple.

He was the kind of man he'd always most despised. He was his father. His father had been a man who'd had a wife he'd run around on, pretending he had no responsibilities. Until one day, his mother caught him and insisted he get help, or she'd leave him. He'd gotten help and died. He was his father. The reason he'd never married. Laura Campbell had probably seen that in him and dumped him before she got permanently hooked.

The breeze was picking up.

Sadness overwhelmed him like those waves that drowned the rocks on the shore.

So then, why did Annie conjure up thoughts of matrimony and the chains of domestic life? He hadn't thought about it—since Laura.

Somewhere a wolf howled in the forest. A motorboat softly puttered back to its dock, running a trail of waves from the restaurant across the lake.

And somewhere deep within his heart, he knew he could never be his father. He could never cheat on his wife.

"Mark?"

Mark spun around, caught off guard by the gentle voice behind him.

"Annie. What are you doing out here?"

She hadn't changed yet but wore a jean jacket over her blouse. His. She looked good in it. Comfortable. Too big, but comfortable like an oversized sofa.

In light provided courtesy of the moon, stars and dock lights, her hair shimmered down her shoulders. There was both delicacy and strength in that face.

"Your mom wants to know if you want your old room?"

She walked past him and held onto the dock posts, gazing out over the lake. "How wonderful it must be to live here," she whispered.

Mark stepped closer, ready to respond. Annie suddenly turned and stepped forward. She bumped into his chest and an electrified emotional current ran across his skin.

But he had no time to reflect on his reaction. Something screeched across the dock. Mark jerked around and watched his dog slide to a halt and slam straight into them.

Mark's feet slipped out from under him. He grabbed at Annie's hand for balance and fell back into the water taking her with him. Lady was the only one who didn't fall in. She woofed, wagging her tail at them.

Shock covered Annie's face. Then she lit up with a child-like mischievous grin. She began to giggle. The giggle turned to laughter, and she was laughing so hard she nearly went under.

Surprised at a side of Annie he hadn't yet seen. He couldn't help but laugh with her.

As Lady continued to bark, Annie threw water at him, and he threw it back, until a blast of cold air frosted him. "Come on. Let's get out of here before we freeze to death." Mark grabbed Annie's hand and pulled her to shore directly under the dock light.

Annie was soaked through. Her hair wet, the jean jacket hung off the side of her shoulders, her blouse and bra clung to her skin.

Mark's body responded. He couldn't help it. He hated her, didn't he—*didn't he*? If so, why did he want her so badly? He moved close-- too close. He wasn't trying to be seductive. Annie wasn't moving away. In fact, she was looking up into his eyes, looking like she was trying to fathom what he was thinking. She moved closer and put her hand on his cheek. They were within kissing distance.

He was still deciding whether he should, when Annie, suddenly seeming to come to her senses, pulled away. She was moving backwards—breathing hard.

Under the light, he caught the astonishment then the longing in her eyes. Mark's libido went into overdrive. He was about to pull her into him and worry about consequences later, when she apparently thought about them now. Her body stiffened. Her expression blanked, and she backed onto the path.

Mark was about to follow, but he stopped. There was absolutely nothing to be gained by pursuing this. Nothing at all.

Annie nodded as though following his thoughts. She turned and walked back to the house, the dog circling her as she went.

Chapter 16

Mark strolled into the corner office he shared with Paul, Lady trotting at his heels. The collie ran to Paul, sat in front of him, wagged her tail then wiggled her butt.

"Hi Lady," Paul said. "Want a scratch?"

"Woof."

Paul rubbed Lady behind the ears and allowed her to lick him on the cheek. Then he gave her black butt a good scratch and told her to lie down.

Lady yawned, curled up under Mark's desk and chomped down on a chew bone.

Paul focused on Mark, his expression full of "what the hell are you doing here?" He cleared his throat and said, "You want some coffee?" He bobbed his head to a full coffee maker in the corner.

"Never could refuse a good cup of coffee." Mark went over and got a cup.

"Donut?" Paul offered, holding up the box.

"Yeah." Mark yawned and grabbed a chocolate donut.

Mark sat back on a chair facing Paul's desk and put his feet up. "And now tell me why when you're supposed to be protecting Dr. O'Brien, you're down here without her, at seven-thirty in the morning."

Mark made a display of looking at the Wal-Mart special battery-operated kitchen clock that was always ran slow. "Seven-fifteen," Mark answered. He took a bite of donut. "Annie's with my mother. They have stuff to do at the hospital." He washed the donut down with the coffee.

"Stuff? What kind of stuff does Annie have to do that can't be accompanied by you?"

"Look, my mother has to check on her patients, and Annie needs to cancel her appointments and pick up her laptop. They're coming here when they're done."

"Oh *great*! So, what happens if someone follows them? Catches Annie alone in her office? What then?"

Mark wasn't used to his mentor's curtness. It was starting to annoy him. "Look, Molly McGuire is on security this morning. She won't leave Annie."

Paul folded his arms. "How do you know that? She probably has other duties to perform."

"Because I asked her to. Molly will escort them back to the car."

Paul's eyes darkened, if that was possible under the dark shadows he hadn't managed to sleep off. "Do you ever follow directions?"

"Yes, frequently. But unlike you, I think I slept a little last night."

Paul put both hands on the desk, looking meaner than a hornet. "What do you mean by that?"

"I mean . . ."

Paul waved one hand at Mark and sat back. "I know what you meant. I'll be honest with you Mark. I'm worried. I couldn't get to sleep thinking about it. And I'm not going to rest easy until Julia and Annie get here."

"Look, Molly's a professional. She's a good shot, and she has a great left hook." He remembered when Molly McGuire decked him when they were in high school. His jaw still hurt when he thought about it.

"I'm not in the mood for jokes," Paul said. "Damn it Mark! If I'd wanted a security guard with Annie, I wouldn't have asked you. Don't leave her alone unless it's with Julia or me."

Mark was starting to get pissed. "Paul . . ."

"Mark, security don't carry guns."

Mark slowly nodded. "You're right. They don't. That's why I told her to bring a stun gun, just in case."

Paul harrumphed. "Stun gun. Need more than that to bring down a lunatic psychiatrist, Mark. Sometimes you have brains the size of . . ."

Mark huffed. Was there no end to the insults? He put down his coffee cup so hard, he spilled coffee on a stack of papers.

"Shit."

Paul sighed. "Don't worry about it. Look, I'm sorry. I didn't mean it. Let's start over."

Mark nodded wiping off coffee from his jeans with a tissue.

"So, I take it, you want to find out what's really going on, right?" "Yeah. There's a lot I want to know about Annie and this ex-husband of hers."

"Do we have an accurate description of him?"

Mark dug out a photo and flipped it over to Paul. "Annie gave it to me this morning."

Paul peered at it. "Looks like the guy wears a disguise without any outside help. Steel gray hair and beard. Prototype professor."

"Annie said his best photos were on his website."

"Okay, but first, I want to make a phone call to the NYPD." Paul picked up his phone.

Mark sat on the corner of his desk and rubbed the back of his ear. "Calling George?"

Paul put his hand on the mouthpiece. "Shhh."

"Morning. Lake Nager Police Department here. Need to speak with your Chief George Masterson. Don't tell me he's not there. He's always there."

Mark said, "Be nice. They may hang up on you. It's early in New York too."

Paul waved him away. "Okay, okay. I want to see if the NYPD has anything on this Duncan Byrne."

"Like the guy's a wanted felon?"

"I doubt that. But, if anyone knows anything, George will—or, he'll know where to get answers."

Paul rubbed his chin. "Half the department owe him favors. Let's see what we can get."

"George. Paul Reinert." He nodded, leaned back as far as his office chair would go and grinned. "Remember me? The one that provides you with two weeks of free vacations every year."

With one hand on the phone, Paul opened his desk draw with the other and groped for his cigarettes. He pulled out a pack, tapped the pack on the desk, until one peeked out, then expertly gripped it in two fingers and pulled.

"Yeah. Just coming to that part."

He cupped his hand over the mouthpiece. "Get on the other line." Mark sat at his desk and picked up the phone. "This is Mark. Met you when you and your wife were out here. How're you doing? Better yet, how's *she* doing?"

"I'm fine, she's fine. Pregnant with our third."

Mark felt a twinge in his stomach. Three children—something he'd never allow for himself. Still . . .

"So, what can the 'big apple' do for the resort town of Nager?" Paul spoke. "Look we have a situation here that might be serious.

Do you know anyone that covers New York University Hospital? Or the Sutton Place area?"

"Well, yeah. One of my detectives transferred from there. Why?"

"I'm interested in finding out if the names Dr. Duncan Byrne or Dr. Annabelle O'Brien ring a bell with anyone."

The man hesitated. "O'Brien doesn't . . . but, wait a minute, Byrne you say? A Dr. Duncan Byrne?"

"That's the name," Mark said.

"Why do you want to know about them?"

Paul answered, "Because his wife, Dr. Annabelle O'Brien recently took a job at the Nager Medical Center here, and someone's pulling some nasty stuff on her."

"What kind of nasty stuff?"

"Anonymous threatening phone calls, slashed tires, vandalized her apartment. Even killed her cat."

An uptake of air. "Aw shit. That's sick." He paused. "But it doesn't surprise me."

A sinking lump formed in Mark's stomach. The NYPD expected this? "How so? I didn't know you even covered that area."

"I don't. But my best detective transferred over here because of that case."

"Why would he do that?" Mark asked.

"Slight disagreement about how the case should be handled." "Wait a minute," Mark said. "What case?"

A shuffle on the other end of the phone, then muffled voices. "Take this will ya?" Slight pause. "I want you to talk to Detective Steve Rodriquez."

"Rodriquez here. What's up?"

"Paul Reinert. Chief of Police, Lake Nager." "Detective Mark Driscoll, also of Lake Nager."

Rodriquez chuckled. "Oh yeah. Heard of your vacation paradise. Got room for another detective up there?" Paul looked at Mark. "Sometimes."

Mark smirked. "You couldn't do without me, and you know it." "So, what do you need?" Rodriquez asked.

"Couple of questions." "Do my best."

Once again, Paul laid out the recent events.

"Oh hell, no. He killed her *cat?* There's a special place in hell for some people." Rodriquez seemed to change gears. "I remember the circumstances well. Last summer. This paramedic from New York Hospital called and asked the precinct to come out and help with an accident in Sutton Place. Very rich-very posh area, east side of New York. He'd reported that a Mrs. Duncan Byrne fell down the stairs in her townhouse when she was eight months pregnant. Her husband found her lying face down in a pool of blood."

Chapter 17

Something vial caught in Mark's throat and spread southward into his stomach. The lump in his throat burned. Annie had been pregnant and had a miscarriage. *A violent miscarriage.*

"Professor Byrne stated it was an accident. His wife went into shock and nearly died. Professor Byrne was devastated—or so he claimed."

Mark honed on "he claimed". Mark knew in his gut something was wrong.

"So, was it an accident?"

"Well, I can't honestly say. My chief assigned me to investigate the case. He had some doubts. His opinion was the same as the medic's. Something wasn't right."

"Why?" Mark asked.

"Well because the stairs had banisters on each side for her to grab onto. The stairs were carpeted so not slippery, and worst of all, the wife had a nasty knock in the back of her head."

"So?" Paul said. "That could have happened in the fall."

"Maybe. But she fell forward down those stairs. Her husband found her *face* down in a pool of blood. If she were knocked on the back of the head, it could only mean someone struck her."

Visions of Annie lying helpless at the foot of the stairs . . . a baby.

Chills navigated up Mark's spine. "So, what happened?"

"Nothing. I investigated. My chief investigated. We asked questions. Apparently too many. Dr. Byrne had connections, one being the DA.

His office told us to close the case—nothing to investigate. The fall had been an accident. I protested. Guess I went a little too high up and ruffled the DA's feathers. I was transferred shortly afterwards. Now I get to work holidays as well as weekends."

Mark started to pace.

Paul motioned him to sit and cool off. "You suspect foul play?"

There was a lull in the conversation. "Well—maybe . . . yes. I'm not easy about it. Mrs. Byrne was so distraught. Wouldn't eat. Couldn't stop crying. The hospital wanted to send her for psychiatric evaluation while she was at the hospital. Dr. Byrne refused to authorize it. He said he was a psychiatrist and could damn well take care of his own wife.

"Sometime after that I heard she'd filed a restraining order against him. Said he was trying to kill her. It was her word against his. Dr. Byrne contended she was depressed and paranoid after the miscarriage. Then, a few months later I heard he'd divorced her."

"He divorced her?" Mark asked, his head suddenly starting to ache. He rested his elbow on his desk and pinched the bridge of his nose.

"That's the official story. The real one is Mrs. Byrne was the one who filed for divorce."

"A lot of conflicting information," Paul said, moving stacks of files from one side of his desk to the other and back again. He frowned.

"Yeah," the detective said. "A lot."

Mark grabbed the phone tighter. "Do you know what happened to him, after that?"

"Well, yeah, as a matter of fact I do. Nothing. He continued as head of his department."

"Oh. Nothing else?"

"Not quite nothing else. Just a rumor that floated in the department and was the brunt of jokes for a while. Apparently, the eminent, squeaky clean, psychiatrist got into a fight with another professor. Officially, the other guy started it."

"Over what?"

"Something to do with stealing his research. He claimed Byrne used it in a paper he published. He could never prove it, but he gave Byrne a fat lip. The other professor was suspended for a week."

Paul chuckled. Mark broke out into a grin that he couldn't help, and Lady softly woofed and went back to sleep.

"How did you find out about all this?" Mark asked.

"I keep a low profile and have spies at the University," Rodriquez said. "I want to find out what really happened that night. If he pushed his wife down the stairs, I'd love to nail the bastard. An eight-month fetus means a murder rap."

Mark shivered with apprehension. "Where is this Duncan Byrne now?" Mark asked.

"I heard he's supposed to be at a psychiatry convention this week."

"So, that would leave him out of being in Nager about now." Mark said.

"Lake Nager? Why would he want to go there?"

"Dr. O'Brien . . ."

"Oh. Mrs. Byrne is now Dr. O'Brien? Oh. Annabelle O'Brien . . ." Rodriquez said. "Sorry. She's going by her maiden name now, I assume."

"Yes. She was hired by our mental health center," Paul said. "Annie thinks her ex-husband might be behind these attacks."

Rodriquez whistled. "Oh brother. Well, judging from some of the things I've heard, it wouldn't be hard to believe it of him. But he can't be in two places at the same time."

"Just out of curiosity," Mark said, "What kind of things have you heard about Dr. Byrne?"

"Besides the fight? You'd have to talk to someone over at NYU, and they might be afraid to talk."

That aroused Mark's attention. "Wait a minute. Afraid to talk?" Rodriguez hesitated. "Well . . . It seems that people who cross Duncan Byrne have unpleasant things happen to them. Not physically. Nothing that would land him in jail. But rejected promotions, cancelled classes, perks that suddenly disappear. Stuff like that. Reading between the lines, he keeps his staff and student assistants on a tight leash. From what I heard, he'd tried to keep tight control over his wife, and she'd started to rebel. He hadn't liked that at all."

"When did they get divorced?" Mark asked, clicking on his laptop.

"After the media got hold of it, New York City separated into factions; men against the women. Very juicy. Duncan Byrne had the best divorce lawyer in the city. When Mrs. Byrne's lawyer brought up the fall down the stairs, Duncan, himself put on a show. He said it was all his fault. He should never have allowed her to go upstairs considering her hormonal imbalance. If he had been there—she'd never have fallen down the stairs. Quite an actor."

"You think it was an act?"

"Yes. I do," Rodriguez said. "I've seen all kinds of acts. This was a beaut."

"So, you think he could have hit her over the head and pushed her."

"I think he's capable of it. But no proof."

"What did Dr. O'Brien say?"

"She had no idea. She thought she'd seen a shadow but wasn't sure. She'd had nightmares about being pushed. But, she had quite a lump on the back of her head."

Mark's mind was racing. The sorrow in her eyes. Now he knew where it came from. Damn it all. Guilt slammed into him. He'd told her to go back from where she'd come, a place where she might be in mortal danger.

"Duncan claimed at the divorce trial that she was prone to clinical depression. That he'd taken her in when her aunt died, because she needed someone to take care of her. And she'd been so depressed while she was pregnant, she could hardly get out of bed. But I doubt that. She never missed a day of work until the accident."

This was a woman who took herself all the way across the country to take a job where she knew no one.

"Right. As I say, I don't know his motivation for wanting to rid himself of a baby and a wife. I don't think there was anyone else in the picture. She wasn't the heiress of a fortune. Still, I'd like to nail the bastard. So, keep in touch. I'll check out the convention. Make sure he's there."

Mark said, "I could come to New York and check it out. He wouldn't recognize me, and unofficially, I could do things that might get you in trouble."

Rodriguez said, "I appreciate the offer, but I have a lot of guys on the streets working with me. I can get one of them over there."

Paul jumped in. "I'd appreciate that. Now, any chance you could fax me a copy of the file?"

"I don't have the file. But I kept handwritten notes. Keep it under wraps though. I'm not sure I should be doing this without an official request."

There was a silent interlude. Mark and Paul said nothing. Soon, the fax hummed and sheets started to flow out. Mark got them and stapled them together.

Paul resumed the conversation. "Got it. Thanks. Just out of curiosity, suppose I could find out myself, but—does Dr. Byrne have a website or a blog?"

"Oh yeah. He has a website. But the interesting thing about it is . . ."

"Yeah?"

"His earliest pages and links referred to articles about general mental illness, neurosis, psychosis. Things like that. The tone changes the day after Mrs. Byrne fell down the stairs."

"Changes, how?"

"He starts making references to murder-suicide. References to death by drowning. Go to the site and see for yourself. Are you familiar with Edgar Alan Poe?"

The hairs stood up on the back of Mark's neck. "Yeah. Very."

"Good. Well, this should interest you then. There's a reference to the poem *Annabelle Lee* that gave me chills. Damned creepy. Come to your own conclusions. Maybe I'm making too much of this."

"Thanks. I appreciate what you're telling me," Mark said. "I'll put George back on."

An exchange on the other end of the phone and George came back on. He said, "You think she's in trouble?"

"Oh yeah. I'm almost positive she is," Paul replied.

"Keep in touch. We'll try to get what we can for you." They hung up.

Mark walked back to the seat in front of Paul's desk. "You think Annie has a paranoid personality or suffers from such bad depression, she's incapable of taking care of herself?"

"Nope."

"Me either."

Paul put in a call to the Hyatt in New York. Within five minutes he had the information he needed. "He's registered, Mark, and according to the desk clerk, his bed has been slept in and he's signed in for all his assigned workshops. So, what the hell happens now?"

"Was he scheduled to speak?"

Paul's eyes never left Mark. Slowly he nodded. "He spoke the first night of the convention. In front of some seven hundred people. It can't be him. Can't be."

"So, maybe we're looking for a hitman?"

Paul typed in Dr. Byrne's website. There, in gothic text was the poem, *Annabelle Lee*. His intent was clear if one could recognize the signs. On the right side was a photo of a painting. A woman with long, flowing blond hair lay face down beneath the water. She was dressed in white, water lilies surrounding her. This wasn't what the poem was really about. But it was becoming clear as to what Duncan Byrne *wanted* to make of it.

Chapter 18

Mark's apprehension turned to anger, then shifted gears into a sheer fright. It appeared there was more to be afraid of than he could have imagined. But still, it couldn't be Duncan. Duncan was in New York City. So, what the hell was going on? A hit man? That didn't fit the profile of murder-suicide if that was his aim.

The two men huddled in front of the computer screen, so engrossed they hardly heard the door squeak open, until Lady scrambled out from under Mark's desk and barked.

Mark turned around so fast, his neck wrenched. A shooting spasm rang along the side. Julia and Annie had come up behind him, peering into the screen.

"My God, don't you women ever knock?" Paul asked, with a growl.

"I'm glad we didn't," Julia replied. "You would have turned this off."

Annie leaned over Mark's shoulder. "My God," she whispered. "That's supposed to be me."

"Annie, you shouldn't see this," Mark said, turning to look at her. She remained composed, but her eyes revealed terror.

"He paints, you know. This is his work." She turned her head away and her gaze fell on the faxed notes." As Mark went to grab for them, she snatched them away and started thumbing through the pages.

"Oh my God." She was standing so close to him, he could feel the heat rise in her, the breathlessness panic in her voice. "You've been investigating *me?*" She was breathing hard.

Mark sighed. "Yes. We are." He looked her square in the eyes. "We need to know about your past to help figure out why he's trying to hurt you."

"So, why in the hell didn't you just ask me?"

Paul said, "We've tried, but you haven't exactly told us everything. Why didn't you tell us about your miscarriage?"

"Because it's none of your business. It's part of my life I'd rather not reopen."

"Annie, it's important," Mark said. "It may be the key to the whole thing."

"No. That has nothing to do with this situation. If you're going to scrutinize my whole background, I'd rather you leave me alone."

Julia was sitting on a desk, drumming her fingers on the top. Her eyes were narrowed. She looked like she was about to explode.

Annie backed away from the desk. "Julia, thanks for putting me up last night. But I think I need to leave."

Mark reached for her. She pulled away. "Get away from me, Mark. Thanks for your help, but I don't need it." She turned and walked out of the office.

Julia muttered, "Well, aren't you two something else? Now you've opened a situation that is such a personal tragedy, I don't think any woman could bear to have a bunch of men scrutinize it like this."

Lady growled at Mark. Damn it. Did females always side with each other?

"Well, why the hell did you just barge in here?"

He looked at his mother. Paul and his dog and stormed out.

Mark caught up with Annie as she was pushing open the outside door. He tried to put his arm around her, but she pulled away.

"No. Leave me alone."

"Come inside, please."

"Mark, I can't. I'm sorry." She started to cross the street, apparently not paying attention to the traffic, because a car stopped short, its brakes squealing. Mark caught her and hauled her onto the sidewalk.

"I hate you, Mark. I need to get away from you and this place."

He spun her around, his hands grabbing her shoulders. When she struggled, he held on. "And, if you left, where would you go then? Don't you think he'd find you again? Damn it, Annie. At least *we* care about . . . you." It had just slid out. He cared about her.

Annie looked at him in shock.

He let go and dropped his hands to his sides. "It's my job to investigate. It's what I do. The more I know, the quicker we'll catch whoever's doing this."

She turned on him. "Whoever's doing this? We know who's doing this."

"Annie. We called New York. Dr. Byrne can't be here. He's registered at the psychiatry convention. He was a keynote speaker the first night. He's been there every day."

Annie's face drained of color. "You're sure?"

Mark nodded. "Maybe he's hired a hitman. Maybe that's why you haven't seen him."

Annie shook her head and looked at the ground as if assessing the situation. When she looked up, she said, "No. He's here. I feel his presence. He might have gotten someone else to register for him. But, judging from that picture on his website, he means to kill me and lay my body into the water. He meant it when he said, 'if I can't have you nobody can'. And Mark," she looked up at him, her eyes wide. "If you get in the way, he'll kill you too."

Mark turned her to face him. "Let him try. As you say, I have a gun. I'm not afraid to use it."

"Damn it Mark—"

"Hi Mark."

They turned in the direction of the new voice. Laura Campbell, dressed in a black silk suit with pearl earrings dangling from her ears, had walked up behind them.

"Girl friend?" she asked. She gave Annie the once over. "Breaking up already?"

Annie coughed. "Hello. I'm Dr. Annabelle O'Brien. And no, you have to be in a relationship to break one off."

The woman smiled. "Touché. A doctor no less." She eyed Annie. "Are you the new psychologist at the Medical Center?"

"Word certainly travels fast," Annie replied. "But yes I am."

"Let me introduce you," Mark said, stiffly. "Annie, this is Laura Campbell."

"I'm Mark's ex-fiancée."

"How have you been, Laura? Heard you got divorced." Mark derived a certain amount of pleasure from saying that.

"Just fine, love. And yes, I'm free." She blinked then raised one eyebrow and smiled. "I heard you're still single too, Mark."

Before Mark had a chance to back away, Laura leaned over and kissed him. Smack on the lips. She flashed a smile. "Maybe you'll remember that. Nice to meet you Annie."

Mark, sickened by the display, abruptly pulled away.

"We're having our fireworks tomorrow night. If you come, you're invited to a light supper and cocktails. You can bring Dr. O'Brien and even Julia if you'd like."

"Thank you very much, Laura, but we have our own celebration on the Fourth." Julia had come up behind them, and her tone implied she'd rather chew glass.

Laura frowned and shrugged a shoulder. "Suit yourself. The invitation stands."

"We'll probably watch the fireworks from our boat on the lake," Mark replied.

Laura turned and stepped back into Mark's space. "Well, if you change your mind, you know where I am. I can give an awfully good party." She ran her finger over his cheek. "But you already know that."

Mark blew out a puff of air. The perfume that had once intoxicated, now nauseated him.

Laura said, "Nice meeting you, Dr. O'Brien." She glared at Mark's mother. "Julia."

Mark knew his mother's expressions well. The flatness in her smile. The narrowed eyes. Nonverbally, she communicated, "Stay away from my son. Stay away from all of us."

Julia pierced her lips together as Laura sauntered across the street toward the Campbell Inn.

Julia put her arm around Annie. "Come on honey. Let's go shopping. If it weren't the best restaurant in town, and if my family hadn't been so close to hers for all these years, I'd never suggest it. But later, we can have lunch at the Campbell Inn, unless Mark decides to arrest you for something." Her smile mocked him. "In that case, I'll bring a bottle of wine, some bread and cheese and we can have a picnic in your jail cell."

"I'm not going to arrest . . ." They left him standing in the middle of the sidewalk, totally off balance, shaking his head.

Paul came out, Lady padding behind him. "So, there they go. I'm wondering if it really is a good idea to leave those two alone."

Mark rubbed his ear. "Your idea. But no. I think they're lethal." He chuckled. "But, as far as Annie being seen in town, I think it's a clever idea. It will flush out her attacker. And, as you said, my mother is a . . ." He looked at Paul. "Does she have a gun?"

"Offered her one. She already brought hers from home."

"That's my mom. Always prepared."

Paul looked in the direction of the Campbell Inn. "Wasn't that Laura I just saw with you?"

"Yep. Invited us and Annie to her annual Fourth of July bash tomorrow. We declined. My mother's attitude is 'whatever it is, I'm going to be doing something else'."

"Mark, you harboring any unresolved feelings toward the lady?"

Mark had to think for a second on that one. Did he still have a thing for Laura Campbell? Her dark eyes, white skin and black hair flashed before his eyes. A beautiful woman. Even more beautiful now than when she'd been in college. But a hardness had crept into her eyes. He realized it had always been there, he'd just never noticed. He shook his head. "I really don't think so."

Paul tilted his brow, looking at him uncertainly, but said, "Good." He patted Mark's shoulder. "So, are you planning on following them around all day?"

"That's my intention. And what better way than to just happen to meet them on the street and suggest we go over to the carnival for some junk food."

Paul nodded. "Yep. Nothing like a good old-fashioned carnival to bring up one's spirits."

"My thoughts exactly." They stared at the receding figures of the two women going into a dress shop.

"By the way," Mark said. "We're having our own cookout on the Fourth. Then we could take the ladies out onto the lake to watch the fireworks."

Paul smiled. "Wish I could," he said. "I have to make sure our volunteer police force is in place. I'm having one positioned over near your house, just in case."

"Thanks. I appreciate that."

"So, I'm going to go back in and make up the duty rosters. See if I can follow up some more with George and Rodriguez. He's supposed to do some more checking into the Byrne-O'Brien divorce. Maybe we'll find something else."

"Good," Mark said. "Meanwhile, I'll tail Thelma and Louise."

Chapter 19

The Campbell Inn stood on a small hill adjacent to the boardwalk and across the street from the Village Green. In front of the inn spread a gravel parking lot that functioned as the village's central and free parking lot. The lot was packed.

Duncan Byrne maneuvered his SUV through the aisles and lucked out. Someone pulled out, and Duncan took his spot.

Crowds were cutting through the lot from the boardwalk to the inn or toward the carnival. On the boardwalk, the people went from shop to shop, entering the bait and tackle shop, buying candy at the fudge store, and standing in long lines at the hot dog and other food stands. Especially the ones that offered elephant ears. Duncan thought he might buy a cherry one and look around for familiar faces.

Duncan didn't like to be wrong—ever. But this time he might have blown it. He'd put the tracking device under Driscoll's car, but his Chevy was parked at the police station.

He'd put a tracker under Annabelle's car but, since he'd slashed her tires, her Impala was at the local garage, which was closed for the holiday. He banged the side of his head with his palm. *Stupid— stupid—stupid.*

He got out binoculars and focused, then settled down and surveyed the territory. No Annabelle Lee. No Mark Driscoll. She was probably hiding out and he was probably with her. Maybe a cabin in the woods somewhere. A little love nest for two. He—

Duncan started to let out a scream of rage and smacked his palm over his mouth.

Back to the binoculars, he focused on blondes in bikinis who resembled Annabelle. No one even came close.

When he was satisfied that Annabelle was not on the boardwalk, Duncan got out his notebook and turned to his checklist. He'd found Annie—check. Found where she lived—check. Made threatening phone calls—check. Slashed tires—check. Put tracking devices under their cars—check. Annihilated apartment—check. Killed cat—check.

Killed Annie—-not yet. Killed himself—not yet. Checkmate—not yet.

He thought he knew where Mark Driscoll lived, an apartment in the same complex as Annabelle. But he doubted she would be there--not after what happened to her apartment.

He'd also followed the signal from Driscoll's tracking device to a location on the lake several miles out of town. Where he'd taken her? His family's home? Now, *that* was a possibility. He'd have to rent a boat to pin down the exact location. He put that on his 'things- to-do' list.

Across the street, the clock on the Village Green chimed one o'clock. A white banner sign read "Nager's Independence Day Carnival" in large red and blue letters. A Ferris wheel churned upward over the tree line. As Duncan got out of his SUV, the muted laughter and screams from the Nager's Independence Week Carnival became instantly annoying. The aromas of cotton candy and popcorn he'd loved when he was a kid, now nauseated him.

So, what to do first. Check in at the Inn, or check out the board walk? He decided on the latter.

Duncan glanced at his reflection in the side view mirror and a prickly sensation ran across his neck. He wasn't sure why, except he had this feeling he was being watched. No. No one seemed to be paying attention to *him*. Annabelle or that detective wasn't in sight anywhere, so what was the problem? But the feeling wouldn't go away.

Paranoia? He hadn't eaten since the night before. On the boardwalk, a hot dog stand loomed a hundred yards away. Better than nothing. He needed to eat.

He blended in with a group of other shorts and sandals wearers. First on the hot cement, then up the three steps onto the boardwalk and toward the concession stand.

He'd almost reached the line when a collie frolicked toward him. The dog stopped, wagged its tail and sniffed his ankles.

Duncan's first instinct was to silence the stupid mutt eternally. Instead, hoping to send it on its way, he reached down—and, the dog growled. Duncan pulled away as though he'd been zapped with a live wire. The wagging tail stopped. The dog's hair rose off its body and it backed up. No mistake. The head was lowered, the teeth bared, the lip curling into its face.

"Lady—come!" A voice yelled from somewhere in the middle of the crowd. The owner appeared and made his presence known. He bent down and leashed the collie. "Sorry. Are you all right? She's feeling way too good."

The man wore a badge on his belt. Duncan would have recognized him anywhere. Mark Driscoll. So, he had a dog, did he? He made a mental note to write that into his notebook for future reference.

When the mutt had been leashed, Duncan started to turn away, when he heard the low throated growl. He whirled back. "Huh?"

The dog had her upper lip raised with a set of brilliant white canines visible.

"Jesus," Duncan said. "You need to muzzle that thing."

"Damn, Lady," Mark Driscoll muttered, looking up at Duncan. "I'm sorry. She normally doesn't react that way."

"Whatever," Duncan replied. "You hold that animal. It's a menace."

Duncan was ready to lay it on Mark and threaten to sue his ass when he realized that Mark might already have his photo. Annabelle had probably squealed to the detective that it was him who was harassing her. And, despite his new identity, he didn't need to call attention to himself, especially to Mark Driscoll.

He turned, and with a sideward glance at the dog, he hurried away.

The parking lot lay at the bottom of steps that climbed up a small hill to the Campbell Inn. As Duncan stood at the top of the porch steps, he could see almost all the shops on the boardwalk, halfway down the street and onto the Village Green. The screen door banged behind him as he entered a vast glassed-in porch that ran from one side of the inn to the other. A perfect place to sip cocktails and watch people come and go.

The lobby was crowded. Mostly with people waiting to get into the restaurant. Above its double glass doors, a sign read, 'No shoes, No shirt, No manners, No service'.

Duncan skirted around the crowd and made his way to the front desk.

A pretty brunette stood behind the registration booth. She had long black hair that swept up the back and wore a black suit accentuated by an American Flag lapel pin. "Happy third of July," she said, much too energetically for his taste. "Can I help you?"

She looked him squarely in the face, and he wondered if she was sizing *him* up. Probably. She had sharp eyes. The kind that didn't miss much. Good. Just the type of person he needed. She'd know the people in town. She might be able to assist him in his final adventure.

"Morning." Duncan broke into a leisurely smile. "Wow," he said.

The woman cocked her head and regarded him. "Wow?" she said. "Not, I'd like a room for the night or reservations for dinner?"

Duncan looked over at the computer, trying to see the names. He couldn't quite make them out. "Both," he said. "I have a room reserved. Name's Edgar Allenton."

She scrolled down on her computer. "Oh yes, Mr. Allenton. You're registered. You'll be with us a week. Corporate rate."

"Yes, that's correct."

"All I'll need now is a business card."

The woman had a dynamite smile, and her eyes sparkled as though she had a secret that she shared with nobody. He'd bet most men would fall under her spell. *Most men.*

He handed her his business card; one of many with fake identification.

"A salesman. Are you here for our Fourth of July Festival?" she asked.

No, you idiot. I'm here to execute my ex-wife.

Duncan mimicked the grins of the tourists. "Partly." He squeezed through his teeth so politely it made his molars ache. "I'm mixing business with pleasure. Looking for some old friends."

"I might be able to help you there. I've lived here almost all my life. I'm Laura Campbell."

"Ah, the Laura Campbell of the Campbell Inn. Owner?"

"In a way. My father owns the place."

"Well, Miss Laura Campbell, if you're not too busy later, maybe you'd like to have a drink with me and tell me all about this lovely town of yours." *And the people in it.*

She raised her eyebrows. Wary, he thought. But interested, by the slow smile crossing her face.

"Unless you're married?" he asked.

"No. I'm divorced."

"A growing trend, I'm afraid. We have something in common. We can commiserate on our marital war stories." He laughed. "Maybe about four or so. I'll still be on duty, overseeing the bar, but I can meet you there."

Laura brushed a stray hair off her neck. "So then, if there's anything you'd like, or anything's not to your satisfaction . . ."

"Oh, I think everything will be to my satisfaction," Duncan said with a smile he hoped suggested leisurely walks on the beach at sunset.

A smile trembled over her lips as she pushed the register in front of him. The kind that suggested, 'Yes. You'll do. I'd rather like a romantic interlude'. She said, "Would you kindly sign here?"

Duncan made sure his hand brushed hers as he accepted the pen.

Pink crept into her face. Yes, here was information for the taking.

She dangled the key in front of him. With a large grin, he picked it out of her hand, holding on just a moment longer than necessary. "I'd like to go and check out the carnival for a few hours."

"Good idea. Best in the Midwest. Would you care to go to your room first?"

"No, but could you have someone bring my luggage up?" He slapped a fiver onto the desk. "It's in my SUV. Would that be all right?"

"Of course."

Duncan gave her his SUV's description. "I'll see you at four then, in the bar?"

She gave him a casual, polite nod then turned to wait on another customer. But he felt her eyes following him as he strolled across the lobby and out the door. Yes. The woman was interested. And he was interested in what she could give him.

Duncan stepped out onto the top of the porch steps when he saw *her*. Annabelle, with another woman, and they carried packages in their arms. That had to be the famous Dr. Julia Driscoll. She looked like the photo on the hospital wall.

His Annabelle looked good. White cotton dress, scoop neckline, spaghetti straps. Sexy, but tasteful. Chuckling, he knew she'd just bought it. He watched them dump the packages into the trunk of a Mercedes, then turn and walk back in the direction of the carnival.

Detective Driscoll and his dog—this time on a leash, strolled behind them. He appeared to be tailing them. Why would he do that? Duncan walked onto the boardwalk and took in the carnival—Fourth of July atmosphere. The shops were full of souvenir hunters, and those searching fishing gear and renting boats for the evening's festivities.

He entered a shop with a sign hanging out front that read *Pop's Boat House. Boats for Hire, Tackle, Bait, Fishing equipment, Beer, Pop, Ice Cream. Guide available. Inquire within.*

A thin, short man who looked like he could have been anywhere from between sixty to a hundred was just finishing up with a customer.

"Sir, can I help you?" He pointed to a duplicate sign from outside. "I'm Pop."

"Pop. Well, well. Do you have a boat I can rent for two days?"

The man scratched his white goatee and slowly shook his head back and forth as though thinking about it. "Well, I *had* them all rented out, I'm afraid . . ."

He put his elbow on the counter and rubbed his ear. "The thing is you see . . ."

Duncan frowned, exuding disappointment. "Aww, no. You see I just got into town—staying at the Campbell Inn over there . . ." He nodded toward the inn.

"Ah, I see. Now, as it happens, the people who were supposed to rent a boat for three days didn't show up. I doubt they'll show now. You might want to pay the remainder of their stay?"

A corner of Duncan's mouth turned upward. Yeah. Sure. Stupid tourist that he was. How much would that cost him? He asked.

They haggled and came to a compromise. So, he'd have a boat for the next few days, so what? He'd gotten what he needed.

He looked into the display case. Hunting and fishing knives. A Gerber AR 3.00 BBS with a serrated edge caught his eye. Easy to open button. Nasty piece of work. He could hear it cut across the throat or cracking through the ribs of some terrified victim. Oh, this was nasty. He could picture Annabelle, pleading for her life . . .

"Sir?" The store owner had his hands on the counter, his eyebrows raised in question. "Can I get this one out for you?"

Duncan's lips spread into a thin-lipped smile. "Yes. I think that will do nicely."

Chapter 20

Annie and Julia walked across the square toward Lake Nager's famous carnival. The one-week wonder of upper Wisconsin boasted of its Ferris wheel, roller coaster, carrousel, bumper cars and a midway.

Somehow or other, Mark, Paul and Lady met up with them as they crossed the green. Somehow or other indeed. Annie suspected she'd seen Mark pass by several shops where she and Julia had been. He'd never actually been in sight as they'd come out, but by the next store, he'd passed by again. And, of course, there was Lady. She was socializing with everyone, apparently well-known and well-liked. A female version of 'hail fellow—well met'.

Annie once more felt under more protection than she liked. She'd always had someone watching over her. Her parents. Then when they'd died in that car accident, her aunt had taken especially good care of her. Even sent her to a private high school in New York City. She'd scraped together the funds to make sure Annie went to NYU.

She'd loved the school. Loved her aunt's townhouse in Greenwich Village, just a short walk away from the school. And when her aunt died, there'd been Duncan who'd swept her off her feet. He'd provided for her, loved her, married her—no sense in reliving everything Duncan had done. It just made his downward spiral sadder.

But, in all this, came the realization that she'd never once been on her own. Never able to make her own decisions. She knew she was a lot stronger than anyone gave her credit—even stronger than she gave herself credit.

So, when the Chief of Police and Nager's premier detective *happened* to meet up with them, she felt claustrophobic. She'd been enjoying Julia's company. And Julia was more than capable. She was a strong woman equipped with a gun she'd taken out of the closet before they left. A gun she said her husband had taught her how to use. So, why couldn't she spend one day—

Annie suddenly realized why it was important to her to spend some quality 'girl' time with Julia. There hadn't been a day since her aunt passed away that she hadn't missed her. And there hadn't been a day since she'd been with Duncan that she'd had a real girlfriend that she could do things with, like she'd been doing with Julia this morning. And now these male invaders were usurping something she'd missed for years.

Oh well. Once again, they were only looking out for her welfare. But she was still pissed that they'd been so brazen about checking out her past, without consulting her. It was as though *she* were the suspect.

By this time, everyone seemed to be in a good mood, even Mark, who cracked jokes. They laughed at almost everything—but she noticed one thing. The men didn't give her much room to breathe. They clung to her like tight-fitting clothing. Every once in a while, she'd pull back to give herself space. But they'd stopped right along with her.

Mark took her arm. "Listen, look for familiarities. If Duncan is here, he might be in disguise. Whatever you do, don't get cornered alone. One of us must be with you at all times. Got that?" His eyes glared into hers like she was a naughty schoolgirl who'd broken a rule on a field trip.

Well bother, that certainly broke her mood. Annie's pride led to a flare up of temper. She pulled her arm out of his. "I got that Mark, loud and clear. You don't have to scold *or* crowd me. Knock it off."

She bounced two steps ahead of him and caught up to Julia and Paul.

He was beside her in a millisecond. "Just let me do my job and protect you, okay? If I lose you, I can't be sure of your safety, Annie."

"So, why aren't I at home, locked in the house?"

Paul grinned and raised an eyebrow. One eyebrow. Annie wondered how he did that. She could see two eyebrows and wide quizzical wide eyes, but one eyebrow? That was talent.

Mark rubbed the back of his ear. "That probably wouldn't be a bad idea." But then he shook his head. "No. Because, you know Duncan. We don't. I want him to try to make a move while we're here, so I'll know what and who we're dealing with."

Paul nodded a confirmation. Annie loved it; the exchanges between these two men. Paul could easily be Mark's father, a role she bet he'd taken when Mark's father had been killed. She looked at Paul and Julia and wondered why they'd never gotten together. It seemed like a natural progression.

Julia stopped the group. "Well, now that we've all agreed to use Annie as bait, if you see Duncan, Mark, you can ram through all these people to get to him."

Paul laughed. Mark rolled his eyes.

Annie giggled. The giggle escalated into a full-blown belly laugh. But the laughter turned into the sharp pain that had become a staple of Annie's physical diet over the past year. Breaths came shallow. She turned her body away from Mark's gaze—not wanting him to see her expression.

But he'd noticed. "What's wrong?"

Tears streamed down her face. "Nothing. I . . ." *Lie, Annie. Lie again.* ". . . laughed too hard, I guess. Have to stop . . . a . . . minute."

Julia said, "Annie, are you . . ."

But Annie bent over, holding her abdomen. A man on the edge of a group of passersby stepped out and caught her. "You all right?"

She was about to say "yes" and "thank you", when she turned into him and came face-to-face with a man about five-foot-eight, with steel-gray hair, a beard and blue-gray eyes. Annie cried out and pulled away from him. He resembled Duncan.

Damn it. Stop it Annie. Just because a man has a beard . . . But at least the pain was gone.

The man stepped away. "Are you all right? You nearly went down there. Be careful. The heat will do that to you. You probably should get into the air-conditioning."

Annie scrutinized him. Although there were similarities, same height, beard, eyes; it wasn't—couldn't be him. His tone quality— vocal inflections and scent were different, but most of all, this man's eyes exuded warmth and concern.

Suddenly Annie realized why, after all these years, she knew what it was about Duncan that made her shiver. His eyes were cold— non-feeling, even when professing his love. As a psychologist, hadn't she seen through him?

But right now, she was becoming a victim of her own paranoia— or something. A man had a beard and she assumed it was Duncan.

"Thank you. I'm fine, now. I appreciate your concern."

"You're welcome. For a minute there, I thought you might have sprained your ankle. Couldn't have that." He turned away and disappeared into the crowd.

It all happened so fast that Annie hadn't noticed Lady standing behind Mark, or Mark holding her there, or the low throaty growl. They turned toward the direction of Lady's displeasure. Just a line of people at a lemonade stand.

Mark loosened the leash. But the hackles on the collie's fur were still up.

The man at the head of the line was the same as the one Lady had been barking at on the boardwalk. The man paid, took his lemonade and disappeared behind a ride.

"Do you know him?" Annie asked.

"No, but Lady hates him and that makes me suspicious."

"How do you know she was barking at him?" Paul asked.

"Because she had a run in with him on the boardwalk." He related the experience. "Anyway, she doesn't like him. And the feeling is mutual."

Julia frowned. "I think we should take our minds off people we don't like for a little while." She pointed toward the rides. "Let's go on the Ferris wheel. Annie, this is a 'must see'. You can look all over Lake Nager and over to the adjoining lakes. You can even see our house."

Mark was grinning from ear to ear, standing at the base of the ride, shielding his eyes from the sun with his hands while looking up at the top. "You know the Ferris wheel was invented by George W Ferris. He made it for the Chicago World's Fair in 1893." He looked at Julia and Annie. "I'll bet you didn't know that, now, did you?"

"I . . ." Annie did know. But she didn't want to spoil Mark's moment. She shook her head.

The gondolas were coming to a stop, picking up two passengers for each car then inching upward to let the next group on.

Mark held the chair and offered his hand. But the pain, as sharp as if someone were slicing her with a knife, returned. Damn it. Annie wanted to hug her stomach. Take pain pills. Drown herself in the lake. Anything to get rid of this.

"Annie, go on," Julia said.

But Annie shook her head trying not to reveal the episode. It was almost too much of an effort to say, "You go on. Someone has to hold Lady."

Paul and Julia got on and their car moved upward.

A boy of about twelve holding a box of popcorn had just gotten off. He looked at Annie. "Hi. I'm Kevin. I'm eight-years-old. Are you Mark's girlfriend?" Without waiting for a response, the boy said, "Mark, can I play with Lady, while you go on the ride?"

A broad grin crossed Mark's face and he nodded. "There," Mark said. "See? You don't have to hold her, after all." He handed the boy Lady's leash.

The boy smiled. "Thanks."

Mark climbed into the next car. He reached out his hand to Annie. "Thanks Kev, I owe you one."

She shook her head. "I'd . . . I'd . . ."

A glint appeared in Mark's eye. "Not afraid of heights, are you?" Pain or no pain, that was a challenge she couldn't refuse.

Chapter 21

Duncan saw the whole thing. He felt in his black leather waist pack for the knife he'd bought in the shop. He managed to get the knife out of its sheathe and ran his fingers over the point, pricking himself.

Damn. Duncan put his finger up to his lips until the blood ceased to flow. But his mind was somewhere else.

She was there. Right by the Ferris wheel . . . and . . . she wasn't getting on. The other two were on. The detective was reaching out. She'd turned pale. Looked like she was in pain again, the symptoms that wouldn't go away for a long, long time. He chuckled. Pain suited her well.

The detective was reaching for her. Annabelle was saying something, backing away. Waiting in line behind them, Duncan inched closer.

The Ferris wheel began to churn. The chair rocked. Duncan started to reach for Annabelle, but the detective got her first and pulled her into the car as the Ferris wheel began its climb.

A shooting pain knocked into his ribs. An elbow. "Hey. Don't cut in line." The woman was big. Bigger than him. Much bigger. He gave her a long, hard, cold-eyed stare. The kind that had sent students fleeing into passive submission. Annabelle had learned to keep her mouth shut when he shot her that look.

The woman immediately backed down. Good. The bitch.

But that was when he heard that damned dog again. A kid was holding her. A *kid*!

"Lady! Stay Lady."

Rage gnawed at Duncan's gut. He moved back into the crowd and away from the devil dog and its young disciple.

How dare that detective snatch *his* Annabelle. He would not get away with this.

They were almost halfway up. The sun reflected off the gondola and Duncan had to squint to see them. But he saw. Oh yes, he saw. Mark had put his arm around her.

Duncan wanted to climb up the steel girders of the ride. To reach them. To tear them apart. To throw them over the edge of their compartment, hundreds of feet to the ground.

Instead, he'd have to settle for adding Mark Driscoll to his check list of things to do.

<h1 style="text-align:center">Chapter 22</h1>

Mark didn't understand his body's reaction to Annie—at all. He'd always been proud of his instincts regarding people. He was usually right. With Dr. O'Brien, he'd taken an instant dislike to her. Now, next to this woman in crisp white cotton, hair that fell down her shoulders and wearing some kind of flower perfume he'd love to roll over in . . . He wanted so badly to kiss her. Part of it, he thought, was that this woman was not Dr. O'Brien. She was Annie to him.

When Annie pulled away from him, he realized he'd been staring at her. His hand had been around her shoulders.

Annie had inched away so her body no longer touched his. She held on to the side of her seat.

He repulsed her that much?

He cleared his throat. "Um . . . Sorry, Annie. It's my protective nature. I didn't mean to crowd you."

Her eyes read 'sure you didn't'. "Look Mark, I don't mean to be rude to you. You've been really wonderful."

Here it comes. Here's where she says I don't like you in that way. Well, God knows I've told the same thing to more women than I can even remember.

"But I need space. I don't want a relationship with anyone. I want to be free of entanglements. I want—I want to be free."

Huh? That had been his line. Mark couldn't help it. He grinned.

Annie looked a little taken back. Maybe she expected him to say how attracted he was to her, expected him to plead with her, tell her that he'd fallen desperate in love with her . . . But why should she expect that? Not all women were head over heels in love with him.

Besides, she was still mad at him for digging out that portion of her life that was intensely private—something, she obviously didn't want anyone to know.

But one thing he did want to know. Why the hell she experienced that pain so frequently. Was it because of her miscarriage? Maybe his mother could help him with that.

The Ferris wheel was coming to the top. "There, over there," he said pointing across the lake. "That peninsula is where our house is, hidden in the trees; beyond that is the lily pond, and behind the house is the driveway that goes out to the highway."

"It's lovely Mark."

But Annie's focus had changed direction. She pointed straight down.

Mark stared at where he thought she might be pointing and finally gave up. "What are you looking at?" Hundreds of feet below, the man whom Lady had growled at was looking straight up at her. Why? But then he saw him move away and head across the parking lot onto the boardwalk where he disappeared as the Ferris wheel descended.

Chapter 23

Mark stood in his boat looking for things he might have overlooked when he'd made repairs, after an overlong and cold winter. He hadn't taken her out yet. Still, wouldn't hurt to check it one more time.

A pontoon drifted slowly by the dock. Mark's head jerked up at the sound, and he reached for a gun that wasn't holstered in his polo shirt. Knee-jerk reaction. He was nervous tonight.

The passengers in the pontoon waved. He waved back.

If it weren't such an important family tradition, he'd keep Annie inside tonight. Watch the fireworks from a bedroom balcony.

Mark shook off the possibility. No. He didn't want to disappoint Annie or his mother after Julia and her friends had gone into so much detail about the fun they had on the boat every Fourth.

Annie. Mark normally didn't notice what women wore, unless the clothes showed off some great female feature. Annie's maroon capri's with matching tank did just that. The dark captured the light of her long braid, hanging down her shoulder, almost touching her . . . He sighed as he checked the life preservers.

His friends had taken to her immediately. He marveled at her social skills and ease at handling strangers. That had never come easy for him. He'd had to work at it, and half the time, he still didn't come across as "charming".

Mark looked at the perfect summer late-afternoon sky. The Weather Channel had been predicting storms, but the system had stalled somewhere in Minnesota. No telling when it would arrive with some pretty nasty weather. For now, it was a perfect night for a ride around the lake. A great night for fireworks.

Someone coughed; something barked. Mark jerked his head around once again, and this time—damn it—it hurt. "How did you two get down here without making a sound?"

Annie's gentle laugh rippled through the air and out over the lake. "Good question. The answer is we didn't. We made lots of noise. You were in a world of your own."

Mark put one hand on his hip, balancing the other on the steering wheel. "I was, was I?"

Lady barked and went into play position, her front leaning on her elbows, her hind end upright. Annie ran her fingers over her jaw and a quirk emerged from her mouth. "Yes, you were." Her voice held decision and humor. "And now, I'm going to sit here and watch you."

A grin overtook Mark. "You are, are you?"

"Yes, I am." Annie inched her way down to sit on the edge of the dock next to the boat. Now, her braid spilled over a white cropped tank top and white shorts that showed off long, long legs.

He sighed. Feelings were emerging from him, he didn't like. His only hope was she'd continue to run from him. Yesterday, the inch she'd moved on that Ferris wheel was as great a distance as if she'd moved out-of-state.

Oh, the irony. He'd wined-dined and slept with a number of women, then when they'd wanted more from him, he'd given them his infamous off-handed comment, "let's just be friends." Now, the women were comparing notes, advising their friends to "stay- away". He couldn't blame them.

But Annie was somehow different. His initial hate had turned around and something quite different had smacked him between his eyes. He wasn't quite ready to admit he was falling for her, but he knew he wanted her and not in the same way as all the others he'd dated. Not even the same feelings he'd had for Laura Campbell. This was somehow, more. He lost the thought as Annie wiggled her toes in the water. Lady settled next to her, her head on Annie's lap. Annie stroked her the way he wished she'd stroke him. *Damn it. No, he didn't!*

He removed his polo shirt to a catcall and whistle. Mark's face split open into a wide grin as he flexed his muscles at her and dove into the water to examine the boat's underside. A catcall. When was the last time a woman actually whistled at him? He swam under the boat.

That's when he saw the bomb. A crude—make-shift device designed to explode when he turned the ignition key.

Holy shit.

He peered at it. Easy to assemble, easy to dissemble, and deadly if not caught in time. "Mark?"

He came back to reality and came up to the surface. Annie was pointing toward the house. Julia was running down the porch steps and down the path.

Now what?

Julia had disappointment written on her face. "Mark, something's come up. I can't go." She stopped and planted her feet on the deck. "There's an emergency at the hospital."

Mark jumped out of the water onto the dock, water spraying everywhere. He slipped into his canvass dock shoes and, squishing in them, headed toward her.

Annie started to get up. "Annie, I need to go up to the house for a minute. I'll be right back."

Julia protested. "Mark, you don't need to stop what you're doing. I just came down to tell you . . ."

Mark took his mother's arm and walked her up the steps to the path. "It's not that," he said, in as low a voice as he could. "I just found an incendiary device under the boat, set to go off when I turn the key."

Julia stopped short. "What kind of incendiary device." Mark pierced his lips together.

"A bomb. You found a bomb under the boat. Oh my God. Does . . ." She turned toward Annie who was scratching Lady behind the ears.

"No. I'm going dissemble it before I tell her. Look, can you bring her into the house on some pretense for a few minutes while I take care of this?"

Julia frowned. "Mark. Are you sure you know what you're doing?" Her tone was throaty, raspy, almost like the growl that came from Lady when she was threatened.

Mark put his arm around his mother. She never ceased to surprise him. A skilled and compassionate doctor who brought babies into the world, a woman who'd toughed it for years with a hard-nosed, skirt-chasing cop who'd raised another hard-nosed, skirt-chasing cop. A woman who played the part of worried mother to perfection. He kissed her on her cheek. "Mom, remember I'm good at this sort of thing. Took a course in bombs 101 in college. And there was that bomb last year—"

"Don't remind me," Julia said. "It scared me half to death."

"Thanks. Don't worry."

"Look Mark, are you sure you and Annie will be safe enough to go out on that boat tonight?"

"Yes. I'm sure. I'll arrange protection for us. Now, you go do what you have to do."

Julia gave her son an affectionate smile, turned and walked down to the dock. She whispered something into Annie's ear.

Annie smiled and returned to the house with his mother.

When they were inside, Mark hurried toward a shed at the back of the house to get some tools. He prayed he remembered Bombs 101.

Chapter 24

"You found an incendiary device under your boat." Paul's voice was unusually controlled—terse. "A God-damned bomb."

"Yes."

Annie and his mother were talking quietly on the porch. After he'd disassembled the device and packed it into a bag for analysis, he'd told her what he'd found. He was sorry he had.

"Yeah. Crude, but effective if activated. Look, I think I should keep Annie in here tonight, don't you?" Mark was pacing back and forth in front of the house.

"Look, for what it's worth," Paul said. "I don't think they'll try anything else tonight. They'll be waiting for an explosion that won't happen."

"That's true." Mark stopped pacing. "You saying we should go anyway?"

"I'd rather you didn't, but frankly I think you should. It will send a clear message that you know what you're doing, and that you're not afraid of him—whoever *he* is."

"So, you're not convinced it's Duncan?"

"He's at a convention in New York, remember? But, yes, somehow I believe he's involved."

Mark huffed out a sigh. He didn't believe anymore that it wasn't Duncan Byrne. Not after all he'd seen. "Yeah, sure he is."

"Anyway, I'm going to send a bodyguard out to protect you. If he, or maybe someone he hired, does try something, we'll be ready."

Someone he hired. That had been running through Mark's mind also.

"Could well be someone he hired. So, a bodyguard? Like who? Everyone's—"

"Me," Paul said. "I'll get one of the summer guys to come along. I want to catch this bastard."

"Oh, this will be fun. A cop patrol running around with semi-automatics. Should make the natives confident in their local police."

Paul laughed and coughed.

"You smoking those cancer sticks again?"

"Hell yes. They've kept me alive. It's the only really bad habit I have." He cleared his throat. "And, if I get sick, your mother can nurse me back to health."

"My mother, huh?"

"Mark, that's a conversation for another day—no year. Forget I said it. Right now, we have to concentrate on a potential killer, okay?"

Mark mulled that around in his mind. He wasn't going to quite forget that Paul had said that about his mom, but he'd decide later what he thought about it. He said to Paul, "I'll ask Annie if she's up to it. If she's not, I'll take the boat out alone." He started for the house.

"Hang on a minute." "Yeah."

Annie and Julia were sitting on the wicker rocker. Annie's face looked pale. She held a glass of gin and tonic, none too steady.

Lady stood in the threshold barking and looking toward the kitchen. Dinner time.

Julia nodded. "I'll be right back. But then, I have to go."

"Wait, would you?" If Annie didn't want to go with him, he'd have her go with his mother to the hospital. That would be the last place he thought Duncan would be looking for her tonight.

"Annie," he said. "How would Duncan know how to put together a bomb?"

Annie shook her head. "I have no idea. I know his penchant for disguise and acting, but . . . well, I had no idea he could do something like this."

Something went off in Mark's brain. It flashed by so quickly, he couldn't grasp the image. He almost forgot what he was going to say.

"Look, you don't have to do this if you don't want. But I'm going out onto the lake tonight like we planned. Paul will be out there shadowing the boat. If you'd rather, you can go to the hospital with my mother."

Annie held a dark, angry expression, but one of determination. "No. I want to catch him. I want to get this over. I'll go with you."

Mark bit his lower lip. He didn't like this—at all. "Okay," he said.

"Maybe, we'll get him tonight." Mark got back on the phone with Paul as Julia reentered the porch.

"Annie says she wants to go."

"Okay. I'll call a couple of my men who are already on the lake to give you an escort. You'll see me in a little while. Is your mother going?"

Mark looked at Julia who was picking up her purse, ready to head out.

"No. She's picked up ER duty at the hospital."

"Good." Paul clicked off.

"So," Julia said. "You're going with Mark?" Annie nodded. "Yes."

"Good luck. Be safe." Julia slammed the porch door behind her then reappeared. "I won't rest, until you're back, so—please call me, okay?"

"Okay," Mark said.

Chapter 25

With Mark steadying her, Annie stepped into the *Sweet Angelina*. She settled into the padded passenger's captain's seat in the front.

Mark held onto the dock and steadied the boat. "Come on, Lady."

Lady was pacing back and forth on the dock. Then she made a run for the boat, tail wagging and—skidded to a halt.

"Lady, come on girl."

Lady came up to the boat and put her paws on the side, barked a few times, then scampered back onto the deck. Then she did something even more puzzling. She howled.

Mark's voice came out thick and unsteady. "Lady? What is it?"

Annie raised her eyebrows. "Maybe she senses the bomb was there?"

"Could be." Mark tried coaxing her again. "Lady, come on, it's okay."

Annie jumped out of the boat and knelt next to the collie. Lady put her paw on Annie's knee and licked her face. "Come on, honey. It'll be fine. You'll see."

Lady didn't budge.

"Okay, okay, don't come then," Mark said giving an impatient shrug.

Mark grabbed two life preservers and put them onto a rear seat. Then he gave Annie his hand again and steadied her as the boat shifted back and forth. Once again, she stepped into the boat and sat. Annie sensed something was still wrong. She felt it in her bones--animals always seemed to know and this one seemed unusually in- tune to the environment.

Several motorboats were already skimming over the water. Mark untied the rope attached to the pier. Lady's increased level of barking spun him around. The dog jumped up and grabbed the rope that Mark was unhitching from the dock. "Lady, let go." He tugged it away. She held firm. He pulled and she let go, growling. He threw the rope inside the boat and turned the ignition key.

"Lady," he shouted. "Go back to the house—now!"

Lady whined and finally gave up. She turned and trotted back to the house.

Mark started backing the boat away from the dock. "I don't understand, Annie. What the hell's wrong with her? I've never seen that dog growl at anything or anybody. In the past two days, she's become a regular Cujo."

Mark was still shaking his head as he backed the boat out onto the open water. He muttered, "She's *never* acted like this."

He wasn't paying attention. The front of the boat scraped the side of the deck.

Good, comic relief. Annie laughed. "Oh good. It's nice to know you're real familiar with your craft."

"Sorry. Worried about my dog . . . something . . . ." He'd been going to say something, but his face softened instead, and he smiled at her. Good sign.

Her mouth curved upward into a playful curve. "So, who's Angelina?"

"Who?"

Annie chuckled. "The name on the boat. *Sweet* Angelina, no less."

"Heh. Oh, *that* Angelina."

Mark grinned. A little jealousy never hurt anything. Always a good sign. "Was the love of my life. She was hot."

Annie's grin faded. "Ah, I see."

Mark pretended not to be looking at her. "Yeah. Miss Angelina McMillan was my first-grade teacher. I had a horrible crush on her."

"No!" Annie giggled, and the boat purred out into the open water. At last. She was beginning to feel good again.

Chapter 26

Adriano Menendez settled on his balcony and watched the sunlight hovering above the horizon. A beautiful evening in Wisconsin. He'd picked his day carefully.

Party boats with revelers passed by the village docks, shooting off fireworks. The police patrol was on hand to slap the idiots on the wrist. But little more appeared to be done. This was a day for celebration.

Some people would have more to celebrate than others.

Menendez moved back to his bedroom where his golf bag lay on the bed. He took out the golf clubs that camouflaged the parts of a long-distance rifle. He'd set up something much more efficient that a bullet that might or might not strike its target at long range. A bomb generally did the trick.

Menendez had a beard, steel-gray hair, gray eyes and a deep grudge. Mark Driscoll had killed Manny, his little brother. He would get revenge on this man if it were the last thing he ever did.

Stupid him, Adriano was still kicking himself. Manny hadn't been ready, but he'd let his brother start his apprenticeship, hoping he'd rise up in the ranks of the drug trade quickly, like he had. He'd thought a small resort town with tourists and little law enforcement would be an ideal start.

The kid shouldn't have been so trigger happy. He didn't have a record and could easily have gotten off with probation. But no, his brother was an impulsive little fool. Always had been. And a little too eager to please his big brother.

Guilt gnawed at Adriano. It had been his fault his brother was dead, but he wasn't about to commit suicide over it. Instead, he'd kill the cop.

He picked up high-powered binoculars and looked across the lake. The Driscoll's place came into view so close he could almost step onto the dock.

The detective had just helped the woman into the boat. The same beautiful girl he'd caught when she'd nearly fallen at the carnival yesterday. But she'd recoiled when she saw him. He wondered if she knew him from somewhere? Maybe on a wanted poster in the post office? He doubted it. If anyone would have recognized him, it would have been the police. He'd covered up his scars pretty well with his beard. Too bad, the woman would have to die too. He didn't care if he killed Driscoll's whole family.

The clock on the green chimed seven o'clock. The town's fireworks started at eight-thirty. *His* fireworks should start any second.

But something was wrong. The boat was in motion. He pulled the binoculars back to his eyes. They were pulling away from the dock. How could that be? Hadn't he assembled . . . Had Mark Driscoll checked out the boat and found the bomb?

Disappointed, Menendez grabbed his golf bag and pulled out the last pieces of a Chevy Tack long-range rifle.

If one method didn't work, he was the sure another would.

He cartel's top hitman for nothing.

Chapter 27

Blue sky and white clouds provided a canvas for a sun that radiated colors of orange and violet. Annie wished she had a camera. She'd simply have to photograph it in her mind. She sat next to Mark in a cabin's chair as he slowed the boat to a troll.

"Over there." Mark pointed to a burned-out shell of an old mansion. "That was built in the early 1900's. The late owners had converted it into a hotel and restaurant that rivaled the Campbell Inn. About a year ago, the place burned to the ground. Arson."

Annie checked it out as they passed. "Shame. Does anyone have any ideas as to who started the fire?"

"We suspected the owners, but they'd been out of town at the time. There were others that would have had motives, but nobody will say their names out loud. I have my suspicions, but I have no proof. So, I won't say what I think."

Soon the ruined shell was almost out of sight as they turned a curve.

The name Campbell came to mind. She suspected Mark thought it might have been someone in the Campbell family or—the owners who'd hired someone to set it while they were away. Maybe they wanted the insurance money to get a clean start into something else. She didn't know the owners, so she kept her mouth shut. A mystery that might never be solved.

Mark tapped her shoulder and once again pointed. "See that farm?"

Annie had to shield her eyes from the glare, but she saw a brick house with low-lying buildings and fencing. Maybe a kennel run?

"That's the Butterscotch Kennels. They raise collies. Lady was born there."

"Oh!"

"It's owned by Laura's aunt. Another Campbell descendent."

Annie tried to cover her annoyance at Laura's name, but didn't seem to succeed.

"Hell, just because I can't stomach Laura doesn't mean I can't do business with some of her relatives."

Annie's body immediately relaxed, but she didn't want to speculate as to why. She didn't care, did she? Hell no. She nodded and looked away toward the other side of the lake.

But, out of the corner of her eye, she caught Mark staring at her. "What actually happened between you and Laura? I know your family doesn't like her, and you shy away from her. What's wrong with her?"

Mark grimaced. "Laura and I went together in high school. I was crazy about her. I thought she loved me. I never understood why my mother didn't care for her and warned me off. I always went my own way, so I didn't pay any attention. We got engaged—set a date. The wedding presents poured in. Arranged for the reception at the Campbell Inn. Bands, flowers, everything. Two days before the wedding, Laura called it off. It was during the tourist season, and she'd met someone else. A millionaire businessman from Virginia. Needless to say, she dumped me."

"Oh my God Mark. I'm sorry." No wonder Mark acted the way he did towards relationships. She couldn't imagine being hurt like that.

"It's okay now. Laura's husband divorced her a couple years later. I'd already gone to college and came home to work as a police officer. She got an enormous settlement and helped put the Inn on the map. Good sense of business; no sense of ethics or morals. I'm glad to be rid of her. For once, I admit, I should have listened to my mother.

She has good instincts when it comes to people. I do too. Just not where women are concerned. Now, I just pull away emotionally, and I don't get hurt."

So much for his story about relationships being dangerous in the profession he was in. Yeah, maybe they were, but that wasn't the reason he wasn't in one now.

Mark wore a rigid, almost stoic expression and seemed to drift into himself.

Annie focused on the other side of the lake. Neat summer cottages with solid forest backgrounds dotted the other side of the lake. Eventually, massive trees replaced the vacation homes. Federal forest lands.

They gently rocked in the wake of other boats as Mark steered into a secluded alcove.

A lily pond.

A cold chill eased its way down the back of her spine. Once she'd loved lily ponds. Her mom had cultivated one in their backyard when Annie was a child. But since she'd seen Duncan's website with the girl lying face down in the water, long, blonde hair matted, billowing in the water and covered with water lilies, all she felt was nauseous. That painting—beautiful, tragic, sad. Duncan may have loved Poe's poetry, but that painting could have been on the cover of a Stephen King or V.C. Andrews novel. Duncan knew she'd look at his site. No—this was meant for her. Its attempt to intimidate–to frighten her out of her wits.

What was even more poignant, this pond looked so much like the one on his website. Had he been here? Seen this? Her heart pounded into a fury. She found herself looking around for escape. Why was Mark taking her here? She looked to him for answers, but his expression had grown stilled. Serious.

"Annie? What's the matter?"

Matter? Good question. What indeed could be the matter? He didn't know. He hadn't turned in here to frighten her.

She smiled to compensate for the shock that surely must have registered on her face. "It's beautiful in here, isn't it?" That was the best she could do. "Such beautiful water lilies. So much like the ones in Duncan's painting."

Mark's face went rigid, and she was instantly sorry she'd said that.

"God, Annie. I'm sorry. I didn't think. I'll turn around . . ."

"No. I can't live my life afraid of everything I come across that reminds me of something my ex-husband might have done."

Mark nodded and visibly relaxed as they turned into the pond. Another boat sat quietly near the edge. A knot of fear coiled up in her stomach. The perfect place for hiding, and the boat didn't appear empty. It rocked at a furious, yet rhythmic pace. She gasped, realizing a small shiver of panic.

"What's wrong?"

She pointed.

But Mark, the dork, wasn't grasping the seriousness of the situation. He was grinning.

"Mark. You don't understand. There's someone in that boat."

"Probably," he said, his voice growing loud enough that the whole pond could probably hear.

Sounds and giggles emerged from the bottom. One human leg propped over the side and two heads popped up and looked in their direction. Mark waved at the couple then turned the boat around.

Relieved beyond words, Annie turned and stared at him. "What is this place? The lake's version of lover's lane?"

He grinned. "Something like that," he said, in a teasing manner. "You came here because you wanted to make out with me? Was that the idea?"

He coughed and rubbed behind his ear. "Well, I don't know. Uh . . . the idea *had* crossed my mind."

"I see. Aren't you afraid I might challenge your motivations?"

"I'm always afraid you'll challenge my motivations, the same way I'm sure you're always afraid I'm about to seduce you."

"Aren't you?"

He stared at her. This time she stared right back. Right between the eyes.

"Yes," he answered.

"Ah. So, the truth finally comes out. For someone who dislikes me so much, I might challenge *those* motivations."

"You don't have to challenge my motivations, Annie. I think you're a hell of a pretty woman and a nice one too. I admire the hell out of you. I don't hate you. I just don't like psychiatrists. That isn't your fault. And, if you *really* want to know the truth . . ." He looked away. "I needed the time off. You were right."

So there. He'd said it.

"Well," Annie said softly, and sighed. "I've finally heard it. Thank you. Maybe someday you'll tell me why you hate my profession so much."

Mark smiled, she thought, in spite of himself. "Maybe, some day. But tonight's made for enjoying."

Leisurely, Annie stretched her long legs and kicked off her sandals.

Mark stretched out his right foot and caught her big toe with his.

Annie didn't pull away. "So, you admire me, do you? And you planned on finding a secluded spot to make out with me, and now your big toe is molesting my big toe."

He started to move his toe away, but she caught it in her foot. "You don't seem to mind it much," he said, leaning toward her. "No," she said. "I don't think I mind it at all."

Then, a motor chugged behind them. She jerked her head around. A boat puttered in their direction. One man drove, the other stood, bracing himself on the windshield. He carried a gun. She tried to speak, but her throat dried up.

Mark took her hand and gave it a squeeze. "Annie don't worry. They're our bodyguards." He waved. "Hey Fred. Glad you're here. This is Dr. O'Brien."

The boat stopped within a few feet of the Angelina.

"Hi, Dr. O'Brien. I'm Fred Goodwin. I generally have Mark's back, when he's not paying attention."

"Very funny."

Annie let out a puff of air. "Oh! We have *bodyguards*." Almost to herself, she whispered, "Thank God."

Mark squeezed again and released her hand. "You're welcome, Annie."

"I didn't mean . . ."

"I know what you meant." Mark's voice was gentle; the glow in his eyes softened his features and made him devastatingly handsome. Yes, she could see why the ladies went for Mark Driscoll.

The police patrol kept their distance and stopped at the mouth of the alcove.

Mark steered out of the lily pond and past them. Neither one waved or spoke as they passed. Then, they were headed back toward the middle of the lake.

<h1 style="text-align:center">Chapter 28</h1>

Mark steered toward the Campbell Inn, to the spot he thought would be advantageous to see the fireworks. Once he seemed to be on safe conversational ground again, he worked up some honesty. "I am attracted to you, Annie. I really am."

A jet boat passed by bringing more and harsher waves. "What?" Annie shook her head. She mouthed. "Can't hear."

He repeated his statement, not sure whether she really hadn't heard, or wanted him to say it again.

Annie said, "Mark you're attracted to everybody. You've probably dated every eligible woman in town." One side of her mouth quivered into a crooked smile. "And maybe some who aren't."

Caught, Mark reached down into the water and shook his hand at her.

She squealed and pulled back.

Embarrassed, Mark laughed. "No, not quite everybody. I'm not that bad. Nor am I dishonest. I don't want to get involved in a permanent relationship with anyone. It wouldn't work for me in my job. It would put the people I care about at risk. It's better to keep emotion out of my life."

Sure. Especially after he'd told her the tale of Laura Campbell. "Do you really believe that, Mark? Or are you afraid. I mean afraid after what Laura did to you?"

She'd caught him, and he was biting his bottom lip. Not a good way of hiding his emotions. Hell. "Does that make me a bad person?"

Annie's face softened. "No," she said. "Just an unhappy one, I would imagine. It's too heartbreaking to imagine a life without love in it. And I imagine not all the women you've dated believed you. I saw one woman who looked particularly wounded when she looked at you. You hurt her, Mark."

He was about to deny the accusation, but he couldn't. He'd seen the look too. He had hurt some women along the way. So, what was he supposed to do, remain celibate?

Hell, romance *had* been in the air. But now, he didn't think Annie would drop dead at his feet waiting for him to kiss her. And it was getting chilly. The sun was just descending over the hills. The red orange was now turning purple and silver, gray. Besides, they had an escort about a hundred yards from them.

It could have been *so* romantic.

Again, the jet boat circled and took off. Again, waves rocked the boat. This time Annie had to hang on.

Mark motored closer to the Inn where his escort joined the two patrol boats that kept the crowd of boaters away from the barge. Then, except for the hums of motors in the distance, everything got quiet. Annie was hugging her knees, a light of anticipation in her eyes. Nice to see her happy. She'd had precious little of that since she'd arrived.

The first of the fireworks shot into the air bringing down an umbrella of pink, blue and green sparks. The crowd shouted to a chorus of "oohs" and "ahs". They developed a kind of choral arrangement. When the fireworks went off, they chanted "ooh." When the colors spread, they sighed "ah."

But Mark hardly noticed the beauty of the fireworks. He was watching Annie. A cold breeze blew over. Mark took Annie's hand. "It's getting chilly. I'll get a couple of blankets."

Annie looked down. She'd been rubbing her arms.

A firework's comet crossed the sky, leaving a glowing trail of white sparks as it disintegrated. Someone shot off a roman candle, which rose into the sky bursting into stars, followed by a softer 'crack'.

Annie's hand landed on Mark's arm. He laughed. "You're not afraid . . ."

"No. Look."

Mark turned and looked where she pointed. A large hole bore through the Plexiglas window in front of the driver's seat. Smaller cracks ran from the center, like small tributaries. Then another crack. This one landed in the back of his seat.

Stunned, Mark fell over, saved from landing on top of Annie, only because he braced his hands on the top of her seat.

"Damn."

Someone was shooting at them.

Another crack coincided with the fireworks and this time it whizzed past Annie's cheek. She cried out, just before Mark pushed her up and over the side of the boat, holding on to her as they fell.

"Hang on to the side rails," he shouted, over the booms of the fireworks. Another shot landing above their heads. "Away from the shots." He looked around from where he thought he'd heard the shots, but it was dark and there was so much noise, he couldn't tell.

More bullets ricocheted off the opposite side of the boat. Mark and Annie hung on to the rail. He wasn't even sure when it stopped. Suddenly, nothing was whizzing past them, or zinging into or off the boat.

Mark swam to the side ladder, keeping himself as low as possible. He turned to grab Annie's hand, and she let go of the rail. But another sharp wave from the jet ski jerked their hands apart. She tried to reach the railing, the ladder, his hand—anything, but the next wave that hit knocked her head against the side of the boat. And she went under.

Life tempted Annie not to struggle. She debated allowing the water to overtake her. She'd banged her head against the side, but that was nothing compared to the abdominal pain that now came back—ripping her apart. She needed air but couldn't have gasped for breath even if her lungs were ready to explode. The sounds were muffled down here. Everything was at peace. Could she be, too?

Annie let herself go. Float wherever the lake might take her. Then Duncan or his henchman could go back to New York and the Driscoll's would be safe. And she—she wouldn't feel anything, ever again. *Let yourself go Annie.*

"Annie," Mark screamed her out of her death wish. Hands grabbed at her waist and pulled—she thought upward, but the darkness made it impossible to tell which way they were going. And then, suddenly the air hit her, and she could breathe again. And it felt so *good*. She couldn't believe that only a few seconds ago, she'd wanted to die.

Someone dragged her from the water and lay her on the floor of the boat. A hazy consciousness overcame her. She heard motors— boats circling theirs. Voices coming from all around. People's distorted faces above her. She gasped and tried to hold on, but she seemed to be floating into darkness. Her lungs. Gasps. The air that wouldn't fully come.

Think, Mark. CPR training. What the hell do you . . . Then, he remembered. He turned her face to one side. Water poured from her mouth. He knelt astride her hips and placed his hand on her abdomen. With the other hand he pressed with quick, upward thrusts. Water poured once again from her mouth and suddenly, she was gasping, pulling herself up, clinging to him, crying, choking, crying some more and finally gasping into normal breathing. She hung on to him, and he nuzzled her wet hair. For a minute, he thought he'd lost her. She'd scared the hell out of him.

Annie seemed to be fading in and out of consciousness. Her shirt had been ripped to shreds and as soon as the air hit her face, a nasty gash started spurting blood. Mark's heart stopped.

One of the patrol boats came alongside. "Everyone all right? What happened?"

"We were shot at. We went overboard to protect ourselves. Annie hit her head."

One of the deputies from the patrol boat had climbed from his boat into Mark's and was kneeling beside her. "Crap. She might have a concussion. We need to get her to the ER."

Mark nodded. "Good. But take her in your boat. I'll meet up with you later. Call 911 to get an ambulance to the dock."

Another cop peered over the side of his boat. "I already did."

Mark smiled. "Thanks. You're the best."

Mark picked Annie up and handed her to one of the deputies in the patrol boat. They sped in the direction of the village docks.

"Who'd shoot at you?" said a man from another boat. Mark didn't recognize him, but it was so dark by now, he only could see a little from the headlights.

"Sick son-of-a-bitch, whoever done that," a woman said. "I didn't think any of us would have an enemy in the world out here on the lake. Unless those drug dealers are following you."

"It's possible," Mark admitted. That he hadn't contemplated. He doubted it, but still . . .

"Just wish they would leave you alone. It's dangerous for all of us," the man said.

"Yeah. Me too," Mark said.

"Well, if you don't need any more help, I'll be getting home too. Too many boats out here, anyway." A man in a third boat didn't offer his name. Mark didn't ask, but he could have sworn he was the same man he'd seen at the carnival yesterday afternoon.

Chapter 29

Menendez had been watching his handy work from his room. Good shot from that distance. But not quite good enough. Why did the bastard have to move at that precise moment? But the fact that the woman had almost drowned gave him some comfort. Now, Driscoll could feel just a little of what he and his family felt when they'd lowered his brother into the ground.

The perpetual lump in his throat rose to a new gag level.

From somewhere in the room, his cell phone rang. Close—where the hell had he . . . It was in his top pocket. Damn. He was losing it.

"Yeah," he said, non-too civilly.

"*Buenos tardes*, Adriano. Carlos Aznar here."

"I know who you are." Menendez held his phone to his ear with one hand, while he was trying to take the gun apart with his other. He gave up on the gun. "*Que pasa?*"

Aznar coughed as though giving up the pretense of politeness. "I *want* you to get the hell out of there and fly down to Mexico. We need you—now. A slight problem with border guards."

Adriano tightened his lip and shook his head as though his boss could actually see him.

After weighing the options as to what a refusal would mean, he finally said, "*Creo que no*. I have a mission I must finish. You understand."

"Por favor." The throaty growl let loose on the other side of the phone, belied the politeness of the nicety. He wasn't asking, he was telling. "I understand, but you must understand. You work for *me*."

"Signor Aznar, my brother—his killer is not dead. The bullet missed."

"Oh? That is too bad. I am sorry. When you come to Mexico, you may practice more on the targets. And . . . do not tell me you missed. This I do not want to hear. Bodyguards and hit men do not miss the target."

Shit. He'd done the unthinkable. Should not have told his boss he'd missed. Such information could prove deadly. "He was on a boat. Beyond rifle range."

"You wait then, until target is in range. A no brainer, si?"

Adriano sighed with relief. "Si, mon compadre. You are right as always."

"No matter. We all can use a day to practice and make plans. The United States Government is once again running interference. We must stop them. So, you come to Chicago. We leave together. *Comprende?*"

"Si."

"I give you until tomorrow night to get here."

"Maybe, if I do ninety on the toll roads."

"Okay then, Sunday morning. No later. I make arrangements. My plane, she flies out Sunday at eleven. *Buenos noches.*" "Buenos . . ."

The phone clicked off.

Menendez glared at his phone and threw it on the bed. He grabbed his binoculars in time to see a boat making its way to shore, toward the docks closest to the hospital. The woman was alive. So was the detective.

Chapter 30

Annie woke in a strange environment. Something wet and stringy tickled her face. Her hair? She was under water. Stems of waterlillies wound their tentacles around her neck, her arms, her waist. A light shone into her eyes with a blinding intensity. The tunnel to heaven? Or the devil. She struggled to get away. Couldn't breathe—her infernal abdomen hurt again. She cried out and—

"Annie. It's okay, honey. Take it easy."

The voice was low and soothing—kind and gentle. The voice of God?

When Annie opened her eyes, it wasn't God nor the God of the underworld staring at her. It was Julia. Mark stood behind her, Paul stood behind him. This wasn't her room. The bed was too small and was surrounded by a high metal frame. She seemed to be locked into this space. Was she confined in the psych ward? Jail? A coffin? It finally came. She was lying in a hospital bed.

Voices, not as pleasant as Julia's, seemed to spurt from an intercom somewhere. Someone calling for a Dr. Something or other. Nothing registered. The intercom voice she related to hell, the people hovering above her, from heaven, so which was it? "Am I dead?" She knew she'd said it, but didn't feel the vibrations, and the people spun away into the distance.

When she came back into the real world, Mark was snoozing in a hospital's version of an easy chair, a magazine covering his face. Paul wasn't there. Julia stood at the foot of her bed.

And her head hurt—throbbed. She moaned.

"Annie?" Julia peered into her eyes with a small pencil-like light. "Uh huh."

Annie blinked and moaned again. "How long have I been out?" "On and off since Mark carried you off that boat." Julia bumped her thigh on the metal frame, winced, and finally pulled a chair to Annie's side, where she sat. She stuck her penlight into her pocket and folded her hands. "I'm glad you're finally with us again."

"With us again?" Annie struggled to think. No. All she could remember was the water. Lots and lots of water. And water lilies.

That was the last thing she remembered before she woke. "What happened? Did I die or something?"

A thoughtful smile curved Julia's lips, but didn't carry to her eyes. "Someone shot at you and Mark during the fireworks last night. You went overboard and hit your head on the side of the boat. Mark saved you before you drowned."

Annie turned toward Mark's direction. "Mark . . ."

Julia put her hand on Annie's arm. "Mark is dead to the world, honey. He's been up all night. You can thank him when he wakes up. Meanwhile, you have me for your doctor and . . ."

Annie smiled. "At least something went right."

Julia nodded. "Paul and his deputies are out looking for evidence and witnesses, trying to figure out where the shots came from. We might find out something later today."

Annie rose to her elbows and focused on the window. A bright light shone through the slats of the blinds. "What day is this?"

"July fifth. Now, lie down," Julia said. "You conked your head pretty good. Thought you had a concussion, but fortunately, you don't. We kept you overnight for observation, and you've been observed. You seem to be okay, although you will probably have a headache for a day or two. Anything you want to know, ask. But lie still. Don't move around."

"Okay." Annie sighed and raised her head to gaze at Mark who was gently snoring.

Julie looked too. "Well, well. Isn't that a romantic picture." Annie giggled then her head hurt again. "Ouch."

"Oh, I'm sorry. I shouldn't have made you laugh."

Annie started to laugh again. Julia put her hand on her arm. "Don't," she said. Julia punched out two pills from a card and handed them to Annie with a plastic cup of water. "Here, take these."

"What . . ."

"Tylenol. Will help the pain and make you drowsy. Sleep is the best thing for you."

Annie pushed herself up and took the pills. Then lay flat again. "When can I go home?"

"Probably late this afternoon." Julia leaned over and fluffed Annie's pillows. "Honey, there is something I want to talk to you about—"

Annie lay back. "What?"

Julia appeared to be forming some kind of question, checked her watch and shook her head. "It will have to wait until later. I have to make rounds."

"Don't you get to go home?"

"I'm pulling double duty. I'll take you and Mark home with me. Then we have some plans to make."

A warning light went up. Plans. What kind of plans? Would they make her leave? She should. The danger she'd put them through, they certainly didn't need. "Plans?"

Julia nodded. "Annie, we're going to get this bastard."

Annie sighed and slowly shook her head. "I'm presenting a threat to you and Mark. I should probably find someplace else to go . . ."

"Annie," Julia said, her eyebrows pushing together. "We've discussed this before. Where would you go? Duncan will find you.

You can't spend your life hiding. You just can't. No. You're here. He's here. He started it. We'll finish it. Period."

Relief caused Annie's eyes to burn. "Thank God. You and Mark are really amazing people, you know?"

Julia looked over at her son who was out for the count. "Annie, Mark can be caustic and a real jerk at times. But, behind that façade, he's a kind man. Sometimes he doesn't want anyone to see."

Annie looked away. Julia was right. Her son didn't want to see, and Annie wanted to know why. Was it only Laura Campbell who had scared him so badly? And why did he hate psychologists? Annie whispered her question to Julia. She was immediately sorry she had.

A watery red ring surrounded Julia's eyes. She looked down. "Annie," she whispered. "In some ways, Mark has turned out a lot like his father. Tom Driscoll was a handsome devil. I was young when I married him, but I knew his downfall. He loved women. As far as I know, for the first ten years or so in our marriage, he never cheated on me, but eventually the temptation proved too much.

"I knew Tom had a girlfriend. Don't ask me how. Wives always know. Intuitively, I suppose.

"Mark was fifteen. He went to the police station one afternoon to ask his father for a ride home. He . . . he caught him having . . . making out with this woman in his office. Mark ran out and bumped into a friend who gave him a ride home. I knew something was up when Mark got home. He ran to his room and slammed the door. He wouldn't talk to me about it. When Tom got home, I overheard them arguing. I walked into the room and told Mark to leave the room. Then I confronted Tom, and he broke down. Told me everything.

"I asked him if he wanted a divorce. He looked shocked—horrified. Adamantly stated he didn't want to leave me. He loved me. Loved me—yeah, right. Then what was he doing with this woman? He poured out excuses. I was never home. My job was more important than him or Mark. I went ballistic. This had been something we'd discussed before we'd even married. He'd known my passion for medicine since we were in grade school. I'd always known his love of the law. I knew the dangers of him being a cop. I put up with his crazy hours, but he cheated on me because of mine. Before he could come up with anything else that might prove stupid or embarrassing, I told him, if he wanted to stay with me, he'd better get counseling. He agreed to it and saw a new psychologist—the kind that watches the clock throughout his sessions."

A rustling and a yawn broke through the sound of Julia's soft voice. Both women looked at Mark who was taking the magazine from over his face and sitting up.

"Morning." Mark stood up and stretched, looked out the window, then turned and sat on the arm of Julia's chair.

"How's the patient this morning?" "I'm . . ."

"Groggy," Julia said. "And hurting. I gave her some Tylenol. She'll be falling asleep soon. I think we should let her go back to sleep."

Mark pinched his lips together as though curtailing something he'd love to say but wouldn't. "Good idea."

"I'll stay for a few more minutes until Annie falls asleep then make rounds. I think Paul may need you. Why don't you go to work then meet us here at around five, and we'll go home together."

Mark formed a lazy smile across his face. "Good idea, but why don't you make your rounds, and I'll stay with Annie."

"Morning." Everyone turned to see a man in a white lab coat, carrying a tray of needles and vials. "I'm here to do the blood workup you wanted."

"Good," Julia said, her expression serious. "Mark, as I said, I think it's time for you to leave. We'll meet you in the lobby at five."

Mark cleared his throat. He didn't look happy. Not at all. Annie focused on mother and son. He didn't want Julia finishing the story about him and his father. That was what this was all about. He'd probably woken up long before he made the fact known. This was information he considered classified—painful.

Annie said, "Thanks for staying here all night, Mark, but your mother wanted a blood workup done on me. Why, I'm not sure. But since I'm going to be stuck by a bunch of needles . . ." She yawned. Her eyes dimmed. "Meanwhile I . . . sleep . . ."

"Annie has to have someone stay here with her. I insist on . . ." was the last thing Annie heard. She felt a sudden prick in her arm. Then, nothing.

Chapter 31

Mark followed his mother out of the room. He started to speak to her, but she'd stopped to talk to the security guard. She'd done that on purpose to avoid talking to him. *Bloody hell.*

"Molly, do me a favor, will you?" Julia said.

"Sure, Dr. Driscoll."

Security guard, Molly McGuire, had blonde hair that she had braided and pinned up like a crown. She'd always worn it that way. He'd made fun of it in high school and that's when she'd decked him. It was on that particular day that Mark had learned infinite respect for his classmate. She didn't look a day older than she had in high school and now, she was pregnant and glowing.

Her husband came up to the ward almost every day when he picked her up from work to brag about their baby's progress and explain the ongoing details of their new baby's room. Everyone liked him—everyone liked *them.*

His mother's voice broke him out of his trip down memory lane. "Stay close to Dr. O'Brien, will you? Don't let anyone in there that you don't know. Her room is off limits to anyone other than me, Mark and the police. If any gifts, flowers or candy come for her, don't give them to her. And I don't suggest you eat or touch them either."

Molly's face flushed. "Dr. Driscoll, I wouldn't dream of doing such a thing."

Julia smiled at her and put her hand on her arm. "I know you wouldn't. I'm just saying, Dr. O'Brien is in danger and we don't want anything happening to her—or anyone else."

Molly blanched and nodded. "I understand."

Mark walked out of the hospital feeling Annie was in good hands.

The small silver alarm clock by her bed read one o'clock. Annie hadn't been asleep that long. Not really. It just felt that way. The sun still shone bright between the slats. She looked around. Empty. No Julia. No Mark. No lab technician. She thought she saw a shadow pass by her room, but she figured it was a nurse, doctor, visitor. She turned over and went back to sleep.

Duncan walked the halls on Annie's floor, wearing beige slacks, green scrubs, a mask that dangled over the neck of his lab coat and a stethoscope he'd stolen from the doctor's lounge.

A security guard with a badge that read 'Molly' stopped him.

He flashed her a dazzling smile and told her how glad he was to be in a small setting hospital, after a grueling four years at Columbia Presbyterian. Then he asked where the men's room was located. The guard pointed and walked away. Duncan ducked into the washroom and waited until it was all clear.

His mission—to get Annabelle out of the hospital without anyone noticing. Not an easy feat. But, if he could get her dressed and wheel her away in a wheelchair, he could easily get her out the hospital doors.

He'd already checked. The detective was gone. Dr. Driscoll was on the next floor down treating patients. The hallway seemed pretty dead after the code blue he'd managed to have called up on the third floor. Duncan figured he had a window of about a half-hour to get her out.

He snuck into her room, careful to leave the door as it had been.

Footsteps. Duncan popped into the washroom and plastered himself against the wall. A shadow came into the room then disappeared back out into the hall. Safe.

He stepped into the room and nodded with satisfaction. Only one bed. Annie lay sound asleep.

Duncan checked the chart at the foot of the bed and flipped the pages. After the medication they'd given her, even if she woke, she'd be so groggy, she wouldn't be functional.

"What are you doing here?"

Duncan whirled. The guard, Molly, stood at the doorway.

The security guard stared at him. "I think you have the wrong room. If you didn't notice, there's a 'no admittance' sign on the door." She placed her hands on her hips and stared at him. "I really must ask you to leave."

"Ma'am," Duncan said, politeness oozing from his voice. "Administration asked that I bring her downstairs. Her relatives are here to pick her up. See? I've come to wheel her down. Except . . ." Duncan made a point to look down at Annabelle. "Nobody said she would be asleep."

Molly took five steps into the room and was almost at the foot of the bed. "Dr. Driscoll is her doctor. She's down the hall," Molly said, her face taut with anger. "Now, until Dr. Driscoll gets back, I have orders to keep everyone out. Everyone. Even hospital personnel. Now, go take care of the patient who really has to go home."

Annabelle moaned, and she opened her eyes. "Who are . . . Mark?" Duncan bent over her. "Dr. O'Brien, I'm here to take you home." But a strange shock of recognition came into her eyes. "What . . . Why are *you* here?" Annie slumped back into her drug induced sleep.

An alarm seemed to go off in Molly's head. She read his nametag. "Marvin." Now the woman's face was livid. "You're *not* Marvin. You don't look anything like him. Listen, get out of this room before I have you escorted out. I mean it. Out!" She elbowed him out of the way and picked up the phone.

Duncan grabbed the receiver from her. Molly made another grab for it, but this time, Duncan wrapped the cord around her neck and pulled. Her cry went unheard. She went down.

She had a small neck.

Voices.

Duncan ducked into the closet and peeked through a crack. "Molly?" A male nurse walked into the room and looked around.

"Dr. O'Brien?" A moan then nothing.

The man walked toward Annabelle. His expression froze, as he looked down at the floor. His dark complexion turned almost white. The man knelt down beside her body so Duncan couldn't see what he was doing. He held his breath.

"*Oh shit, no!*" He called someone on his pager. "It's Molly." His voice broke. "I . . . I can't get a pulse. She's lying on the floor. We need a code blue." He paused. "Code Blue," he screamed into the intercom. "Get a doctor. Molly's not breathing!"

As the man bent over her body, Duncan took the split second of opportunity to leave the room.

But nobody was paying attention to him.

He watched as attendants on the floor rushed into Annie's room and suddenly a "code silver" blared over the loudspeaker.

Duncan sauntered toward the elevator and nearly bumped into Dr. Julia Driscoll.

"Sorry," she said. She was breathing hard. "Emergency." She took off down the hall in a run. Duncan waited for the elevator, took it down to the lobby and walked out of the hospital. As he drove from the parking lot, Mark Driscoll and another officer peeled in the entrance. They parked in Duncan's space.

Oh, the irony.

Chapter 32

Duncan sped out of the hospital grounds, down Forest Avenue to the highway and North toward Two-Lakes Campground, his main base of operations.

He had to think. If that damned security guard hadn't come in, he'd have Annabelle. He fantasized about what he wanted to do to her when he tied her to his bed. His mind became so obsessed with her body, he started shivering. He couldn't wait to get to his RV, and he pulled onto the service road that led down to the lake.

As soon as he was sure nobody could see him, he undid his pants, massaged and fantasized. But he didn't limit his fantasies to sex. He'd already moved on. Even drowning no longer appealed to him. He wanted to slowly choke the living daylights out of Annabelle while having sex with her. He could picture her repulsed and terrified expression mixed with fear—orgasm and death wrapped into one nice little package. He wanted . . . The tension in his body was building to a ferocious level.

Even rubbing and pulling didn't seem to be giving him relief. He envisioned her stripping for him, layer by layer, showing him all those female delights he'd loved so much. She opened her legs to him, and spasms broke out.

Spasms. Thank God. Maybe he'd find that relief now. He wanted to scream from his frustration.

She'd scream too when he banged himself into her as hard as he could—then put his hands around her delicate little neck. Oh, the terror in her eyes as she realized she was going to die.

Finally, that liquid fire inside him that had smoldered for so long started bubbling to the surface and exploded like lava erupting from a volcano too long lying dormant. He screamed out his frustration and rage.

Duncan lay in a stupor, his sex scent floating everywhere until he opened the windows and let it disintegrate into the air.

When he finally could drive home, he stumbled into his RV, poured a glass of Johnny Walker Red, settled into the sofa and thought. He'd killed a woman. He hadn't wanted to kill her. But it wasn't his fault. She'd interfered. People must understand that nobody can come between him and his Annabelle. *Nobody.*

What God has joined, let no man put asunder. And that included Annabelle herself.

Chapter 33

At two in the morning, Annie woke and realized two things. She was no longer in that God awful hospital, but lay in her own bed at the Driscoll's, and her headache had finally disappeared.

Except for a half moon peeking its way inside the room, the only light source was a collie-head night light plugged into a socket.

Annie got out of bed and slipped on her robe.

Disturbed, Lady stood up and shook herself, her tail wagging. "Shh." Annie pointed her finger to her lips and whispered, "Go back to sleep, little girl. I'm just going onto the balcony for a minute."

Lady grunted, circled three times and lay down, but her head was still fixed on Annie.

Annie stepped onto the balcony. The night was quiet, except for the rustling trees and the occasional plop in the lake. A distorted light from an almost full moon bobbed over the water with the ripples. A nice night.

God's country, this beautiful place. A piece of heaven.

Even Mark seemed to change overnight.

When Annie had gone to bed after the sad, quiet trip home from the hospital, Mark insisted on carrying her up the stairs then sat beside her on the bed.

"You didn't have to . . ." Annie said. "But frankly, I'm glad you did. My head is starting to pound again."

Mark examined her face. "I wanted to make sure you were alright." Mark pulled out a pill card from his top pocket. "My mother told me to give you two of these. They will knock you out. When you wake up, the headache will probably be gone. I could stay here with you, sleep in that chair over in the corner."

He wanted to sleep in a hard-wood rocking chair all night. She smiled. That really was sweet of him.

"Mark, you don't have to stay with me all night. Really."

"I know." He shook his head and stood. "I just wanted you to know I care about you . . ." His voice got softer. "Now, I'm going to let you get some sleep. I'll be across the hall if you need anything."

Lady padded into the room and looked at Mark, then at Annie. Mark knelt beside Lady. "Stay here and guard Annie, okay girl?"

The soft expression on his face made him one of the most handsome men she'd ever seen. Strange. She hadn't thought he was that good-looking, but now . . . No wonder half the women in Nager were in love with him.

A woof and a half a sneeze brought Annie back into the present.

Lady settled across Annie's feet.

Not only Mark, but the other Driscoll's were becoming as dear to her as her family.

And that was why she had to leave. The realization struck her in the face like cold water from the lake. Once more, the people she loved would disappear: her parents, killed in a crash, her Aunt who succumbed to cancer and Duncan overtaken by mental illness.

Tears burned her eyes and started to trickle down her cheek. She wiped them off with her sleeve.

Duncan—overtaken by madness? Were there clues she'd missed? Had *she* been so obsessed with her work that she hadn't paid enough attention to his abnormal behavior?

Now she wondered if he had stalked someone else in his life he'd claimed to love. Or . . . was he a sociopath? The perfect husband when she was eager to do his bidding. But, once she came into her own with a baby on the way, he had been threatened and his true personality emerged. But killing that woman? That cop who Mark knew and respected.

She had to leave. Now—right away, before Julia and Mark were up and tried to stop her. If she moved on, Duncan would either follow her or go back to New York, where the NYPD would surely deal with him.

Her instincts shouted she shouldn't go anywhere without concrete plans. Nonetheless . . . .

A letter. She had to write that letter.

She turned and barely missed stepping on Lady. The dog scrambled to her feet, following Annie inside.

Annie opened her laptop case and pulled out a pad and pen.

Dear Mark and Julia,

Please know you're the best friends I've ever had. Your generosity has surpassed anything anyone could have done, or even been willing to do, during such a crisis in my life.

With a heavy heart I have to leave without saying goodbye. If I did, I'd never be able to go and I'd put you in more danger than you are now.

Make no mistake, Mark. I believe it's Duncan who's stalking me. Not a hit man. I think if you check his hotel in New York, you'll find he's substituted one of his graduate students to attend the conference for him. You might ask the NYPD to do a room check at night.

I'm so . . . so sorry about Molly. She did not deserve to die. There's going to be so much grief in this town. All because of Duncan . . . and me.

To put anyone else in danger would be unthinkable. Please forgive me for leaving without your knowledge. I know you'd never let me go, and I'd never want to leave you and this beautiful place.

I'll be with a friend who Duncan doesn't know. She's moved to the mountains in Canada. By the time Duncan figures out I'm no longer here, I'll be long gone—and, as there's no longer a tracking device under my car . . . he won't be able to find me.

I want you to know, you have become as dear to me as any family I've ever had. Thank you.

Mark, we've had our differences. I hope in some way we've reconciled them. I have more respect for you than any man I've ever known. You have so much to give a woman—as a husband and a father. I hope you find your one special person. You're a good man— kinder than you even know. You deserve happiness.

Take care friends. With any luck, I'll find my niche as a counselor at some small-town hospital in Canada, kind of like Nager.

I'll miss you.

Love,
Annie

Annie propped the letter against her pillow. She pulled on jeans, a tank top and jacket then surveyed the rest of her closet.

She hadn't bought as much as she'd originally thought. By the time she'd finished packing, her duffle bag was only half full. Now, to find a way out.

She slowly pulled opened her door. Across the hall, Mark's door stood wide open, and she heard the rustling of paper. Too bad. She'd hoped he'd gone to bed. Only God and Mark knew why he hadn't. She retreated and closed her door again.

The situation called for a little creativity and that might entail climbing down from her balcony. She stepped outside and looked around. A post ran straight down from the bottom of the floor and hitched onto the house where it reached the porch. If she could grab hold, make it down to the top of the porch, without breaking her neck . . .

Thump.

The noise sent her heart racing and she whirled around. Just Lady trotting across the balcony, her tail wagging.

Annie let out a sigh of relief, then knelt and took Lady's face in both her hands. "Lady, I'm going to miss you, girl. I wish you could have met my cat, Nemesis. I think you'd have gotten along." Annie sniffed back a tear and enclosed both arms around the dog's furry neck. "But you're going to have to be quiet for me now, okay? No barking—please?" She pointed Lady back to the bedroom and closed the sliding glass door behind her. Lady scratched herself, then turned and jumped back on the bed. All Annie heard were crickets and an occasional car horn from across the lake.

Now to climb down.

A shadow crossed the path outside the house. Her heart racing, Annie crouched and peered through the bars. Paul's deputy emerged from around the house and headed toward the porch. The screen door closed under her.

Annie had the sudden claustrophobic feeling she was under house arrest and all they'd left out was the ankle bracelet. They probably *should* have put one on *her*.

Feet shuffling into the house from the porch. Only the barest of sounds.

A faint voice from the back of the house. "Who's there?" Julia's voice.

Annie's heart stopped. She was sure of it.

"Just me, ma'am. Getting some coffee so I can stay awake."

"You scared the hell out of me."

"Sorry, ma'am. Didn't mean to do that."

"As long as you're here, I might as well pour a cup for both of us."

Then nothing more.

Not *too* far to the ground. Annie threw the duffle bag and her purse onto the ground and hung the computer case over her shoulder, praying its weight wouldn't knock her over.

She reached down and grabbed the post, then climbed over the railing. Wrapping her legs around the post she inched her way down, pulled by the eight pounds of her laptop until the post melted into the house. From there, she jumped and landed on top of a clump of pine needles. Nothing broken—nothing hurt, the computer hadn't even touched the ground. In fact, it had been so easy, she wondered how well protected the house actually was.

Home free—almost.

Now, to get to her and motor out of there without being heard. *Good luck.*

She made it in record time. Throwing everything in the back seat, she eased in and pulled away without incident.

Chapter 34

Mark was frantic. The deputy kept trying to leave the room—leave the country, but Mark kept going over and over, why he'd gone inside, fallen asleep and let a slip of a girl outfox him.

Julia said, "It wasn't his fault. I got him a cup of coffee and kept him talking so he wouldn't fall asleep. This was *my* fault."

No, it hadn't been. The deputy had known better.

They'd read the letter, seen her empty closet. Mark had never been so angry in his life. He almost *felt* like letting her go. If Annie didn't want to be here with them—then damn it, let her get on with her 'normal' life.

He paced around the dining room table, dog at his heels.

Good luck, sister, if she thought she could have any kind of life with that maniac running around.

He stopped and put both hands on the back of a chair. No. She couldn't survive out there alone, and he knew it. He pounded his fist on the back of the chair. *Damn her.* And, he'd been awake, typing on his computer right across the hall from her. Still, she'd slipped out. He was as much to blame as his mother and the deputy.

In the end, Lady had been the one to wake the household. She'd been the one in Annie's bedroom. *He* should have stayed in the room with her.

"Detective Driscoll, Mrs. Driscoll," the deputy said, looking down at his shoes. "I'm sorry, but it's possible she'd slipped out before I came in for coffee. I'd been patrolling all night. It's possible. Everything seemed normal—quiet. Look, I would have seen her if she'd walked out the front. Maybe the back?"

"No," Julia said, leaning her back to the wall. "I sleep in the room next to the back door. If anyone tried to come in or out that way, I would have heard. I'm a light sleeper."

"So how did she get out?" Mark asked. "How? She couldn't have flown out of the balcony." No, the jury was still out as to whether she was an angel or devil, but she *was* wingless.

"The balcony." Paul stood in the doorway. "I just circled the house. She shimmied down the post and must have jumped to the ground. There's fresh set of footprints embedded in the pine needles."

"We have to get her back," Julia said. "But how? Didn't you take out that tracking device she had in the car? Besides, Duncan was the only one who could have tracked her."

"Not necessarily," Mark said, a sudden grimace appearing across his face.

"Huh?" Paul looked puzzled. "What do you mean?"

"I put another device under her car when I got it back here. I can follow her from my car, and I'm going now, before she leaves the state."

Apprehension clouded Julia's eyes. "What if she doesn't want to come back?" she asked softly, sinking into the dining room chair.

Mark sat next to her and took her hand. "Then, I'll just have to charm her into coming back, won't I?"

Paul coughed. "I'd say you have a big opinion about your influence on ladies."

"And, you'd better not say anything to her you don't mean, Mark. I will not have you breaking . . ."

Mark stood and shook his head. "You two have a rather sordid impression of me. I swear I will not do anything to hurt Annie. I'm going to find her. Right now."

"I'll go with you." Paul turned toward the porch.

"Paul, with all due respect, I think I'll go alone. I'll keep in touch. See you later." Mark brushed past Paul and stepped onto the porch.

Paul grabbed his arm. "Mark . . ."

"Paul let go. I'm going alone. There's a few things I need to clear up, and I can't do that if you're along."

Paul let go and backed off. "Okay."

Chapter 35

Two-Lakes Campground. RV's keep right. Cabins keep left.

Annie pulled off the highway and onto a gravel driveway that led to Beaver Lake.

She wasn't as wide-awake as she'd thought. She'd fall asleep if she kept going on this one-lane highway with nothing but her headlights. She saw the office and headed in the opposite direction way down the lane into a clump of trees that overlooked the lake. It would be beautiful when the sun came up. She'd heard that Beaver Lake fell into Lake Nager through high waterfalls, something she'd been meaning to see. Maybe tomorrow morning before she left.

She snuggled into a blanket and pillow she always kept in her car and fell asleep, sure she'd done—was doing—the right thing.

Dreams raced by. Dreams of happier days. Dreams of Mark and his mother. Dreams of Mark's handsome face behind a glass window. He was knocking. And knocking. She couldn't quite reach the doorknob. The banging now became incessant. Annie woke and realized this hadn't been a dream. She jumped and screamed, then saw Mark's face plastered against the window.

Damn it. Was the man psychic? How had he known where to find her?

She shook her head, waved him away and started the motor.

But Mark wasn't taking no for an answer. He stood directly in front of her car so she couldn't move forward. When she checked her rearview mirror, his car backed up lengthwise across the road. No escape. She was indeed a prisoner. That man didn't need his house guests to wear ankle bracelets.

Annie opened up the door. "Okay, you obviously aren't going to get out of the way, so get in, if you want to so bad." Her blood pressure rose, and her heart raced as she realized what she was planning. As soon as Mark moved from the road, Annie gunned the motor. But before she could drive away, Mark opened the door. Half of him leapt inside and grabbed the steering wheel from Annie. He was able to break inches before they hit a towering oak tree with a base large enough to demolish a semi, let alone her small car.

"What the hell are you doing?" He pulled up the arm rest, bumped Annie over and into to the passenger seat.

"Ouch. Damn it."

Keys. He took them out of the ignition and put them into his left pants pocket. She couldn't get far without those.

"Mark, you just ruined my hip for my entire life."

"Good," Mark said. "Now, we need to talk. Why the hell did you run? You could have killed us both just now."

"If you hadn't gotten in the way I wouldn't have."

Mark turned to her and folded his arms. "What's the big idea?" "What Mark? Look, I think everything I needed to say, I wrote in the letter. What more needs to be discussed? You're not going to lock me up or anything, are you?"

"I'd like to." Mark blew air from clenched lips. "My mother is frantic with worry, and Paul is about to call out the state troopers, trumping up some charge so he can bring you to jail and throw away the key."

"Why would he want to do that?"

Mark couldn't believe this. He wasn't getting through, damn it. "Annie—*why*? Because it's better you're being in a cell than buried in a coffin six feet under."

Annie shivered. "Oh Mark, don't . . ."

He bit his lip, fuming, trying to get this across. "Don't what? Tell you the truth? You're damned good at telling me the truth, but you don't like it much when someone gives you a good dose of truth serum."

"Hmm." Annie chuckled—once. "Touché."

"Yeah, right. Touché."

He needed to turn away from her; needed to tell her what was in his heart right now. And, he had to be sincere, otherwise, she'd leave, and Duncan Byrne would find her. He thought Annie's future, and possibly his, depended on her staying. But, with Annie staring at him, how the hell could he go on?

"You can certainly write a good line, but you're very good at expounding on your feelings, and then running away. Good job, Annie."

"Mark, please."

"I want you to know something. We've had our differences in the past, but I've grown to really like you. I wanted to get to know you better—even possibly . . . I mean when this is over."

Annie shook her head. "I don't want any more blood on my hands. I can't stay here."

"Honey, you're not responsible for anyone's death. Look, if you stay, we might be able to catch him before he kills again. If you leave, he'll follow and be out of our jurisdiction. We won't be able to protect you, and you'll have to go through this all over again somewhere else."

The first light of dawn was rising. And what he saw saddened him. Annie softly crying.

Mark pushed up the arm rest and moved in toward her, taking her in his arms. "Baby don't cry. It's going to be all right. I'm not going to let him hurt you." He put his lips against her hair.

"Mark, do you really care about me? I mean really?"

Did he? Did every woman in town know about his exploits with women?

He pulled away. "Look Annie. I have a rotten reputation. I'll be the first to admit it. But I've never in my life lied to anyone I've ever dated. I care about you—a lot. There's only been one other woman I've cared about as much, and she didn't deserve it. Just like I said in the boat, I like the hell out of you and . . ." Should he say it? Supposing she didn't reciprocate? *Go for it Mark.*

"And?" Annie repeated.

"And I think I'm in love with you," he said. "There, I've said it, and it's up to you to step on my heart if you want."

Annie put her arms around his neck, and he felt the swell of her breasts against his chest. Her lips were soft against his cheek. "I'm not a woman who steps on anyone's heart, Mark. I care about you too—but you don't know me."

Mark's lips brushed her hair. He whispered, "I know enough. I don't fall lightly, Annie. I never have."

Annie pushed back, then turned and got out of the car. What the hell? Running again. She sat on a log by a stream that connected one lake to the other. The sun started to peek up over the lake.

"Annie don't run. Please." Mark went over and sat next to her.

They sat in silence watching the water and the breaking dawn. "Mark, tell me about your father."

"My father?" Where did that come from? He didn't want to rehash this over again.

"Mark, I know you were awake when your mother told me about Tom Driscoll and his girlfriend."

Ah. The hospital. Mark nodded. He'd just told Annie he loved her. He needed to be honest with her about himself, his dad. Make a clean sweep of this.

"Your mother said she would leave him unless he saw someone professionally."

"Yes, you're right." Mark took Annie's hand. "My father was running around. I don't think he loved anyone else. I think he was trying to escape from the real world. Part of the problem was me."

"You?"

"When I was in high school, I went a bit wild. I started hanging with some kids from Brighton who were majoring in Theft 101 and went on field trips stealing candy from local grocery stores."

Annie chuckled. "Sorry. Your choice of words. I'm glad you can poke fun at the situation . . . at yourself."

"Well, I get my witty sarcasm from my mother."

"Go on," Annie said.

Mark nodded. "Okay. He caught me and my buddies one night. The others ran. I refused to give my father their names. I think he admired me for it, but it didn't help me. He put me in jail overnight. Funny thing is, I loved him for it. I've never forgotten. Never got into trouble again. The next day he went to see the hospital shrink."

"The clock watcher." Annie smiled at him, but not a fun—ha ha type of smile.

"The clock watcher." Mark spoke softly. "I guess the session got intense." He forced back the emotion in his voice. It became toneless. "That damn shrink, dismissed my father right in the middle of his experiencing a mental breakdown."

"Oh Lord, Mark. How did you find that out?"

"From my mother. My mother has ways of finding out. The hospital fired the psychologist."

"He deserved it," Annie said. "They should have revoked his license."

"After my father left the hospital, he got a call to check on a 7-Eleven—a robbery in progress. I don't know, I think my father thought it was me again. He wasn't prepared for what he found. Instead of a bunch of misguided kids, they were crazed crackheads looking for drug money. The bastards gunned him down."

Mark wiped his eyes with his arm. He couldn't help it. All this crap had been building inside him for years.

Annie had finally done it. She'd made him spill his guts, something he didn't think anyone could make him do.

Annie leaned over to him and pulled him in her arms and held on. A loving gesture—not at all sexual. Still, the brush of her cheek against his, the faint scent of gardenia and peach shampoo and the electricity he found present in her body, brought about an intensity he hadn't felt, maybe ever.

Mark caught her mouth and kissed her. And he felt it. The 'it' factor he'd been told about but had never experienced. His heart raced, not from the torture of the memory, but from her.

"Mark," Annie whispered. She pulled back for a minute, looked him in the eyes then kissed him back. First, soft and gentle, then becoming harder. Her heart raced against his. His body started to betray him—he wanted her, right there on the pine needles by the lake with the sun coming up. Wanted to feel himself driving into her— loving her—And her making love to him.

But Annie pulled away. Mark thought she might run again. "Annie?"

She didn't move away, but she might as well have. Her mind had drifted miles from him.

"You don't know me."

Annie wasn't sure how much she trusted Mark. With her life, maybe, but not with the kind of information she was about to tell him. He'd experienced enough emotional trauma for the moment.

She stood and walked to the road, thinking. Mark caught up with her and grabbed her arm.

"Annie, you can't just walk away after a remark like that. I just spilled my guts to you, now you're going to run away again?"

She shook her head, but still couldn't get up enough courage to look at him. "I'm not running away. Some things are just too difficult to talk about."

"Yeah," he said. "No shit. I just laid something on you I haven't told *anybody*. Play fair with me."

She had to concede. "I know. I know."

He muttered something that sounded like "Damn" under his breath and walked back to the car.

She followed.

He had his hand on his car handle. "Annie, do what you want. I'm going home. I want you to come with me—but I have no right to stop you from leaving."

She'd hurt him. He'd trusted her, and she hadn't trusted him. She came up and rested her back on the passenger door next to him.

"The reason I left without telling you was I knew if you'd asked me to stay, I wouldn't have thought twice about staying."

"I'm asking you to stay."

And there it was. He'd told her he'd fallen in love with her, she'd fallen in love with him too. But a relationship with him—with anyone, would do more harm than good.

"I need to tell you something. I have little experience in love affairs—none. Duncan swept me off my feet with his kindness and mentoring, not passion. I haven't dated anyone else since high school."

"You don't have to."

"Yes, I do. I need to tell you something that might make you change your mind about me and the future."

"What the hell could it possibly be, Annie? Did you shoot someone?"

Annie laughed. But it was hollow. "No. I didn't shoot anyone."

"Then?"

"I was eight months pregnant. So excited about the new baby— thought Duncan was too. He put up an excellent front, I guess. I had no idea—" No idea Duncan was a monster who hated children. Annie started to relive the memories and lost her sense of the present.

"He acted fine at first. We worked on a project together. I interned and collaborated with him while he taught and saw patients. I was happy—thought we were happy as a couple. But little by little—I didn't see it coming—he started removing me from my friends. The psych department suddenly canceled my study group meetings with other students with no explanation. We started working together privately. Duncan accused me of having an affair with someone in my study group. Somehow, in his mind, he thought the baby was not his. After I convinced him he was, indeed, the father, he accused me of loving the child more than him. But I never thought we weren't safe."

Annie had to stop, the emotion had overtaken her voice. Her body started to shake with the memories.

"Go on," Mark said gently. He took her hand, and she held on— tight.

"Friends held a shower. Fathers are not supposed to attend these things, but he insisted. As everyone fawned over me and the baby, hardly any of the women paid attention to Duncan. Apparently, he needed to be the center of the universe. I've seen it grow over the course of the years. I didn't think it had grown so bad.

"One day when I wasn't feeling so hot, I stayed home. Duncan left for the university as usual, I thought. I'd been sleeping downstairs, but when I felt well enough, I went upstairs to take stock of what we had and what we still needed for the baby's arrival." Oh God, did she have to go on with this? The shadow—the hand—the fall—the blood. *So much blood!*

Annie caught hold of her emotions and continued. "When I came back downstairs. Well, the staircase had two banisters that supported my weight." Shivers at the memories. She had to rub her arms to keep warm, but even that didn't help. Her teeth chattered.

"I never had a chance to grab them. I saw a shadow come out of nowhere, and something hit me in the back of my head—hard. Then, I felt a push. I flew off my feet and straight down. I woke up in the hospital." *So much blood!* She couldn't get it out of her mind.

"God. He hit you on the back of the head then pushed you down the stairs," he whispered. "He pushed . . ." Incensed, he pounded his fist against the car. "That madman killed your child—and almost killed you."

Annie nodded. "Yes, but there's more. In the fall, I damaged my insides pretty bad. I still suffer from excruciating pain—"

Mark had the grimmest expression she'd ever seen on him, and he didn't seem to be breathing as he followed her story.

Here it comes. This is where I botch any chance I might have with him.

She looked away, out over the water, feeling his body touching hers as they stood next to each other. "Mark," she said quietly, "I can never have children again."

Dead silence. Annie huddled in her arms, and when she felt his arm wrap around her shoulder, she bolted back to her car.

"Annie!" Mark shouted after her. "Annie, it's . . ."

She stopped and turned. "No Mark. It's not okay. I'm not a good candidate for a long-term relationship, I'm sorry." She ran to her car, got in and searched for her keys, ready to leave Nager. But she couldn't. Mark had her keys.

Mark sat enclosed in a fog of horror. What kind of monster could do that to a pregnant woman? Hadn't he realized she could die too? Stupid contemplation. Of course, he had. That was his intent all along. But why? If he were so jealous, he'd have reason to want the baby dead, but not her.

He had to get Annie home. She needed to talk to his mother about this—see if anyone could do anything to relieve the excruciating pain she suffered. He'd seen it. Hadn't known it for what it was but knew something was very wrong.

The car hadn't moved. He smiled and patted his pocket. She couldn't get far without these.

Chapter 36

In the Two-Lakes Campground, campers slept off a three-day binge of Fourth fish boils, boozing and boating. Drunken laughter still emanated from a campsite down the way, but Duncan surmised those people wouldn't notice him.

He popped out his blue contact lenses and substituted the brown. Then carefully combed down a blonde wig. Good thing, The Community Players. He could make up disguises with the best of them. Even his own wife hadn't recognized him at the hospital. Although she'd sensed his presence. Yes. He definitely thought she'd sensed him.

Duncan befriended his neighbors, a couple who couldn't stop bragging about their two adorable blonde-haired, blue-eyed little girls. Two bitches who'd grow up to be whores of hell. No matter. He wouldn't be around to witness that happy event. But he would be around to watch after his neighbor's campsite and their red Ford Aerostar while they went on a camping expedition. Yep. He sure would do that. He would baby sit their keys—gladly.

Then the idea popped into his head. Except for his grievance with Annabelle, he'd never thought of killing. But, that cop . . . she'd just been in the way—an accident. That had started something so strong in him, he didn't think—or even want to stop. He needed to kill another blonde. Call it a blood lust, he thought. Tonight, he'd begin a new career.

Tonight, he'd become a serial killer.

Duncan drove out of the shadows and onto the highway leading around Lake Nager into Brighton. As the street curved away from the lake, trailers lined the narrowing road, which had turned from asphalt to gravel.

He'd heard about this shabby section of Nager Township. Best kept secret in the area. Where the bars stayed open all night, and where the whores hung out. He drove up to a shack boasting a neo sign flashing Shady Lake. Shady Lake. Yeah. Shady all right.

Somebody came flying out the door. "Go home. You're stinkin' drunk," came a voice from within. Raucous laughter cut off when the door slammed shut.

He chuckled and got out of his van. Just the place.

The man bumped into him. Duncan nearly gagged from the stench of the liquor and his body odor—something between urine and vomit.

"Sorry captain," the man said, saluting. He grinned and showed half a mouth full of teeth—half black.

Duncan didn't know whether to deck the guy or drown him.

A woman walked out of the bar as he was about to enter. She had long blonde hair and a pretty face. Young. Maybe seventeen, eighteen. She could have been Annie when she'd been younger.

Red polished fingernails wrapped around his arm, and he smelled a hint of cheap perfume. "Hey you." Her voice was sexy, sultry—put on.

"Is Benny bothering you?" she asked. "Well . . ."

The girl's eyes raked over him. Like he might be her next breakfast. "Hang on," she said. "Let me take care of Benny."

"An Aerostar, Captain?" Benny said, looking at the van. "A vintage. Don't make 'em anymore."

Duncan smiled. "No, they don't," he said.

The girl was still looking him up and down. Surmising how much money he had in his pocket, Duncan figured.

Benny suddenly lurched away from them and ran to the back of the building.

"He has to pee," the girl said.

Duncan controlled his disgust. "Figured as much."

"What about you?" Her expression read seduction, her eyes read money.

"Me?"

"You . . . uh . . . want to party?" she asked.

He stepped back and casually leaned up against the light post. "Party huh?"

She smiled and pushed aside a see-through over shirt to reveal a halter top made of nylon. Her nipples showed through. She was primed.

"How much party?" He wanted to know.

"That depends on how much cash you have."

"Can I see a little more of what I'll be buying?" he asked.

The woman smiled, batted her eyelashes, and hooked her arm around his. She walked him over to the car—into the shadows and pulled up her top.

He nodded approvingly. "I guess playing with those for a while might be worth something at that. How much?"

"You're not a cop, are you?" Her eyes darted right and left as though giving herself an escape route.

"Hardly," he said. *A cop wouldn't be doing what I have planned.*

"Fifty."

"Get in."

When she'd slammed her door shut, she said, "I know a spot where we can have complete privacy. You'll love it. We can even go skinny dipping."

"Skinny dipping? Sounds like just the thing. Show me how to get there."

As they pulled out of the drive, he checked back to see if anyone had been watching. The drunk had already gone. Nobody was outside. Good.

"What's your name, honey?"

"How did you know?" she asked, laughing. "Know what?"

"That my name is Honey?"

He grinned cheerfully. "I'm psychic. Honey, I'm Edgar."

"Pleased to meet you, Edgar."

I'll just bet you are.

She directed him past the three bars, one grocery store, a row of trailers, then onto a side road that led down to the lake.

They stopped in front of a shed that looked like the big bad wolf had huffed and puffed and blown the place to smithereens. Two Porte-potties added a touch that exhumed a stench so pungent that Duncan coughed and turned in the opposite direction, a hand over his mouth. God, this woman was so tacky she'd take a trick here? Take him to a grassy toilet? Who did she think she was? Or rather, what did she think he was?

The toilet. He couldn't stand that smell. His long-haired blonde society mother had locked him in an outhouse once for an entire night. The ceiling made a home for spider webs who occupants delighted in crawling all over him all night. He'd been six. He shook with remembrance. Spiders. He hated spiders.

The only saving grace was a long stretch of grass leading down to a sandy beach. From there, he could see across the narrow end of the beach to the Campbell Inn.

Honey put her arms around his waist. "Sorry about the smell. The people of Lake Nager look at us as poor white trash and the parks don't bother to clean out the Porte-potties."

"No shit," Duncan said. Any sexual drive he had before, temporarily disappeared. But sexual drive was not why he was here. And the drive to kill grew stronger by the minute.

"You want to go skinny dipping?" she asked. Duncan laughed. "Does that come with the price?"

"Sure does," she said. "Come on. Last one in the water . . . and all that." Within seconds, Honey had shed her clothes along the beach.

Perfect. Duncan could enjoy the sex then give the bitch the surprise of her life. Instead of strangling her, he'd just hold her under water and drown her. She was so petite, it wouldn't be hard at all.

Duncan undressed and the two of them jumped into the lake.

Within a few feet they were up to their waist.

Honey started to swim out. Duncan followed, grabbed her at the waist and pulled her to him. His hands explored everywhere until they rested between her legs. Then his fingers were inside, and Honey groaned. Duncan wrapped her legs around his waist, then took her and enjoyed every minute. Under the half moon, Honey could have been Annie. She looked like her. Duncan closed his eyes and pretended. Finally, when his body exploded, he cried out her name—" Annabelle."

Honey slid out and treaded water. "Who?"

Duncan pulled back a little. "Annabelle was my wife. She died recently."

"I'm sorry," Honey replied. "You can pretend I'm Annabelle if you like."

"I'd like to call you Annabelle, if you don't mind," Duncan said.

"Sure. I'm here to please you."

And you will Honey-Annabelle. Believe me. You will.

But Honey got out of the water and began pulling her clothes on. Duncan watched her—couldn't believe she'd given him so little.

He'd thought she was having fun with him. "Come on back in here." He half-ordered.

"That will be extra."

She'd just royally pissed him off. He could almost feel his hands around that pretty little neck of hers. "How much more—and what will you give me in return?"

Duncan walked out of the water and shared her space of dripping water. He was hard again and didn't like it. He'd never thought of himself as a sexual being. Maybe it was the thought of throttling her that was turning him on.

"Give me a hundred, and we can stay out as late as you want.

You can *do* anything you want," she whispered.

That was about the dumbest thing she could have said. Duncan smiled. "Sure. That will be just great. Lay down on the grass and spread your legs. I'll show you some tricks I'll bet you've never learned."

"That sounds like a challenge." She pulled him down with her.

He asked her all too politely to take him in his mouth and she complied beyond his wildest imagination. Then he entered her again and soothed her hair out of her eyes. He pumped into her, and his hands reached her shoulders, then up. They were on either side of her neck. Honey was getting close to an orgasm of her own. In another zone. For a split-second Duncan thought she was so good, she should be saved.

Even he didn't realize what was happening until it was too late.

Slowly, his thumb moved forward and squeezed. Hard.

The shocked look on her face was worth the admission price he had no intention of paying. She blanked out before she could scream before she could struggle.

Honey-Annabelle was no more.

Duncan drove the van out of the park. He still needed to clear up one piece of business. Bernard Benny.

Chapter 37

Annie lay on a lounge chair looking at the sky with its puffy, *Please Don't Squeeze the Charmin* type clouds and the boat-to-boat covered lake. The afternoon sun beat in through the screen porch. A hot, lazy day. In the middle of the lake, kids jumped off and swam around a stationary raft. Life appeared to be a typical, normal vacation day in the Two-Lake Countries today.

Annie didn't think her life would ever get back to normal, before someone either drove a bullet through her head, strangled her, or successfully drowned her. A paradoxical thought for a beautiful place like this. Beautiful Lake Nager. Swimming, camping, hiking and murder. Oh yeah. Just great.

Mark and Annie had driven home from the upper lake around six in the morning. When she got back and saw the worried looks on Julia and Paul, she told them how sorry she was. She thought the note would explain all, thought it was for the best, but on reflection, maybe it hadn't. Sad that she'd caused such an upheaval, she went to bed.

Now, they all congregated on the porch. Mark stood with his back to everyone, appearing to watch the lake intently. Paul paced the floor and Julia watched them all from the rocker.

Paul stopped in front of Annie and said, "You understand that protecting you is our job, don't you? Catching this creep is imperative before any other young lady is killed."

Annie nodded. What else could she do? He was right. Paul reached in his top pocket for a cigarette.

"Paul, you'll kill yourself if you don't stop smoking so much. But, if you must, please take it outside away from the porch." Julia's voice was sharp with disapproval.

"Sorry." Paul put the cigarette back into its box, the box back into his top pocket.

Mark finally turned. "Annie and I had a long talk about this," he said quietly. "I don't think she really wanted to go anywhere, did you?"

Annie shook her head, but still couldn't bring herself to look anyone in the eye.

"Good," Paul said. "That's one worry off our hands." He put his thumbs in his pant belt loops and tried to look severe. "You had us scared half to death."

"Paul," Julia said. "I think Annie knows that. What she did was for our safety, not hers. I think she was brave to take that stand."

Paul opened his mouth.

"Although." Julia continued. "I think it was a lousy idea, and I'm glad she's back."

"Thank you," Annie said, not sure anyone even heard her. "I'm sorry for creating another mess for you. I really thought it would be easier—safer for me to be gone."

"What was the last thing you remember when you were in the hospital?"

Damn. She didn't want to go through this again. How could she remember anything when she was sleeping? "I remember Julia and I were talking, somebody with a white coat stuck a needle into my arm, something about checking my oxygen level."

Julia nodded. "I had to make rounds, and Mark went to work. We had Molly guarding Annie's room."

"I could have sworn I woke up and saw Duncan hovering over me—but it wasn't Duncan. It was someone who looked different."

Mark and Paul made eye contact.

Paul asked, "Do you remember any other dreams you had?" Annie nodded slowly. "Yes. A woman struggled with a man.

They were in a hospital room. Then, she was looking down at him from the ceiling while he choked her to death. Somehow this doesn't make sense. Maybe she fell to the ground, and he was on top of her. I don't remember anything else." The urge to throw up grew in strength. Annie resisted. "My God, she was blonde." It must have been the security guard who'd been watching my room.

Paul nodded. "Annie, I think you must have witnessed what happened." He urged. "What else do you remember?"

"Just a tall black, male nurse bending over a body lying next to my bed."

"Do you think he might have been responsible?" Mark asked.

"No. He was talking through his pager, calling for a code blue. Then all hell broke loose, and they wheeled me to another room. That's all I remember. I'm sorry."

"So, who the hell was it?" Paul asked, frustration written over his face.

"Duncan," Annie said. "It was him."

Paul cleared his throat. "Maybe. We'll find out for sure tonight who the devil is at that convention."

"And if Duncan is there, then we have a hired gun," Annie said. "A . . . hired gun?" Mark blinked his eyes at her and shook his head. "Um . . ."

But Julia was shaking her head. "I doubt a hitman would have flattened your tires or killed your cat. Hitmen usually do the job they were paid to do, then leave. This spells revenge."

Mark was staring open-mouthed at his mother. "How the hell do you know that?"

"Well, don't you agree?" she asked.

"Yes, in fact, I do. I don't think it's a hit man either."

"Did they find any fingerprints—I mean other than the ones that were supposed to be there?"

"They won't find any," Julia said. They all stared. How did *she* know?

"Why?" Paul stopped his pacing.

Julia said, "Look, gloves are for the taking at the hospital. Every room has a box of rubber gloves. I'm sure he took a pair and put them on."

Paul's cell phone went off.

"Yeah?" he said. "This better be good."

His face turned red, then white. Annie thought all he needed was a little blue and he'd be as patriotic as Nager.

"When?" he asked. "Sure." He nodded his head. "How long has she been dead?"

"Dead? Who's dead now?" Mark asked.

Annie huddled into her cocoon again. Someone else had died. Connected to her? She should have *left*. She stared at Paul who was now focusing on her. Of course, it was connected.

Paul nodded and clicked off. He put away his cell and gazed into space. "What the hell is going on here?"

Annie wasn't sure he was talking to them or to himself. "What?" All three asked in a chorus.

"Another murder. In Brighton. Mark, get your gun. We have to go."

He turned to Annie and Julia. "Ladies, I don't want to scare you . . ."

"*But* . . ."

"But I don't want you going anywhere. Stay inside with the doors locked. You'll have a security guard patrolling the grounds again, until we get back."

"Who was killed?" Julia asked.

"Her name was Honey. She hung around the Brighton bars."

"I know her," Julia said. "She has a young daughter whose father is in jail. Honey turns tricks late at night to support her child."

"How do you know that?" Mark asked.

"Because Julia knows just about everything that happens to everyone around Nager," Paul said. "Now come on." Three steps and he was at the porch.

"I've had just about enough of bombs and guns," Annie said. "And just about enough of Duncan. I feel like going out and finding him myself."

"You'll do no such thing," Mark said, reaching for a hook around the inside of the house door. He pulled out a hip holster and put it on, checking the gun for a clip.

"Honey wasn't killed with a gun or a bomb," Paul said. "She was strangled. Her body washed ashore."

Annie remembered the painting on Duncan's website. She shivered and wrapped her arms around her knees. "My God, don't tell me she was blonde."

Paul shrugged. "I don't know. We'll find out soon."

Mark knelt in front of Annie. "Honey, if this is connected, we'll find out. We *will* catch this guy."

Annie nodded. "I know you will."

Mark took her hands and kissed them. She smiled. That they'd catch him, she had no doubt. Whether they'd do it in time, was another story. *A whole other story.*

"Come on Mark." Paul was halfway out the screen door. Mark got up and stopped, shaking his head. "I don't understand this. He follows no particular pattern. He scares Annie with pictures of a drowning blonde girl under water lilies then he goes ahead and tries to shoot her. Then he strangles a security guard and a prostitute."

"He went to the hospital to kill me, didn't he?" Annie asked.

"I'm not going to lie . . ." Paul began, then stopped when Julia glared at him.

"And I think Molly saved your life," Julia said.

If she'd said anything else in the entire world it wouldn't have had more effect on her than that comment. "Yes, and it cost Molly her life." The guilt she'd tried to hide just came out anyway.

Mark stopped at the doorway and turned back to Annie. "None of this is your fault. Don't ever think it is. This is the work of a mad man. Or . . ." Mark hesitated, and his face clouded with uneasiness. Then he put his hand on the porch doorknob, ready to leave.

"Or?" Annie asked.

Mark let go and turned back. "Oh crap. Maybe this isn't the work of one man. Maybe we have two killers in Nager."

"Oh great. Just great." Julia rose and stomped into the living room.

"Oh Mark," Annie whispered. She rose and searched for something suitable to say. Then she simply said, "Please be careful."

She turned and followed Julia inside.

Chapter 38

Mark got into Paul's car, and they squealed backwards down the driveway until they reached the highway. Then they peeled forward onto the almost deserted asphalt and headed toward the other side of Lake Nager and Brighton.

"So, what have we actually accomplished? What do we know? We have two murders and one attempted murder. Possibly Annie— but possibly me." Mark blew through his mouth at that thought. "Annie's had threatening calls made from different stolen cell phones from several states. All calls recorded on several transmitters around here."

Paul fixed his eyes on the road. He held onto the steering wheel so tight, his knuckles turned white. "We won't know anything until we confirm that Duncan Byrne is actually at that psychiatry convention. I called the NYPD last night and his room has been slept in, he's checked in for messages and, several professors have said they've seen him."

"Uh huh. Did anyone bother to check the handwriting against Duncan's?"

Paul shrugged. "Yes. It's being analyzed. It's too close for someone who's not a hand-writing specialist to notice the difference. And that's another problem. Nobody has actually *spoken* to Duncan."

"I'll bet though," Mark said, "there's someone walking around that convention who could be a dead ringer for him."

Paul chuckled. "And, unless that fool is real careful—he may very well end up *dead*."

"So, what we're saying is—"

"Duncan Byrne is here in Nager and is crazy as a loon." A muscle flicked angrily at Paul's jaw. He was breathing hard.

Mark turned his head toward the window. He didn't want Paul to see the fear in his eyes or the trembling in his hands. This was Annie's life he was talking about—maybe others. Mark was a good cop, and he knew it. But this had become personal. He might not wait for a judge and jury if he found this bastard.

"I'll bet he's shaved the beard," Paul said. "He's probably changed his hair color and is blending in with the tourists. And even though he might have been only after Annie, I think he's expanding his repertoire."

"He's turning into a regular serial killer."

"But we don't know that. As yet, we can't prove Duncan killed Molly, and we don't know he killed this Honey woman. Or shot at your boat."

"I don't get it. Besides the drug dealer incident, the only killings we have around here are hold-ups with thugs who panic and shoot."

Paul nodded. "You're right. I wish they would catch that look-alike in New York."

"It shouldn't be that hard. Do they have someone standing by his door, waiting until he comes back?"

"Look, Mark, I know this is hard. There's no reason to be staking out Duncan Byrne in New York. Rodriguez is doing this as a favor. There isn't even anything illegal about him sending in a double to attend this convention. In fact, the only probable cause we have here is threatening phone calls. We have no one named Duncan Byrne here and nobody who looks like him."

"But we do have a killer. And, because of the nature of the crimes and the killer's MO—blonde hair, strangulation—I think we have probable cause."

They kept quiet for the rest of the ride. Both wore grim expressions; both lost in their own thoughts.

What's the clue, here? Where are you Byrne? What do you look like?

As they passed into the city limits, Paul put on his siren. People stopped and stared. Paul *rarely* had on his siren. Soon, they found several cars following them. The local version of ambulance chasers; the cop copyists.

A police car loomed up ahead, closing off the gravel road that led down to the lake. Paul waved, and the police moved, giving Paul enough room to bump down to Brighton's version of a park.

The stench hit Mark full blast from those damned Porte-potties. Didn't anyone ever clean them up? He made a mental note to ask. But right now, he focused on a man, a boy, a couple of cops and something lying on the ground.

A body lying on the ground.

"Why can't we see?" The boy, Mark determined to be around nine or ten, was asking the cop. The cop was flushed, flashing angry glares at the older man.

"What seems to be the problem here?" Paul asked.

"We found the body, and *he* put a tape around it and won't let us go down there," the boy said.

"That's his job," Mark said. "You might mess up the evidence and then we couldn't catch the killer."

"But our boat is down there. Can't we at least get our boat and go home?" the man asked.

"Sir," the deputy said. "They were fishing. Trolling along the shore and found the body floating in the water. Mr."

"McGinnis," the man said. "Michael McGinnis. My son is Jeffrey."

"Right . . . He called from his cell phone about a half-hour ago. I've taken their statements. Names, address and telephone number."

"Tell you what," Mark said. "After they've searched your boat, I'll have one of our men take it down the lake to a little alcove. You can—"

"Searched our boat? For what. *We* didn't do anything."

"I understand," Mark said. "But we have to investigate everything. That's procedure. There's a path you can walk through to get there. Is that fair enough?"

"I suppose so," the man said, not looking like that was fair at all. "Want to see the body!" Jeffrey whined.

Lord preserve him from amateurs, especially kids. The forensics van was pulling down the driveway.

"Dad! Just like TV. Can we watch them work, huh?"

"Son," Mark said as gently as he could, considering he'd like to throttle the boy about now. "You and your dad can read about this in the papers later, okay? You have to go home now."

"The papers?" The boy looked around. "I don't see . . ."

But another van followed the forensic team. The local TV station. Oh God, would there be no end to this interference?

"Can we be on television?"

The team ran out of their van. One started filming, while the other stuck a microphone in Mark's face. Mark frowned, his most professional murder frown. "You understand, this scene is being investigated—so there can be no professional comments at this time. This family was out trolling and found the body. They can tell you more than I can right now. I just arrived. Haven't even seen the crime scene yet. The chief of police, Paul Reinert is standing over there. You can ask him questions when he's ready. Meanwhile, I have to go investigate." He shrugged his shoulders and smiled his you-know-how-it-is smile.

As he was leaving, a reporter already had a microphone in the boy's face. The kid's expression turned ultra-serious. "My name is Jeffrey McGinnis. We found a body in the lake."

Paul caught up to him and they went under the tape together.

Mark glared back at the reporter. "Little Jeffrey is having way too much fun."

"How the hell did the reporters get here so quick?" Paul asked. "I'm thinking McGinnis probably called them before or after they called us."

"His fifteen minutes of fame."

"Precisely."

Photographers were taking pictures of the body. Evidence gatherers were screaming not to screw up their crime scene and Mark was staring down at the nude body, shaking until his teeth chattered. "Oh shit," he said.

Mark had gotten used to dead bodies through the years. Gun shots, strangulations, even a hanging or two. But this was different. This was something that made him want to throw up.

The girl had long blonde hair. From the back, the killer might have mistaken her for Annie.

"Oh shit. No." Mark knelt down beside the body, touching nothing, but thinking everything.

Paul took Mark aside.

"Mark, Annie and your mother aren't safe. Look, we can handle things here. Take my car and go back home. Our deputy can't be everywhere at once. When I get back, we'll have some decisions to make."

Mark didn't have to be told twice.

Chapter 39

The news repeated the same stories over and over. The war in the Middle East, the street gangs in Chicago, guards killed at the Mexico-United States border.

Annie paced in the living room.

Lady tried to keep up with her, gave up, jumped up on the sofa and made a nest of a blanket. Soon, she was snoring.

Julia put on Mozart's *Eine Kleine Nacht Musique* softly then poured a glass of wine, but it wasn't working. Annie gulped the wine like it was water.

"That won't help. You'll just get drunk."

"Promise?" Annie said, only half listening to what Julia said and to what she'd replied.

Julia didn't laugh back, and she wasn't smiling. Her eyes had a sadness in them, and although this was a time for fear—Annie sensed this would be quite a different topic.

"Honey sit down. We need to talk."

Annie's heart sank. Every time her mother had said that, something bad had—or was about to happen. Annie sat on the sofa next to Lady.

"Something's bothering me." Julia continued. "Concerning your health."

Oh God. Either Mark had told her—or— "What about it? I don't have any more headaches. Except for being a little stiff, I feel fine."

"That's not what I want to talk to you about."

A twinge of disappointment settled over her. She'd wanted to hide this and didn't seem able. "Mark told you?"

Julia's eyebrows shot up, but other than that, she held her surprise very well. She pulled a rocking chair across from her.

"Told me what, Annie?"

"Oh, well . . ."

"When you tell Mark something in confidence, it stays in confidence. So, no. I don't know what you told Mark. I wish you'd tell me, though. What's causing these sudden pains?"

Annie opened her mouth, denial on her tongue.

"Oh honey, you can't hide something like this. It shows all over the place. If you don't want to tell me, fine. But don't deny it's happening."

"It's happening. When it comes, it hurts pretty bad."

Julia nodded. She looked like she dreaded what might be coming next.

"Look, it's not a life-threatening illness. But it is terminal in one sense. Look, Mark is the only other person, beside my doctor in New York who knows. This is what I know."

Annie poured her heart out to Julia for a half hour. She went through her marriage, the near accident at the subway station, the fall down the stairs, loss of her child and divorce. She left nothing out, including the bruising to her uterus and the permanent scar left in her mind. That she could never have children.

Annie honestly didn't think she had another tear left from this, but she was wrong. Julia brought over a box of tissues.

"That was why you wanted to leave New York and come to Nager?"

Annie nodded. "It seemed ideal. A place I could do the type of work I really wanted to do, counsel people in trouble, and get away from the world that had cause such tragedy." She tried to fight off that raw primitive grief that racked her body and soul. She shook her head. "I was wrong. That world followed me here."

"Annie," Julia said gently. "That world will be caught and brought to justice. But your uterus can heal. It may take a long time, but there's no reason to think you can't have children. Look, do I have your permission to talk to your doctor in New York?"

Surprised, Annie almost smiled. "Of course, if you think it might do some good."

"I don't know what it will do, but it's a start. Then let's get some X-Rays and find out just where we're at?"

"That's fine, Julia. I appreciate your concern about me."

"Was your husband always this abusive?"

"No. He never laid a hand on me. Controlling, I guess he was, but I always wanted to go in the direction he wanted me to. I didn't even notice."

I didn't even notice. Not until that hand came down on my back and pushed.

". . . In local news. The body of Honey Wright was found in a Brighton Park this afternoon by a fisherman and his son. Police are . . ."

Annie and Julie immediately focused on the TV screen. Mark was talking into the microphone, telling the news team and viewing public, there was nothing to report yet. But a close up revealed the woman's long blonde hair. Annie moved closer to the screen and touched where the hair lay wet and mangled.

"Annie. No."

Annie shook her head repeatedly. "No. No. She's blonde like me. Long blonde hair. Molly was blonde like *me*. My God, he's going after blondes, Julia.

Julia turned off the TV. "Sit." She poured another glass of wine and this time didn't say a word when Annie gulped.

Annie put down her glass. Supposing it *wasn't Duncan?* "Nobody will be safe until this person is caught. Whether it's Duncan or someone else. I'm assuming it's him, but supposing it's not. Supposing it's another Ted Bundy who happens to have a thing for long-haired blondes instead of brunettes with their hair parted down the middle?"

"God, I hope not. Whichever it is though, you're not safe. It's a damned good thing we have Lady, a security guard and me."

Annie crossed her legs and leaned forward. "You?" she almost laughed. "That's strange company you've put yourself in."

Julia smiled. "Absolutely. I can shoot a gun with the best of them. Remember, my husband was a cop—and a good one. He taught me. Speaking of which," she said, rising and going into a small study off the living room. "Can you shoot?"

"No," Annie called back. "At least I've never tried."

Julia came back carrying a pistol. "No time like the present. Come on. We'll go into the basement. My husband had a pistol range set up down there."

A pistol range. They had a pistol range in the basement.

Mark screeched Paul's car to a halt in the driveway. Then heard something that scared the shit out of him. Gun shots.

He saw his deputy racing across the lawn.

"When did this start?" Mark asked as they took off up the porch steps.

"I heard the first shot a few seconds ago."

They crammed into the doorway at the same time. The security guard deferred to his boss. Then they were creeping down the stairs, guns drawn.

Mark pointed and stopped. He almost dropped the gun. His mother was behind Annie, steadying her hand as she aimed for a target.

"Oh my God," he said.

Both ladies wore ear plugs and didn't turn around. Annie shot and missed the bull's eye, but at least made the second ring.

"Take out the damned ear plugs," Mark screamed.

That they heard.

"Oh, hi Mark," Julia said. "Why are you two pointing guns at us?"

"Because we thought someone was shooting at *you*."

"Well, as you can see, sweetie, nobody was. We were shooting at a target. I thought, considering the circumstances, it would be best if Annie learned to shoot. She's making very good progress."

Mark shook his head, trying to keep from laughing. But this was too serious for that. "I thought you'd just started."

"Well, we had, but Annie has a very steady hand. I don't think it will take her long at all."

His mother! Would you believe this? "Mom, can't you let me manage the business of taking care of Annie?"

Julia took the gun from Annie and put it down. "No dear. You know Mrs. Clinton's philosophy . . . 'It takes a village'. Well, this is our village right here."

Actually, his mother was right. The more Annie learned self-defense, the better off she would be.

"I don't suppose you've taught her karate," Mark said. Julia shook her head. "Not . . ."

"Not to worry," Annie said. "I already have a brown belt in karate."

Mark looked at her and just gaped. He couldn't help it. "You have a what?"

"A brown belt in karate," Annie said, sweetly. "I took a class at NYU. Duncan insisted. Of course, that was when we were first married."

"I see," Mark said.

"Sir." The security guard tapped him on the back. "Since you're overseeing gun shooting and karate, can I just go back to staking out the house?"

"Yeah, sure," Mark replied. "Whatever." Karate. The woman knew karate.

Chapter 40

Mark was on the phone with Rodriquez, trying to listen, talk and get up the wooden basement steps without stumbling and falling onto his knees. His imagination still hadn't cleared from the visions of his mother showing Annie how to shoot. "Paul's not here. This is Mark Driscoll."

"Mark? Sorry, thought I'd gotten Paul's number." "No, but that's okay. You got my cell. What's up?"

"I have information for you."

"Thank God for that. Hang on. I'm at home. I need to find some privacy." *It's about time.* His attitude was coming out, and he knew it. If he wanted anything, he'd better act a bit more friendly.

"Look, amigo. Sorry. Our precinct has been kind of busy with a car bombing."

That tidbit pounded into Mark's brain. Car bombings. CNN News reported that several people had died on a busy New York City street when a suicide bomber blew up his van. The street had looked like a nightmare in Iraq. "Oh shit, I'm sorry. By comparison, a serial killer looks tame."

"Serial killer you say? And here I was thinking about getting away from it all and moving to Wisconsin."

"We could always use good detectives up here. We'll find the money for you."

"Good. I might take you up on it. Live in one of your campgrounds during the summer. Move to town in the winter and go skiing. Sounds pretty good to me." He paused. "Now, tell me about this serial killer."

Mark looked through the open office door at Annie and his mother. Julia was showing Annie a semi-automatic from his father's gun collection. She'd pulled out a clip and was showing her how to load them. He thought they might not hear his conversation on the porch. Maybe. He moved out there.

"How much has Paul told you?"

"Since our last conversation? We've been on the phone several times a day. I heard about someone attacking you and Dr. O'Brien while you were in your boat." Deep sign from his end of the phone. "I heard there'd been a murder, that it hadn't been Dr. O'Brien and she was home and was okay. That's all I know."

"Someone strangled a security guard at the hospital and a prostitute in an outskirt village of Brighton. They both had long blonde hair."

Rodriguez groaned. "As does Dr. O'Brien."

"We're anxious to catch this animal. I thought he might be this Duncan Byrne, but now . . ."

"But now?" Papers rustled over the phone. "I have news for you. Duncan Byrne is not at the convention. We found the guy who was using his room."

Mark's heart did a summersault and toppled all the way to the floor and back. "That right? You got him?"

"Hell yeah, we got him. Hey, amigo, you can't be surprised by this. We're the NYPD. We always get our man."

"No. I didn't mean to doubt New York's finest. I even expected it. But it's just so bloody awful hearing it said aloud."

"I know exactly how you feel. Kurt Adder was a grad student of Dr. Byrne's who was promised an A on his dissertation if he went along with this, and an F with the promise of bringing to light a shady past if he didn't."

"A shady past?"

"The guy had been a heroin addict."

"Oh hell. So, Byrne blackmailed him into doing this."

"Yep. Adder said it didn't sound like such a bad assignment considering he could use Dr. Byrne's charge cards and go off to any workshops he wanted. He wanted an A and didn't want the world to know he'd been addicted to heroin."

"That would have made a future for him difficult," Mark said. "Byrne is a slime ball, and I hope he rots in hell." Yeah. He really did wish he could unleash the devil upon Duncan Byrne. "Does this guy know where Byrne is?"

"No. Neither does his housekeeper, anyone at the university or acquaintances at the convention. They all thought Kurt Adder was Duncan Byrne. He'd come into workshops late and eat out so nobody could talk to him."

"So, now we know where Duncan Byrne is…."

"Not exactly, Rodriguez," Mark said. "He's here, somewhere in Nager, but disguised and nobody has seen him. At least not as Duncan Byrne."

"Look, I'd like to come help you catch this bastard."

"You'd be welcome, believe me. I speak for Paul too. And, if you need a crime Byrne committed in NY, I think I can safely say, we suspect him of the attempted murder of his wife and the murder of his unborn daughter."

"Damn," Rodriguez said. "I nearly lost my badge because I pursued that. Wait a second." A file slammed then he was back. "Let me get back to you." Rodriguez clicked off.

<h1 style="text-align:center">Chapter 41</h1>

Duncan needed information.

He'd spent the morning talking to groggy-eyed and hung-over campers who were actually up after the campground's all-nighter fish-boil. Nobody had heard anything. Big surprise. Thank God for drunken stupors.

No cops had been around yet either. Maybe they hadn't found the body. He arranged to have brunch with Laura Campbell. If anyone knew what was going on, she would.

As he drove out of the campground, a police car drove in. Okay. So, unless someone had been caught in an alcoholic binge or a drug raid was imminent, they'd found the body and were investigating.

Duncan stopped a few hundred yards ahead as the police car turned toward the office. Wouldn't hurt to find out what they wanted. On the other hand . . . He drove onto the highway into Nager.

A red minivan. Had anyone seen it in the vicinity of Brighton? He doubted it. Everyone had been inside, except an old drunk, who'd been too curious for his own good.

Duncan sat with Laura Campbell on Campbell Inn's outdoor patio, soaking in the sun. On this glorious July afternoon, Lake Nager was probably as full of boaters and swimmers, as it was with bass and perch.

Laura wore black Capri pants and a white halter tie top. Her dark hair hung down her neck in a thick braid. A stunner. Too bad he wasn't looking— He'd bet though, she'd love to come to New York. Maybe after his mission? He leaned back in his chair, stared into the dark eyes of Ms. Laura and realized that could never be. He'd be with Annabelle under the murky lily pond. Probably fending off the restless spirit of his mother.

"It's sad," Laura said. "Molly McGuire was one of my best friends in high school. She put herself through school . . ." Laura looked like she might cry. Almost. Not quite. "She was pregnant for God's sake. Her husband adored her. Why her. It's not fair."

Duncan took Laura's hand. "Life isn't fair, Laura." *The fact is that if you had a remote inkling of who I am and what I'm doing here, you wouldn't be alive to talk about it either.*

"Well, I'm doing what I can for the family. We're hosting a reception after the funeral. Everyone will be invited. Including you if you want to come. Edgar, I know you didn't know . . ."

Duncan squeezed her hand. "Of course, I'll be there for you Laura. Anything you'd like me to do, just name it."

"Thank you. That means a lot."

A waiter brought a gin and tonic for Duncan and a Margarita for Laura. They sipped and watched the crowded lake.

"I haven't seen much of you for the past few days. Too bad you had so much work to do," Laura said. "We've finally had some beautiful weather."

Don't pry, Ms. Laura. Don't pry.

"I'm working on a project now. I'm close to the end. Just a few odds and ends, then I'll be totally free. You can show me around town."

Laura nodded, but her focus was on the Driscoll's house on the peninsula. She picked up a pair of binoculars that every table had chained to a leg of the table.

"See someone you know?"

"Yes. Some friends. I'm wondering why they have cops hanging around the grounds."

"May I?" His hands reached across the table.

Laura handed Duncan the glasses. Sure enough. A different deputy. A woman this time, walking the perimeter. He wondered if whoever took a shot at Mark Driscoll on the Fourth, might shoot the deputy down. Interesting concept. Would make for a good show.

He'd thought about that. Apparently, he wasn't the only one trying to get at the Driscoll family.

A shadow covered the table. Duncan and Laura looked up into the face of one of Nager's permanent deputies.

"Howdy, Miss Campbell."

Laura beamed. "Hi Fred."

The bitch was flirting. These women were alike. They couldn't even keep their minds on the man they were with for one damned meal.

"What brings you here? Business or pleasure?"

Fred Goodwin put his hat onto the table. "Sorry for interrupting. Important." Fred interrogated Duncan with his eyes. His discomfort came close to the way he felt when he'd run into Mark and his damned dog. What the hell. Did they take courses in Greeting- Intimidation 101?

Duncan reached over and shook the man's hand. "I'm Edgar Allenton. Glad to see Nager's so well protected."

Fred shrugged. "I hope so. That's why I'm here."

"Oh, about poor Molly?" Laura looked around for a waiter. "Do you want a drink?"

The deputy shook his head. "Can't. I'm on duty. And no. Not specifically about Molly. This is another one."

Laura's turned pale and shook her head. "What in God's name is going on here? Ever since . . ."

"Ever since what?" Duncan prodded.

"Nothing," Laura said. "I shouldn't have even thought it." She turned her attention to Fred, who was looking out over the water. He didn't appear to want to continue the conversation.

"Why are you here?"

"Earlier this afternoon, a young woman's body was found near the park in Brighton."

Laura looked down and shook her head. "Who was it? A tourist? A boater who got out of control? A suicide?"

"Ms. Campbell," Fred said, "I'm sorry. Don't do this to yourself. Honey Wright was found face down in the water by a fisherman and his son. She'd been strangled, but the final cause of death, they think was drowning. They won't know until the autopsy is complete."

"Oh, my God," Duncan said. "Did you know her, Laura?"

Laura shook her head. "Only a little. We hung around in different circles. But everyone around here, outside the tourists knows everyone else pretty much. Honey had a lousy life. She's worked for me as a waitress for a while, then I guess she decided she could make more as a prostitute."

"Oh," Duncan said. The word made him want to go ballistic. He'd learned to control it well.

Fred said, "Look. We think it's someone who might be after Dr. O'Brien, the new psychologist at the hospital. We're checking handwriting samples, so I'd like to take your books with me."

"My books? That's impossible," Laura said. "No. We need those books for auditing purpose."

"You'll get them back, I promise," Fred said.

"Laura, if you'll excuse me for a minute, this conversation should be a private one and I have to use . . . Well, I'll be right back."

Laura and Fred were arguing when Duncan left and headed for the men's room, detouring by way of the desk. The clerk was helping a family with their luggage, the book unattended.

Duncan flipped to the page where he'd signed and tore it out, careful to wipe down the rest of the book from any fingerprints he might have left. He stuffed the sheet into his pants pocket and met her on his way back outside.

"Sorry," she said. "I'll be right back. They want to compare some handwriting samples."

"Sure. I'll be enjoying my drink and looking at the scenery through the binoculars."

Especially the peninsula.

<h1 style="text-align:center">Chapter 42</h1>

After a futile day of investigations into the tourists of Nager, Mark was exhausted, and the day wasn't over. The clouds on the horizon pushed the sun beneath the earth. The sun protested spewing forth a few streaks of purple and orange. Mark's muscles protested too, but little good it did them. Mark swallowed the last two Tylenol he carried in his jean's pocket, downed them with a beer and watched Paul drive his mother out of her house and into town.

The two women in Mark's life were driving him crazy. They simply didn't want to follow directions. They second-guessed everything he and Paul ordered them to do.

So maybe police procedural-style hadn't been the best tactic in the world. But they knew he and Paul were scared to death for their safety. Didn't they? They knew that he and Paul would do what was in their best interest. Didn't they?

Oh crap. He was turning into a macho asshole. Women like Annie and his mother did not take kindly to male dictators. Period. He should have known better.

Paul's car faded into the darkness of the tree-lined driveway. Soon all Mark saw were red taillights and a blinker indicating a right turn—toward town and the hospital.

His mother had been pissed when told she should pack a bag and stay at the hospital for a few days until they caught this maniac. She'd pointed out the man was not after redheads and Annie could use all the help she could get—especially a woman friend, and especially a friend who knew how to *shoot.*

Yeah, but although a serial killer might be after blondes, if this one had a grudge against Mark, he might get even with *him* by harming his mother. After Molly's murder, the hospital had extra security guards on duty. And, with a threat looming over the head of Dr. Julia Driscoll, those guards would take turns keeping her in sight. Whether she wanted them there or not.

He looked up to Annie's bedroom balcony. She was glaring down at him. Damn it. He'd pulled apart the distaff team of Thelma and Louise and Annie was pissed. For God's sakes, the woman trusted his *mother* more than she trusted *him.*

"Annie," he yelled up at her. "Get off the balcony. I'll be right in. We can talk."

"I don't particularly want to talk to you right now." "Shit, Annie!"

Annie put her hands on her hips and huffed. Then turned around and disappeared into her bedroom.

He had chills every time he thought about Honey's corpse and how much she'd looked like Annie from the back.

He wanted to get Annie out of the state. If possible, into Canada. But, as she was the only one who really knew Duncan, she needed to remain.

A police squad car pulled into the driveway and Fred emerged carrying a briefcase. Mark hoped that meant good news. The guy had been traipsing all over Nager today. Maybe he'd come back with something useful.

Fred gave Mark a friendly salute. "So, we're making this our temporary headquarters? Good thinking Mark. We can keep a twenty-four-hour watch on Dr. O'Brien, and she won't have to be confined to the police station."

"That was my plan." As though he could keep Annie confined *anywhere.* Still, now he could feel free to investigate on his own.

"Besides, Julia promised she'd made sandwiches. Her sandwiches are famous."

Mark mustered up a grin. He wasn't feeling all that cheerful, but a little comradeship couldn't hurt in a dire situation.

Soon three unmarked police cars lined the driveway. Paul, Mark and seven deputies were seated around the dining room table spreading out the notes they'd gathered, trying to keep them free of mustard or mayonnaise.

Annie wasn't invited, but she made her presence known at every given opportunity. When Simone Glen, the only woman detective, suggested she stay, Mark threw up his hands and made room for her next to him.

In one day, they'd hit all campgrounds, motels, inns and bed- and- breakfasts in the area.

They compiled a list of a hundred or so from New York. Most were families, so he figured he might be able to eliminate them— although not necessarily.

Annie looked at him like he had three heads. "My ex-husband has a PhD in psychology, and he's a master in disguise. The man would know how to get a phony driver's license if he wanted. Look, Duncan has a lot of resources at his disposal, just like Kurt Adder who posed as him at the Psych Convention."

"Well, look. Here's something." Fred pulled out the Campbell Inn's roster and opened it to where a recent page was missing—torn out. "I called Ms. Campbell about it and she denied any knowledge about any missing pages. They'd just recently audited the books. She thought maybe the log pages had skipped a number."

Mark looked at him and ran his finger over the jagged edge. "I doubt that. Someone tore out this page."

"Well, yeah," Fred said. "Hm, maybe ye ol' Campbell Inn is doctoring their books?"

"That would be good news," Annie said. "But I don't think this missing page has to do with defrauding the IRS."

Everyone turned to her.

"Oh bother," she said. "We know someone at the Campbell Inn tore out this page. Most likely Duncan. If not, you have another problem on your hands. You can poll the room numbers that aren't listed in the book. It's a possibility Laura will remember who belongs to what room. But that will take some time we don't have the luxury of wasting. Or . . ." Annie pushed her hair behind her ears. "I can pinpoint the perp for you. Plain and simple. Either way, it looks like you're going to need me."

Mark glared a tiny little hole into her. "Damn, Annie, you've been watching too many cop shows."

"I don't know, Mark," Fred said. "I think this woman of yours has a good point."

Mark threw up his hands. "We'll see."

"Okay guys, if this is it, we'll touch base tomorrow. This is about as much as I can stand tonight."

Seemed all right with them. Within ten minutes, they were out of the door, into their cars and gone.

So was Annie. She'd hightailed it to her room before the last one had left.

Annie sat cross-legged on her bed, answering e-mail. She heard movement coming from the doorway and gazed up at Mark leaning against the door. His expression gave the impression of sadness—profound loss. She suddenly knew what he was going to say.

"I think it's best if you let me drive you to your friend's place in Canada. Let us handle catching criminals."

He turned on a small brass lamp and turned off the main ceiling lamp. The hallway provided the only other light and they sat in semi- darkness.

Annie stared at Mark for a moment. She was about to say that was a good idea. She'd been saying that all along. But the truth was, Annie didn't want to leave the Driscoll's and even more, didn't want to leave Mark. She really liked him. Maybe even loved him a bit.

Her mind went back and forth on that one too. She couldn't give him what he'd eventually want from a wife. That is, if he wanted a wife at all. Maybe it would be better if she did leave.

She sighed. This was for the best. "Okay," she said. "But instead of your driving me all the way to Canada, why don't you just drive me to the airport, and I'll fly up there. I'll give my friends a call."

Mark frowned and paced the hall while Annie spoke to her friends. Something still bothered him. That is, besides Annie leaving. About the gun shots. It didn't fit.

A long-range rifle had fired that shot. The casings hadn't been found. Mark suspected they wouldn't find them anyway. They would be at the bottom of the lake by now. Those shots could have been fired from the lake or from the ground, or from one of the rooms in the Inn for that matter.

It had been the perfect psychological moment, the exact moment when everyone had their head turned toward the sky.

He'd been sure Duncan had arranged this. But now, he was no longer positive. He was here, of that he was sure, but Duncan's MO did not fit the shooter profile.

Mark desperately needed to go to bed, his head felt heavy, his eyelids drooping, but he knew no sleep would come tonight. He wanted to go down and sleep on the porch, but that would be a stupid idea, in case someone was waiting to take another shot at him.

Shot at him.

Wait a minute. Wasn't it *Annie* they were after?

The bullet pierced the back of *his* cabin seat. Not hers. Maybe the guy hadn't been a bad shot after all. Maybe, it was just dumb luck that Mark had moved when he did.

Mark grabbed onto his bed post. His knuckles turned white. Why him? Retaliation? One of the dead boy's family out to get revenge? Mark thought about Paul's wife. It had happened before.

<h1 style="text-align:center">Chapter 43</h1>

Mark's restlessness got the better of him. He walked past Annie's room, she held the phone out to him, shrugged and pointed. Apparently, she hadn't reached her friends yet. He mouthed, "I'll be across the hall."

He started for his room, but changed his mind, walked downstairs and pushed the porch screen door hard.

The *Angelina* gently bobbed up and down on rolling waves coming into shore. A dull pole light dimly illuminated the dock, but outside of that, only a moon and the stars that peeked in and out of the clouds and the blinking lights across the lake provided a beacon down to the water's edge.

Mark was at a crossroads, and he knew it. He didn't want Annie to leave any more than he thought Annie wanted to go. The truth was, he'd fallen for her—hard. Suddenly, everything he'd thought was important in a relationship, wasn't. It didn't matter if she couldn't have children. He just wanted to be around her. Even if she was a bit of a pain in the ass sometimes. Hell. So was he. So was everyone who was interesting. The tragedy here was, if Annie left and if Duncan went after her, she could never return. She'd always be on the run.

"Hi. I thought you were in your room. Why . . ."

Mark whirled around. In fact, he nearly jumped out of his skin. "I'm sorry if I startled you." Annie wore a long white cotton nightgown with blue ribbons laced in the neckline and a blue shawl around her shoulders. The moonlight cast a silver hue through her hair as it hung over the shawl.

"Annie," he said. He wanted to yell at her, and at the same time take her in his arms and protect her—love her.

His mouth went dry. He wanted her, couldn't have her. So, he did the only rational thing he could. He got good and mad. "What the hell are you doing here?" His voice came out gruffer and more unnatural than he intended.

Annie's eyes opened wide. Her mouth flew open. Then her eyes locked into his in mortal combat mission. "Wow. What the hell is wrong with *you?* I thought we had things to discuss. I just got off the phone— My friends are away on vacation. I . . ."

"Wait. Back up a second." He took a step closer and grabbed her arm. "Coming out here was the stupidest thing you could have done. What if someone was—is, out here watching the house. Watching for *you.*"

She tried to jerk away, but he held fast. "Mark, stop it. You're hurting me."

Shit. He was shaking her. He pulled away in mid shake, horrified. He'd never shaken a woman before in his life.

"I'm sorry, but if I'm to protect you, I have to know you'll play by the rules."

She didn't look at him but stood next to him and stared out over the lake. "Are there really rules in this game? Does Duncan have rules?"

Mark was silent. She was being totally irrational here. "Damn it Annie—killers don't have rules, they just—"

Annie appeared not to have heard him. She continued to stare. "You saved my life," Annie said. "In many ways. I'd be dead if it weren't for you."

"Yes," he replied softly.

"You know, they say once you've saved a life, you're responsible for that life forever." Her voice sang like the warm tones of a cello.

Mark smiled. He wanted to say he'd like to take on the job permanently. However, he didn't. Instead, time for some cold hard realism. "Old wives tale. Besides, I am responsible for you. It's part of my job description, saving damsels in distress."

A passing cloud shrouded the night sky. He strolled to the edge of the dock, Annie close behind. The scent of her body drove his body hard against his jeans. Painful. She was driving him crazy.

"And am I a damsel in distress?" she asked, that cello tone sultry and seductively low.

He turned and put his hands on her shoulders. "You are the most competent, intelligent woman I've ever known, Annie. But at this very moment, you are a damsel in distress. And a stubborn one. I'm honor bound to protect and keep you alive. But if you put yourself in dangerous situations where I can't defend you . . . God I don't know what I'd do if anything happened to you." Shit. That hadn't come out like he intended.

"What are you saying?"

Mark shook his head. "I don't know what I'm saying. Maybe, once this is over . . . Maybe we can . . ." Mark turned away, away from this siren that sent his libido into overdrive.

"Maybe what?"

Damn it. He *knew* she would ask that. He wasn't ready to use the word *relationship* yet. He wasn't ready to use the word *love* yet either.

He put his hand gently on her arm and went back into neutral territory. "Look, I'm sorry. I didn't mean to manhandle you, and I sure as hell don't mean to scare you, but somebody's trying to *kill* you, if you haven't noticed."

"I've noticed," she replied.

"Finding Duncan is the most important thing we can do right now."

But no matter how he tried to keep his mind on business, he gazed up and down the bodice of her nightgown. The outline of her nipples pushed at the cotton of her gown. He stood inches from her, his body in sexual agony. He had to control this. Had to.

What was worse, Annie noticed. He wasn't sure whether she was blushing or giggling, but he wanted to do what he'd done with girls when he was eight. Tickle them. Whatever possessed him, he didn't know. But he did just that.

Annie broke out into a grin and was about to say something when he tickled her. She yelped, moved back and started to laugh.

"I swear Annie O'Brien, I'm going to throw you off this dock."

"You'd better not." She challenged. "I'll pull you in with me."

"Oh yeah? Is that a threat?"

It was déjà vu. First night all over again. When Lady had knocked them into the water. Annie grabbed Mark around the waist and jumped. They made a hole where they landed, tsunami waves hurtling over the dock.

"Cooled off yet?" she asked.

He splashed water at her. She splashed back.

The water came up to their waist—approximately. Didn't matter though, they were thoroughly soaked. Mark pressed himself up so close to Annie's back, she gasped. The cold water had done nothing to alleviate the strain of his erection. She moved back into him, and he couldn't hide it from her.

She turned into his arms, laughed then looked serious. "Oh Mark, I'm sorry. I didn't realize what this . . ."

"Annie, it's okay." He caught her around the waist and held her close into him.

Wet hair rested against wet cheek. His lips caressed as they traveled up her neck to the back her ear, where they rested. He nibbled. She was so close. So clean, the smell of lake floating up and down her skin. Female, vibrant and infinitely sexual.

He quivered at the thought of thrusting himself between her legs, inside her . . . .

"Then you don't hate me anymore?" she whispered. Her body molded into his.

"Hate you? Lord no," he whispered, his arms locked under her breasts. "There's a fine line between love and hate, Annie. And what I'm feeling for you is far from hateful."

The cloud had drifted away, and the moon appeared, brightening the dock with its crescent.

"You have to know I don't hate you."

He turned her into his arms and caught the bottom side of her chin with his finger, forcing her to look at him.

Annie asked, "Do you love me? Is that what you're saying?" Mark stiffened and Annie pulled back.

"Hell. I've put us both on the spot now, haven't I?"

Mark kissed her cheek, drowning in that wonderful scent. But he couldn't say it. Why did everything have to be so damned *complicated?* "I don't know, Annie. What do you mean by love?"

"This." She kissed him.

Mark knew at that moment he was drowning in love.

Chapter 44

One minute Annie was in the water hanging onto the dock. The next, she had an arm around Mark's neck, being kissed Hollywood style.

Oh my God. I didn't know people really kissed that way. Except in the movies. More.

She was about to kiss him back when a pistol shot brought her back to reality. Two pistol shots. She let out a short screech before Mark covered her mouth with his hand.

"Shh," he whispered. "Hang on to the dock, I'll be right back." Mark ducked under the water and swam to the other side of the dock.

Once more, the pistol cracked. "We have you covered. Come out of the water with your hands up."

A woman's voice. "Get out here now!" Her voice was gruff, angry, authoritative. Annie hoped with all her heart she was one of the good guys.

"Officer Glen. It's me Mark. For God's sake don't shoot me."

"Oh, good God. Mark! What the hell are you doing out here?"

Annie heard splashing and assumed Mark was getting out of the water. She couldn't really tell what was happening, just that Mark knew the woman. Annie waded to shore. A young female deputy, holding a pistol at her side, grinned from ear to ear.

Annie didn't think it was quite that funny.

"Sorry Dr. O'Brien. I'm Deputy Simone Glen." She started to laugh, then giggle, then stopped. "Sorry. I think I'll go check the back of the house. Uh . . . I think it needs checking. I never thought I'd find you . . ." She giggled again. "here. All wet. Wait 'til the guys at the station hear about this."

Mark and Annie stood together at the edge of the dock, drenched and dripping, watching the fading figure of Nager's queen of pistol-packing deputies, the African American beauty, Simone.

Annie didn't have much time to think about her. Without warning, Mark lifted Annie into his arms and was carrying her toward the house. Her fingers must have unbuttoned his shirt because it flew open when he butted her bedroom door open with his hip and deposited her in the bathroom. Already, a pool of water grew at her feet.

"Well, this is romantic," Annie said.

Mark turned on the light. "Yeah, isn't it?" His gaze hit her face then fell to the ground and back. He was inspecting her.

"You see something you like?"

He grinned. "Well, yeah. I mean, cotton doesn't hide much when it's wet."

Heat rushed up into her face. "Oh, bother! Now, you're embarrassing me. You're wet yourself. Why don't you go dry off and let me change."

"Well, hell, Ma'am. I thought you'd let me dry you off." Mark sat on the edge of the bathtub. "It would be fun. Trust me."

"I don't doubt that."

He took her hand. "You know, you really should get out of that nightgown. You'll catch cold."

Annie pulled back and put her hands on her waist. Catch cold. "Uh . . . Mark. In case you haven't noticed, it's about eighty degrees. I doubt I'm going to catch cold."

Mark raised one eyebrow. "Modest, huh?" The monster was playing.

"Modest?"

"Okay, look I'll change and let you dry off. But I'm warning you now, I'm coming back and . . ."

He's coming back.

That thought was enough to give her heart palpitations. She'd never been with anyone but Duncan before. What would it be like to be with Mark? Duncan had been passionate, but never very loving. He could be harsh to brutal at times and at others, tender and loving. There was never any way of knowing with Duncan. Her heart beat faster. She tried to control her breathing. Would it hurt? Her insides had been so damaged when she'd lost her child, and the after-math pain came so frequently, she wondered if allowing him inside her would cause the pain to return—even worse. God, was this a stupid idea? Well, whatever it was, she wasn't about to back out.

She dried off and put on a pale lavender nightgown that fell to the ground but left little to the imagination.

Mark came back in ten minutes wearing pajama bottoms and a T-shirt. He wasn't smiling. That wasn't good. She thought he'd at least wear a happy face. Not a good sign at all.

Annie didn't wait for him to come to her, she went to him. She lifted one hand to explore his face, to run her fingers across his stubble of a beard, but he caught it and brushed his lips against her fingers, one by one. The caress was light, the impact devastating. Their eyes locked before he patted her hand and let go.

Mark looked away. What the hell had she done now? The man was starting to cool. Unfortunately, *her* body was on fire.

Annie tried to release her fingers, but Mark wouldn't let go. "Mark? What is it?"

Mark shook his head. Trying to make a decision? Was he going to *back out?* Mark Driscoll, king of Nager's eligible studs?

Annie held her breath, taking only shallow pants as needed.

He turned back to her and pulled her close to him, brushing his lips against her cheek. Loving, gentle, and damn it—platonic. Just like that, the passion was gone.

"What?"

He let her go and sighed. Sad and resigned. A sign that the evening had just ended before it had really begun.

"I want you, Annie," he said. "Badly. Probably more than I've ever wanted any woman."

"But?" Annie ventured into the realm of disappointment.

"But I can't do this," he answered. "I know I come on as some would-be Casanova, but there are boundaries. I'm about to cross mine right now. You're under my protection Annie. It wouldn't be right."

"Oh!" She bit back the bitter tears of disillusion. "I'm your job."

He looked back at her, staring. For a minute, she thought she noticed him waver, but then he shook his head. "No. You're more than that. Much more. God knows I want to. Maybe under different circumstances. Another time, another—"

Damn him. She lashed out at him. "Mark. Stop. You don't want me, so don't pretend. I can take no. But, damn it, don't romance me, whisk me up to my bedroom in your arms, then push me away. It's not only hard on my body, but it's brutal on my heart."

There, she'd said it. And she felt the rest of it following. She couldn't hold back. "You really are a heart breaker, you know that?"

Mark grabbed her hand. She jerked it loose.

"You've made your point. I'm a job. You either don't want to get involved—or you don't want me."

"Annie!"

"Mark, please just get out of my room. I don't think I can handle seeing you right now."

Annie grabbed the robe from the corner chair and put it on, covering every inch she could.

She thought she caught the corners of Mark's lips turning up for a brief second, but then his face went as expressionless as before.

"No, it's not that way at all," he said, his hands up in protest. "Look, I was caught in . . . I mean you were so beautiful in the . . . I mean."

Her cell phone rang. She grabbed it off the nightstand. Mark turned to go.

"It was many and many a year ago, In a kingdom by the sea,

That a maiden there lived whom you may know By the name of Annabelle Lee."

Annie's heart raced, pounded with the sound of Duncan's voice. "Duncan."

Mark had just reached the threshold. He stopped and turned.

"My beautiful Annabelle Lee," the voice whispered. "You know I don't hold this against you. It was the baby who took you away from me. And now, roué's, cads would devour you if you let them."

Her body temperature cooled until she had goose bumps up and down her arms. Her insides shook. *The baby took you away from me.*

Mark was by her side, listening on half the earpiece.

"And I'm glad you weren't killed while you were out on the boat. But that detective, my dear Annabelle. He must go. This is your very last chance. You may return to me and we can pretend this never happened. I'll take you back to New York and we'll go back as we were before."

"Duncan, I'll never come back. Why don't you go back? It's over."

"I miss you." His voice rose higher in pitch, became almost whiny. "I miss you. I told you before. I intend to get you back, and I don't care whether it will be dead or alive.

"You know, you're so beautiful standing in your bedroom wearing that negligee. Pale lavender, my favorite color on you Annabelle. I can picture your breasts bare, ready for my touch. Instead, you let that detective in your bedroom, looking at you, touching you. I can see you together in your bedroom right now. Annabelle, don't become a whore for him." He hung up.

Annie cried out and without thinking raced to the balcony.

Marked grabbed her before she could reach the threshold.

"No, Annie. No!" He almost threw her away from the opening. He peered out. Then he closed the sliding door and pulled the curtains.

When he turned back, Annie was still shaking. "Where was he?" she whispered. "Where was he?"

Mark took her in his arms. "Anywhere. On the lake, across the lake looking through binoculars, even on the path. Who knows?"

She lay against him, allowing his lips to caress her hair.

"Don't go anywhere alone, Annie. You understand? Nowhere." He let her go and started to walk to the door.

"Mark," Annie whispered. "Don't leave me. Stay here—with me tonight."

He turned and stared.

"Please."

He nodded. "Okay, but we're sleeping in my room."

Chapter 45

nnie followed Mark next door to his bedroom. When she reached for the light switch Mark pulled her back.

"No lights," Mark said. "It's better he doesn't think you've moved from your room. I'll leave the door open a crack. Just get into bed."

Annie obliged. The bed was high and piled with pillows and comforters. So, the Spartan detective who worked the streets, slept in his car or didn't sleep at all half the time, the man with the rumpled hair, really did like the finer things in life. Well, good for him. She hadn't taken him for a comfort type of guy.

She wasn't sure she could handle a night next to Mark without badly needed physical relief. Her body still hadn't recovered from the smoldering expression in his eyes when he'd seen her standing on the dock, wet and exposed. When he'd kissed her, or when his lips had touched her neck, or his fingertips had grazed her breast.

But the hot tension he'd created, he'd splashed away with ice cold reality. She was a job, and he'd be jeopardizing her trust if he were to make love to her. He was making that abundantly clear.

What a crock. The man had gotten to her. Up until a few days ago, she hadn't even liked him. Suddenly, she'd discovered what all of Mark's other women knew. The man was hot. Sexy, *smoldering* hot. And he'd played her. Come close, but not too close. Look but don't touch. Love me, but don't expect love in return. Except his other women at least had the privilege of having sex with him. She hadn't even had that. Damn him.

So how would a night of no-touching play out? And could she handle this?

She sat on the edge of the bed. Mark pulled out a gun from his jacket pocket and put it on the bedside table. Then he took out his cell phone and punched numbers. "Simone," he said, slightly pulling back his curtain. "We just got a call from Duncan. He's somewhere where he can see into Annie's room."

"Okay, good. But watch yourself." He clicked off.

"Simone's calling one of the summer volunteers to come watch with her. He's bringing along his guard dog."

"That makes me feel better, but what about Lady acting as a guard dog? She seems very protective."

"Lady would bark her head off, but she isn't trained. She'd get in the middle of things and get hurt. Too soft to be a really good protection animal. I'd rather her stay closer to you. Speaking of which, where is Lady?"

"She was downstairs earlier, curled up in the corner. She didn't come out with us."

"I'll be back in a minute. I want to find her and bring her up here." Mark waited as Annie slipped under the covers then was gone again.

Annie tried to shut her eyes and rid herself of Duncan's sing-song whisper. His painting of her lying face down among the lily pads haunted her. The only thing worse she could think of was being entombed with that psychotic psychiatrist.

When Mark came back, Lady padded behind him. She jumped on the bed as Mark closed the door. Lady licked Annie's face while darkness engulfed the room.

"Lady, where have you been, girl?"

Lady woofed and whined a bit, then settled down at the foot of the bed.

"Simone locked her out on the porch. She wasn't sure she should be inside but didn't want her getting hurt wandering outside."

"She usually sleeps with you?"

"When I'm here, yes. Otherwise, she sleeps downstairs."

"Ah." In his mom's room.

Mark plopped his body onto the bed and swung himself under the covers.

She turned toward his movement, as he banged into something hard—something like a skull.

"Oh damn—shit that hurts." Mark put his hand over his forehead.

Annie scooted back onto her knees, her own forehead aching. Leave it to her—trying to be romantic and knocking her love interest in the head. "I'm sorry."

Lady suddenly stood up, shook herself and pounced between the two of them.

"*You—lie down. There.*"

Anne could hardly make out Mark's movements, but the dog obeyed and went back to her position.

He chuckled as he groaned. "No. It's all right. I'm so used to diving into the middle of the bed, I didn't think. Look I'll stay over on my end." He was whispering. There really wasn't any need. There wasn't anyone else in the house.

They talked. Really talked for the first time. About old movies, books, his mother, her parents and life on Long Island. His job, her job. They avoided past relationships and the immediate horrors. At times they brushed up against each other and both pulled away. But after a while, they pulled back less and less, and they continued to talk a hair's breadth away. And then, Annie's voice started to fade out in the middle of sentences, and Mark started to yawn. Both turned and barely mumbled, "Good night."

The steady ticking of the wall clock, the rustling of the trees from outside and Mark's soft breathing lulled Annie into a deep sleep. And for a while, she knew nothing but the lake, fireworks, Mark's hands messaging her shoulders, moving down and covering her breasts, his thumb circling her nipples, causing them to harden. Like he was hardening against her stomach. Then, his lips covered hers, hot breath spreading its warmth down her body until it spread to her belly and became an ache that reached down between her legs. He was pulling her nightgown over her head, standing back, stroking her with his gaze in the moonlight. She couldn't move, only will him to lay her down, run his fingers and his tongue over every inch of her skin, until he buried his fingers inside her.

Then she was lying on a pine bed, a moonbeam streaking his hair. And he was honoring her silent plea. Kissing her nipples, stroking her inner thigh. Splaying his hand until she parted her legs and—a black shadow covered them.

Annie woke with a start.

Mark mumbled, "What's wrong?"

She was shivering. From an erotic dream turned nightmare? She was wet between her legs, and her breasts ached. But she wouldn't give him the satisfaction of confiding in him. "Nothing," she whispered back. "Just a bad dream."

He pulled her close. His lips rested on her cheek, his chest warming her, the even rhythm of his heart lulling her back to sleep again.

This time she lived in a house with Mark, and she carried his child. They were happy, planning for the baby. She had to get something from the basement. Then just as she reached the top of the stairs, the shadow again. A hand touched her back—and pushed. Her hand caught the railing, but the thrust was too strong, and she tumbled down the stairs. She lay on the concrete, unable to move. Blood. So much blood. She heard a baby cry. It came from somewhere close. She tried to move toward the sound but couldn't. And then knew why. The sound was coming from inside of her.

Then she was awake and screaming. "Annie?" Mark turned on the bedside light.

Annie's panic attack struck hard. She couldn't breathe. She leaned over the bed, trying to catch her breath, and the pain in her abdomen came again and doubled her over. Then Mark was picking her up, holding her against his chest.

"Annie. What?"

"Nightmare . . ." Her teeth chattered.

"Come on lay down. Tell me about it."

It took a few minutes, but when Annie gathered her wits to speak again, it was about the happiness of an eight-month pregnancy. Duncan backing away from her, becoming distant—remote. Then one day, when she was at the top of the stairs, a hand on her back. The push. The blood on the floor. Then she was crying. And she couldn't stop.

Mark held on and she sobbed. All the pent-up emotions, the horrors, the fears all culminated at that moment.

"Annie, it was just a dream. You're all right. I'm here. No one can hurt you." He massaged her temples as he crooned, calming, soothing, relaxing.

She turned so their foreheads were almost touching. She whispered, "But it was a reenactment of a real event. A murder that happened. A murder he'll never be charged for, and I can't get it out of my mind. The police still think it was an accident. But it wasn't. I hate him for this. Duncan murdered my little girl." Oh damn. It hurt. The sequence of events, the pain in her stomach. Memories. "And he didn't even care if the fall killed me, too."

She covered her face with her hands and lowered it to her chest. Hiding it out—hiding him out.

"It's not enough he's destroying everything that is me, now he wants to wipe out my existence. I'm so frightened."

"Annie, when I get my hands on that bastard, he's going to wish he was never born."

Annie moved over and knelt beside him. She kissed his cheek. Warm. Gentle. "Mark, I need you."

"Honey, you've got me."

"No, I don't mean that. I mean . . ." How do you ask a man to make love to you? She'd never done it before. Never had to. Now If he rejected her . . . Well, so-be-it. "Mark, make love to me, please."

"Are you sure? I don't want to take advantage of you when you're so vulnerable."

"Please take advantage of me," she replied. "I need to be loved tonight. To feel the warmth of another human being inside me. To be kissed like the world was coming to an end and to be caressed like I was the only woman left on earth. Mark, I want to be loved by you."

He lost his breath. Not once in his long years of dealing with women had anyone put her desires in such a warm and tender way.

Chapter 46

Duncan was playing a complicated role in Nager. That of tourist, Edgar Allenton, a successful software executive from California. He was keeping two residences: the Campbell Inn for convivial companionship and his RV at Two-Lakes Campground for outdoor living.

Hiding out on the patio, watching the early morning water, he waited for Laura Campbell to meet him for breakfast. The waiter brought him coffee and the morning local paper.

Front page headlines mentioned bombings in Baghdad. On the home front, guards on the Mexican border, guards had been murdered in the past couple of days. Authorities suspected a Columbian drug cartel. He flipped the page. There it was on page three: Local news read: *Does a serial killer stalk Nager?* How irresponsible. Now, every blonde in the county would panic.

He turned to the obituaries. A whole column was devoted to Molly McGuire's memorial service. Only a one-liner about Honey Wright, mother of a little girl. Poor Honey. He wondered if anyone would even bother to go to a prostitute's funeral. Maybe a drunken father or mother. Maybe a fat slob of a sister with four screaming kids. Life was so unfair, he thought. She was, as he'd so often written about, an invisible street person. Her poor child raised in brutality. She'd probably end up in the same profession.

He sighed as Laura Campbell made her way through the restaurant toward the patio. It was time to put on a sympathetic happy face.

This reception would be his ticket to his and Annabelle's destiny. *Life everlasting, amen.*

And Ms. Campbell would help him play out his charade until he could arrange a ruse, distract the others and capture Annabelle. And he'd do it at Molly McGuire's memorial service reception. Nobody would notice in a crowd. According to Duncan, that was a psychological fact.

Duncan rose as Laura approached. He kissed her cheek. They sat, and Laura leaned across the patio table.

"The arrangements for the reception are coming along, don't you? think?"

"I think, you're a very astute businesswoman." Her face clouded. "You don't think this seems self-servicing, do you? I'd hate people to think . . ."

Of course, it's self-serving. You're only worried about what the community thinks of you.

Duncan said, "There's nothing wrong with what you're doing." He patted her hand. "It's a wonderful gesture for Molly and the community. And I believe you're a very good woman."

He lied.

"No, I'm not," Laura said shaking her head. "Thank you for saying that, but I'm as self-centered as they come."

"We all look out for our own interests to a certain extent. And when we do something that hurts someone else, we embrace the hurt, grow from the experience, then we move on. Believe me, you would not be offering The Campbell Inn for Molly's reception if you were selfish."

Laura studied the table. "Would it be wrong of me to want to set this up for an ulterior motive?"

"You have an ulterior motive for doing something nice for people that are hurting? Well, maybe you do. But you would still be doing something nice for those people, wouldn't you?"

"Yes, I suppose so." "Can I help you with this ulterior motive?" Laura shook her head. "I don't think so. I don't know how you could. You see . . ." Laura told Duncan about her past relationship with Mark, how she'd dumped him for a millionaire from Virginia, and in turn, several years later her husband divorced her for another woman. She'd made a virtual fortune in the settlement, and when she'd come back, she'd taken over the Campbell Inn from her father. But, although the community still flocked to the inn for her father's sake, many shied away from her.

"Look, if I thought you'd stay here, I'd really go for you in a big way. But, honestly, I don't think you're interested in me that way."

Duncan Nodded somberly. You're right about that honey.

"And you'd be right. Because I'm still not over Mark. We belong together. I know that now. But . . . well, I was hoping that with this reception, I could get to talk to him. Really talk to him. I'd need someone to corner Annie O'Brien to succeed."

Laura continued pouring out her heart, or the part she wanted him to know about. And, unless he was very much mistaken, he'd fit somewhere into this.

And something else about Laura. Her *eyes*, he thought. No emotion there. Yes, something missing.

When the waitress brought his pancakes, he ate while Laura picked at grapefruit.

A good act Laura Campbell had going. He knew exactly what she was going to want him to do. And it would play into his plans perfectly.

Between bites, he said, "Laura, listen to me." She gave him her full attention.

"Do you really want Mark Driscoll?"

Laura nodded.

"Maybe, because you can't have him?"

She jerked her head backwards and looked at him? "Because I can't what? I can . . ."

He raised both hands, palms out. "No, no. You couldn't have him. Men have big egos. Leaving a man like Mark Driscoll at the altar leaves him vulnerable, exposed. Afraid to commit again. But maybe it's time to extend the olive branch. How close is your family to his?"

Laura rubbed her chin and frowned. "We used to be close. Not anymore. I can hardly blame them, I suppose."

Something came to his mind—maybe the good part of Duncan Byrne that still existed. "You know, they say you can never go back. You realize your relationship would never be the same."

Laura nodded slowly, and a tear trickled down her cheek. Fine, but it wasn't in keeping with the hardness around her mouth. Yes, he thought. She would get Mark Driscoll back then when somebody else came along, she'd dump him again. He'd known women like that. Many of them had been in his care. As sick as his obsession with Annabelle was, that was one thing she never played with. His softness changed in a split second. No, she'd just cheat on him on the side. Then bow out with a divorce. *Only, she didn't want him back. Focus Duncan. Focus. Another problem. Another relationship.*

Laura had been staring out across the water, toward the peninsula, Duncan bet.

She nodded. "I know that. Nothing ever stays the same."

"So, you don't just want him because he's with someone else now?"

"He's not with someone else," Laura said. She got up and Duncan thought she might walk away. "Please, sit. I didn't mean to get you upset. I just wanted to point out that seducing a man because you can't have him might not be the best reason in the world. Are we in agreement with that?"

"Yes."

"Good. Give Dr. Driscoll a call and remind them of the reception after the funeral."

"Okay, what else?"

"Laura, this is what we're going to do. I guarantee it will work if you hold up your end."

Duncan stood on the patio watching Laura leave.

So, the ball is in now rolling downhill and cannot be stopped. Payback will be hell, Ms. Annabelle.

Chapter 47

Annie and Mark emerged from the saddest funeral she'd ever experienced. First off, none of the bigger churches would take Honey Wright, a penniless girl who sinned for a living. Christ the Savior Evangelist Church semi-graciously gave in when the funeral director mentioned SEC was their last hope. Annie wasn't so sure the preacher was happy to be their last choice.

The affair had been somber as expected, but fuller than Annie anticipated, until she realized most of the congregation were on-the-job police force. *Poor Honey.*

Surprising, Laura Campbell sat alone in the back. After one glance toward them, Laura avoided eye contact and kept her focus on the preacher expounding Honey's good qualities, of which he knew almost none.

Laura waited on the bottom step of the old, wooden church with the peeling paint.

"Hi," she said. "I'm glad somebody came that I know. This was so awful. I didn't know if I could get through it."

Mark didn't say anything.

Annie replied, "Yes, it was so sad. Poor girl."

"Annie, Molly's funeral is tomorrow."

"Yes, I know."

"Annie, I'd like for you and Mark . . . and Julia to come to the reception we're holding over at the Campbell Inn. Would you come, please?"

Mark studied his hands.

Annie glanced at him out of the corner of her eye and realized he wasn't going to give any more to this conversation. "I would love to come, Laura. Thank you for inviting me. I'll speak to Julia. Mark . . ." She turned to him, putting him on the spot. "Mark will have to speak for himself."

He gave Annie a dirty look then suddenly became charming. "Of course, we'll come, Laura. I believe most of the hospital staff and police department will be there. Molly was very popular."

"Yes, she was," Laura replied. "Yes, she was." She turned toward the parking lot. "I'd better get back to Edgar. He's helping out at the inn."

"Edgar?" Mark asked.

Laura smiled and blinked a couple of times. "He's staying with us for a while. He's a salesman from California. A *nice* guy, for a change."

Laura turned and walked toward a black SUV. A vehicle that didn't look anything like her Mercedes.

"God, I'm glad we're back," Annie said. She crossed over the threshold into the living room and removed her black suit jacket, then spied the flashing red light of the answering machine.

"Message," she said, pointing.

"Yeah." Mark flopped on the sofa next to the telephone, ignoring the thing. Instead, he focused on Annie and took her hands, pulling her down next to him. "Annie. You're an amazing girl. You looked death in a face so much like yours. You didn't falter—not once."

Annie shivered.

"I'm sorry. I didn't mean . . ."

Years of pre-med came and went like the flash in a camera. "I've seen murder victims before. But I have to say seeing someone so young and pretty, die so horribly." She caught another vision, this one of strong hands closing around the dying girl's neck.

She curled up closer to him and leaned on his shoulder. "Poor kid. And, the make-up artists didn't hide much, did they?"

"Money talks, Annie, especially in the funeral business. They could have done a better job with her. But Honey Wright was only considered a hooker in Brighton."

"Mark!"

"No, I was going to say, she was only eighteen. A decent kid. She'd gotten hooked up with a slimy bastard who beat her. He got caught robbing a currency exchange where he killed one of the clerks and is serving life in the big house. Honey tried waitressing and wasn't any good at it."

"I don't know much about Brighton. It looks downtrodden with all those shacks along that dirt road. But from the bars we passed, I'd say most of the action takes place at night."

"Yeah. It can get pretty rough. Those girls take a chance every time they go off with someone."

Mark crooked his finger. "Come sit on my lap. I want to hold you."

Annie crawled into his lap. "I want to be held."

Mark started to reach for the answering machine, but Annie pulled his hand away and put her arms around his neck.

"I want you to concentrate on nothing except me." She kissed him behind his ear lobe.

"Hey," he whispered. "I'm not going to be able to control myself.

"Really? Is that a promise?" But her emotions vacillated between the sadness left over from the funeral, her desire for Mark and the opportunity to forget. She shivered. Mark covered her with his arms and erased the goose bumps.

"This is serious Annie. I don't want to scare you, but did you see the bruises on her neck?"

"Yes. I saw. Scary way of life, being a prostitute. That poor girl had no other skills, so she invited in men who could easily overpower her.

That's how so many girls get into this business. They have or feel like they have no other choice."

Mark nodded and pulled her down into him, holding her.

"It just was no way to end up." Annie sat up and looked at him. Her mouth dipped into a frown. If Duncan had his way, he'd choke the life out of *her*.

"Why didn't anyone hear her?"

"Hear her? Bloody hell, there wasn't anyone around to hear her." "This must have been someone she trusted. They'd had sex and before she knew what was happening, he strangled her." "They actually had sex?"

"Hell yes."

Mark leaned over and pushed the message button.

"First message," the robotic voice said. "Hi, Julia-Mark. It's Laura."

Annie scrambled up and sat on the edge of Mark's knee. "What the hell does she want now?" Mark said.

The machine continued. "I just wanted to remind you about tomorrow's reception after Molly's funeral. The weather is supposed to be atrocious, so dress accordingly. I'd really like you to come. I have some interesting people Annie might be interested in meeting." Pause. "Your friendship has meant a lot to my family over the years. So, let's not be enemies anymore, okay? I'll be looking for you. Oh, and I invited Paul too. He said he was coming."

"Paul didn't mention that to me." He blinked off the phone. No more messages. "Her whole attitude is strange."

"Mark, should we go?"

"Yeah, I think we should. Duncan might be staying at the inn."

Somehow Mark envisioned the man who'd been with Laura. The same man who Lady had disliked. The man drove a black SUV. And, he had a name. Edgar. Now he had to find out his last name. If this were Duncan, Annie should have recognized him by now, if she'd gotten close. Or . . .

Softly he said, "Annie, Duncan might not be the one. He could have hired a hit man."

She paled briefly, then shook her head. "I don't think so."

"Why not?"

"Because Mark, I think this Honey Wright was a dress rehearsal for me. A simple practice session. That's why. I doubt Duncan has ever killed anyone. A hit man probably wouldn't have missed in that boat. He wouldn't have aimed at you in the first place. No, I'm sure it's Duncan. He's sophisticated, well-spoken, and Honey probably thought she had a possible sugar daddy. She went with him and killing her was the easiest thing in the world. She never saw it coming." She let out a long sigh. "I think we should go. If he's in Nager, he'll be there. It will be close quarters. I'll see if I can spot him. And you and Paul will be around."

Annie lay back into Mark, their cheeks touching. She whispered, "I want this over this, Mark. I want to love you without worrying that someone might be watching, waiting—"

Mark smiled and said, "This might not be the time to tell you, but I'd really like to screw you right now."

"Your mother's coming home."

"Hell. I'm twenty-nine years old, and I'm worried about my mother catching me?" He chuckled. "So, what do you suggest?"

Annie popped up and pulled him up. "I've never had sex anywhere other than the bedroom. You live in the middle of the woods on the edge of the lake. Isn't there somewhere more creative we can go?"

"More creative? Outside?"

"I know . . . but . . ."

"Annie, there's poison ivy in the woods. Trust me. I know." Annie laughed. "Oh, you do, do you?"

"But. we *can* get creative on the floor of my bedroom. I'll show you positions you've never even dreamed existed."

Her mouth quirked with humor. "Ah, you so sure about that?"

"Oh? And how would you know?"

"My Kama Sutra is almost worn out."

Mark laughed. "It is huh?" Then he tickled her. Annie squirmed and tickled back.

Mark couldn't stand it anymore. He reached under her silk tank top, felt the fullness under the lace of her bra, reached back and unhooked it freeing her breasts. He lifted her tank to her neck and explored her with his hands, his mouth.

"Umm." Annie moaned. Her nipples had just flown to attention. A car crunched over gravel in the driveway.

"Oh shit," he said. "I feel like a bloody teenager." He picked her up, carried her up the stairs into his bedroom and kicked the door shut.

Chapter 48

Mark was on a mission. Last location of the day—The Campbell Inn. Paul and the deputies would have covered every motel, inn and campground in the Two-Lakes County area. If he didn't find some sign of Duncan soon—

He climbed up the porch steps and immediately knocked into a florist carrying a potted plant. The man obviously hadn't seen Mark, nor anything else, because when he stepped aside with a gruff "Excuse me," he banged his hip on a wicker porch chair.

Hmmm. Graceful.

Mark maneuvered around waiters carrying trays filled with stacks of china. Staff members hauled freshly cut flowers into the restaurant area. An overly animated Laura Campbell, surrounded by men in dark suits, pointed to a program and was engaged in a heated discussion.

As usual, Laura looked gorgeous. She always did. She wore a black dress that looked "designer" and a string of pearls Mark surmised had not come from K-Mart. And an expression that stated, *I'm the boss. Don't mess with me. What a mistake I nearly made all those years back.*

This morning he and Annie checked out the Two-Lakes County Campground management office. As they wound their way around the grounds, they found a red van parked in the trees between a camper and an RV. The manager told them the family came up from Illinois every year and were away on a week-long camping trip. However, a man next door who had an RV was looking after their campsite. Mark checked the list. The RV belonged to Edgar Allenton of California. He owned a black SUV, and he was parked next to a campsite with a red Ford Aerostar. Coincidence? Mark didn't believe in them.

Paul assigned Fred and Simone to drive to Brighton and follow up with Bernard Benny. By the time Mark dropped Annie off at his house, they still hadn't returned. He sure didn't want to take Annie on this one last call. Fortunately, his mother was home and as he left, they were downstairs shooting up the basement—again. *Damn.*

So here he was.

"Excuse me." Mark elbowed his way in front of one of Laura's associates. "Sorry to bother you, Laura, but this can't wait. I'll be over there." He motioned with his head toward the reception area.

Laura took a deep breath and adjusted her smile—from animated into bland, turning to a you're-bothering-me frown.

Mark turned and bumped into an artist's easel with a large photo of Molly McGuire. His sadness hit him almost as hard as the side of the easel. Blistering anger surged, and he almost forgot the dull ache in his side. He wished he could enforce the Golden Rule to a man like Duncan. Choke the living daylights out of him.

He lounged against the reception desk, one foot crossed over the other, arms folded.

As Laura approached, she flashed him a smile, her former *I'm too busy to be bothered*—gone. "Well, well, well," she said. "What brings you here? I thought you'd be home getting ready for the funeral."

"I came for the list of names Deputy Goodwin asked you for."

The pleasure she'd shown when she'd approached disappeared, replaced, once more, by annoyance. "I've got what you want, and I don't see why you have to be so formal. Everyone calls him Fred."

"I'm here on business, ma'am." Mark knew that would get her.

He wasn't disappointed.

Laura clucked her teeth.

A waiter came up to the desk. "Ms. Campbell, the man from the Nager Florist shop needs to find out where he should put the potted palms."

Laura's smile twisted into something not so pleasant. "Tell him this is an emergency, and I'll be there in a minute. Don't bother me again." Her voice held an edge that threatened to deal a sharp verbal blow. The waiter hurried away.

"Now," Laura said, pleasantly. "The list." She reached down under the counter and pulled out a log sheet filled with hand-written names and identifying information.

Mark scanned the names. No Duncan Byrne. No New York addresses, telephone numbers or license plate numbers.

Laura had done one thing he appreciated. She'd requested their professions, and they'd given her their business cards. He looked through them, smiled and nodded. "Good going. Thanks."

But not a psychiatrist in the house. So, what had he expected?

That the man was stupid enough to advertise his arrival?

He looked at the make and models of the vehicles. Hmm. Four black SUV's. That held some interest.

Bloody hell. Look at this. An SUV owner named Edgar Allenton registered at the inn was also registered at the Two-Lakes Campground. Possibly a coincidence. Although, vacationing in town and having a small campsite someplace else was not unheard of, it was the first lead of any kind he'd had.

"This Mr. Allenton."

Laura cocked her head. "What about him?" *That* received her interest.

"He's a salesman?"

"Yes. From California. Why?"

"Does he spend much time here? I mean at the inn?"

"I couldn't really say. Mark, you know I don't make my guests sign in and out."

Mark coughed. "Sarcasm doesn't become you Laura."

Laura played with her hair until black curls fell over her shoulder. "Maybe not, but why do you want to know so much about *him*?"

Damned flirt. Mark remained silent.

Laura shifted positions and looked uncomfortable. Patience was a virtue in police business.

"Okay. This is what I know about him," Laura replied. "He's in Nager mixing business with pleasure. He has friends here, and he's courting clients. Anything wrong with that?"

"Not particularly. Just looking at all strangers coming through here—not an easy thing when it's Fourth of July and we have hundreds, maybe a thousand extra faces. You know what I mean? We're trying to find a killer, Laura, and we have a small police force. We need citizen's help. You mingle with your guests. What do you know about him?"

"Not too much," Laura said. "He's from San Francisco. Travels all over the country—"

"What does he sell?"

"Software."

"What kind?"

Laura's eyes widened, her face went blank. "Uh . . . I'm not sure. Educational, I think. Why? Is that important?"

Mark shrugged. "Don't know. Maybe not. Do you know if he's driven a Ford Aerostar since he's been here?"

"No. As you can see." Laura pointed to the make of car. "He drives an SUV. In fact, I haven't seen one of those in years."

"No. Not many around. Do you know if he's staying anywhere else while he's here?"

"Anywhere else?" Laura shook her head. "I don't know. He said he has friends here."

"At the campground maybe?"

"Why do you want to know all this?" Laura asked. "Wait, wasn't a red mini-van seen at the bar where Honey was . . . uh, drinking that night?"

"Yes."

Laura leaned over the desk, so that one hand brushed against Mark's arm. "So, the only one who came forward was the old drunken fool, Bernard Benny."

"How did you know that?"

"Well," Laura whispered. "I just heard that he drank too much. Someone in Brighton found his body in the lake. Drowned."

Now it was Mark's turn to be surprised. "Drowned? Bernard Benny is dead?" *Oh crap. Erase one witness.*

Laura pulled back. "Look, I only heard it from a local town gossip. They said it was an accidental drowning. I believe they took him to the medical center."

Oh boy, wait until the chief hears about this.

Mark backtracked to why he'd come. "Look, I'd like to meet this Edgar Allenton."

"Please not today. Not until the funeral and reception are over."

"Laura. I want to talk to him *now.*"

"I . . . I don't know where he is *now.* He should be here this afternoon. I'll introduce you, and you can take it from there."

"Good." Mark turned to go. "See you later."

As he walked through the double doors and out into a drizzle, Mark pulled out his cell phone. "Paul," he said.

"Yo," Paul said. "What's up?"

"Did you know ol' Bernard Benny was found dead this morning?"

"Say what? I must be getting wax in my ears. I thought you said Bernard Benny was found dead."

"You heard right. Who responded to the call?" "Wait. Fred just walked in."

Mumbles from the other end of the cell phone. "Damn it!" Paul exploded.

"It's true I take it?" "It's true."

"You realize," Mark said. "Benny was the only one who could spot a red Aerostar in Brighton that night."

"Yep. Just as a matter of procedure, has anyone talked to the owner of the van?"

"They're supposed to be out on a week-long camping trip in the wilderness with their kids."

"Shit. Maybe they're not. Maybe they were out killing."

"Maybe this perpetrator just rented a mini-van.

Sure Paul. Are you *losing your mind?*"

"No. Maybe. Just figuring out some stuff."

"Paul, did Fred check to make sure there were no other witnesses?"

"Yeah, he did. Nobody saw nothing. Nobody ever sees nothin' in Brighton. Except ol' Benny."

"And the Brighton crowd will make sure they see even less now." He clicked off and walked down the steps and headed toward his car.

Damn, damn, damn.

Chapter 49

Duncan slid from behind the restaurant's double doors. Mark was walking out of the inn holding a cell phone to his ear.

Hope he trips.

Duncan had heard every word. Driscoll was getting too close for comfort, at least for this stage of his perfectly thought-out murder-suicide plans.

Fortunately, they wouldn't try talking to him until the reception. He'd avoid Mark, then rescue Annabelle from Mark's clutches before the arrogant son-of-a-bitch had the chance to confront him.

His mind skipped to the days ahead. This afternoon. The bumpy ride against across the lake. First choking then drowning Annabelle, letting her gently enter the next world, then allowing himself to slip into the deadly abyss holding her hand.

Bodies flown to New York City. A dual funeral at Trinity Church opposite the new One World Trade Center. He'd made the prior arrangements and paid dearly to assure there would be no mistakes. He'd be buried with his two women. His mother to the right of him, his Annabelle to the left.

"I'm sorry sir, the restaurant is closed for . . ."

Duncan whirled. He hadn't heard the waiter approach. How dare he interrupt his thoughts? How dare—

The waiter paled and backed off. "Sorry, sir. Just doing my job." The man scooted out of there before Duncan could respond.

I have to be careful. Keep a low profile until after tonight.
Nothing must be allowed to go wrong.

Duncan walked into the crowded lobby and nearly ran into someone rolling in a long pin-board with photos of every aspect of Molly's life, including wedding photos, baby pictures, graduation from police academy posters.

Sad, she had to die. Wrong place at the wrong time.

Would the police try to break into his RV? He'd locked it up tight. He doubted anyone would get in without a sand blaster and a search warrant. He doubted they'd get to it so quickly. No probable cause. Not yet.

But they'd get there soon.

His mind drifted back to the overheard conversation. So, he hadn't gotten to that stupid drunk fast enough. He should have drowned him before he'd had a chance to talk. But then, he mused, he was too busy killing someone else.

He thought it time to put Plan B into action. It might take that and more to get Driscoll away from Annabelle for the necessary length of time.

He quietly approached Laura at the reception desk. She was frowning. "Look at this. They misspelled . . ." She looked up and smiled. "Oh, Edgar. Sorry. This has been such a hectic day."

And it's going to get more hectic as the day goes on, Ms. Laura.

"Can we talk in your office? What I have to say to you is very private. But it's something you should know. I've put it off far too long."

Duncan sat across the desk from Laura and pulled out his trump card.

Edgar Allenton, Private Investigator, Radcliff Building 3400 West 45th street, New York City.

Laura frowned. "I don't like to be lied to Edgar. I don't like it at all. Your license says California. So, from which state are you?"

"I have licenses in five states. My firm sends me to California, Florida, Illinois, Wisconsin and New York. New York is our headquarters."

"I see. So, why are you *here?*"

"I'm looking for someone." "Really? Who?"

Duncan pulled out a photo of Annabelle. "You recognize her?"

"Dr. O'Brien? Of course. What do you want with her?" The volume of her voice escalated.

Duncan, now Edgar Allenton, leaned forward in his chair and leaned on Laura's desk. "Her family—her husband—"

Laura's eyes widened in astonishment. "Excuse me? Husband? Annie O'Brien is married?"

"Thought that might interest you."

Laura leaned, arms folded. "She's married?" she repeated.

"Yes. She's married. Her husband and her family hired my firm to bring her home. Otherwise, authorities will be forced to arrest her."

"Wait a minute. Arrest Dr. O'Brien? For what?"

"Look. Promise you'll help me?"

"I don't know. If she were wanted for anything, why wouldn't the hospital have a record of it? They check backgrounds."

"To be honest, the DA filed charges after she left New York. Her family asked the NYPD to give my firm time to persuade her to come back voluntarily."

"So, you're saying, Dr. Annie O'Brien is married and wanted in the state of New York?"

Duncan AKA Allenton nodded slowly. "That's what I'm saying."

"Do you mind me asking what she's wanted for?" "Will you help me?"

Laura nodded. "Okay."

Duncan leaned forward, conspiratorially. "Normally yes. But since you intend to cooperate with me, I'll tell you. About a year ago, Dr. O'Brien lost a child in a fall down the stairs. She was eight- months pregnant."

"No!"

"She told them, she'd tripped, and the medical reports stated accidental. It took a while for the baby's autopsy report to come in. When it did, her system was filled with anti-depressants."

Laura's face reddened. "The bitch. How could she?"

"Indeed." Duncan crossed his legs. "Then after some probing, the detective in charge found out that Dr. O'Brien had been making statements about the inconvenience of a child. There had been arguments. Her husband wanted her to quit her job and stay home with the baby. She'd stated emphatically she wouldn't. Her husband decided to let it rest until after the child was born. Apparently, Dr. O'Brien didn't."

"That's murder," Laura said.

Duncan AKA Allenton nodded. "Look, you want Mark Driscoll back, that's obvious. I'm giving you a chance to do that if you'll help. You'll have plenty of time to talk to Mark. But don't talk to him about this, understand? If I can't bring her back, I prefer to talk to the police chief myself. This may be painful for Mark." Laura nodded. "I understand."

Chapter 50

At two-thirty, when the funeral started, a gentle summer drizzle floated to the ground. By four, when it was over, the sky was dark steel, and the streetlights shown on mini lakes all over the pavement. You couldn't see two feet in front of you through the dense fog and blistery rain. Luckily for most folks, they'd parked across the street at the Campbell Inn and had only a short walk.

St. James Episcopal Church was one of Nager's gems, the oldest church in the community. All the major happenings—baptisms, confirmations, first communions, weddings and funerals of the Nager elite happened in one of three sites. St. James, the Lutheran Church down the block, the Roman Catholic Church around the corner and the Synagogue. The same people generally attended the main events in all three locations and all deceased were dispersed from Klaus' Funeral Home across from the hospital.

Annie took Mark's arm and walked down the freshly painted wooden steps. She was thinking contrasts. Molly—Honey. Unlike the cheap plain pine box, with a few almost-wilted flower arrangements and one uninterested pastor at Honey's funeral, Molly's family and friends had planned the biggest funeral Nager had seen since Mark's father died. The local flower shop had donated their services and probably half their stock, as did the minister, the Very Reverend Father Charles Grant. Father Grant had christened Molly, baptized Molly, gave her first communion then married her to her now distraught husband.

Molly McGuire was loved, and Nager would grieve. Honey Wright would soon be forgotten.

Annie's umbrella turned inside out from the wind. Mark shielded her with his coat, but it still didn't do much good. He was all for going home and skipping the reception.

"We have to go," Annie yelled while they avoided puddles trying to make their way across the street.

"Why?"

"Because you promised you'd go, and because you have to talk to Edgar Allenton. If you don't tonight, and Laura tells him of your interest, he may be gone tomorrow."

"Maybe I should have Simone take you home and stay with you, honey. You'd be safe there."

"If he sees I'm not here, he'll find his way to your house. No, Mark, I'll be safer in a crowd. Besides . . . I can identify him." Although she hadn't seen him once. Not to recognize.

"True."

They ran up the Campbell Inn porch steps and stepped into the already crowded lobby. Annie put her hand to her chest. "We made it," she said.

"You can say that again," Julia replied, coming up behind them. "I haven't seen a sky like that in years."

Family loyalty, love, warmth. Something she'd resigned herself she'd never have. Then Julia hugged Annie, and for an instance, Annie felt she belonged to them.

"Listen, the county issued flashflood warnings," Paul said, his ear attached to his cell phone.

"The highway down by the service road's vulnerable," Mark said.

"Should we leave?" Annie said. "Is the house okay?"

"The house is fine," Julia said. "We're on high enough ground that we don't have flooding problems. Not everyone along the lake is that fortunate."

As they moved into the restaurant, Annie peered out the picture windows and onto the lake. A stroke of lightning plummeted into the middle. "How far would you have be, in order to be electrocuted?" she asked.

"Don't know," Mark said, shaking his head. "Maybe about fifty feet? Why? We're not going out on the lake."

"Studies show about thirty feet, but I believe you could be killed up to fifty," Paul said.

Julia took her arm. "Not to worry. We have a lot of storms here. We haven't lost anyone to lightning in years, and everyone knows enough to stay out of flashflood areas." She walked Annie over to a wall of paintings, Mark following close behind. "I wanted you to see this. We have quite an artist's colony in Nager. Our lake is famous for its landscapes."

Seven oil paintings framed in gold gilded frames hung on the wall: Lake Nager, the waterfall connecting highland Beaver Lake with the lowland Lake Nager, Two-Lakes country forest, the Campbell Inn painted from the water, the lake at sunset, a summer's day with boaters and fisherman, and the *lily pond*.

The lily pond. A beautiful mixture of vivid oil colors of summertime. The water a bright translucent blue mixed with hues of sea green and brown mud. Centered with white and pink water lilies.

Annie's imagination ran wild. She saw a body with long golden hair, floating under the water surrounded by beautiful flowers.

Annie's breath seemed to leave her body. The blood drained right out of her face. She felt dizzy. Disoriented. She groped for Mark's arm for support.

Mark pulled her close, wrapped his arms around her upper chest and kissed her cheek. Warm, accepting, loving.

"Baby, what's wrong?"

"That painting."

Julia was staring intently at the painting. "Lovely, isn't it? That was done by a Lake Nager artist."

Annie caught her composure and bottled it—tight. "It's so real, you can almost pick up a rock. Smell the water lilies. Reach into the water." And a realization hit her right in the stomach. "That's our lily pond."

"Yes," Julia replied. "It is."

Julia caught the eye of a group standing across the room. "Listen, I *have* to mingle." She waved to the group. They motioned her over. "Annie why don't you come over with me? They're physicians at the hospital. I'd like you to meet them."

"Wait," Mark said. "Hang on." He got on his cell phone. "Fred, where the hell are you?" Pause. A strange look came over Mark's face. He rubbed behind his ear. "You've got a what? How the hell . . .? Get it fixed and get over here right away."

"What's wrong, sweetie?" Julia asked. "Fred's got a flat."

Annie looked around. "Mark, there's Simone."

"Good," Mark said. "We'll turn you into a detective yet." He dialed across the room.

"Simone, I want you to shadow Annie. Go where she goes. Even into the ladies' room. Don't lose sight of her. And if there's any sign of Duncan, call."

Paul said, "There go Thelma and Louise."

Mark howled. A group of people turned and stared.

Paul poked his arm. "This is a solemn occasion. You're not supposed to laugh."

"Oh yeah. Sorry."

Simone met Annie and Julia and joined the hospital staff. Mark breathed a sigh of relief.

He made a note of the people in the group. The mayor of Nager, who wore a politically somber expression, a couple of doctors and nurses Mark knew. They stood deep in the forest of other people, Mark didn't know. They could have been Campbell Inn patrons. But there was one who interested him. A man who wore a dark navy suit, had blond hair and wore glasses. The man on the boardwalk.

Chapter 51

They left Mark standing by the painting, watching Laura Campbell inching her way over to him. As he was trying to think up an excuse to move, a mental light bulb went off. *Bloody hell. I have to talk to her. She's got to point out Allenton.*

As she closed in on him, Molly's family caught up with Laura. Molly's mother took Laura's arm, and they turned and walked in the other direction.

"I don't mind telling you Mark, I'm nervous. Warnings up all over the place," Paul said. "Don't know how long I'll—we'll be able to stay."

"We? What about Annie and my mom?"

Paul shook his head. "Simone will stay with them. Simone's a sharpshooter, your mom knows kick boxing, right?" Paul grinned.

Mark nodded. "And Annie's a brown belt in karate. The two—no three of them are lethal weapons."

"Nager's own Thelma, Louise and Simone."

And Mark noted, Paul's gaze zoomed right in on his mother. "Look I gotta talk to Laura. I'll get you a beer while I'm over there."

"Sounds good to me," Paul said.

Mark signaled a hello to Annie and Simone then meandered toward the bar. The area was packed with Nager's elite. Laura's waiters and waitresses wore black slacks and white shirts and blouses. They passed out appetizers and took orders for drinks.

And the rain kept coming down, like somebody had turned on a faucet and forgot to turn it off.

"I've got something for you," Paul said, charging up, then grabbing a beer from Mark.

Mark raised his eyebrows. "That quick?"

"Uh huh. That drunk in Brighton had been thrown out of the bar the night he died. He'd been barfing at the back of the bar when the red van pulled up. He saw Honey with this guy."

"No kidding."

"We have another witness."

Mark was finally able to smile, even if it was only half a smile. "Who?"

"The bartender. The one who threw old Ben out. He talked to Fred this morning. Said he felt terrible."

"Okay, so he felt terrible. What did he see?"

"As I said, the red mini-van, and the driver who picked up Honey."

"What did the guy look like?"

"Said it was dark. But he thought he had blond hair and a mustache. But he recognized something about the car. It had stickers all over the place. Yellow ribbon, American flag, support our troops, and Wisconsin Dells."

"Sounds exactly like the same vehicle that's parked next door to Edgar Allenton's RV. But . . . according to the campground manager, Allenton has blond hair, and he wears glasses, but doesn't have a mustache. But . . . bloody hell. Mustaches are easy to put on and take off."

Mark drank his beer, his eyes surveying the room, never letting Annie out of his sight for more than a few seconds.

Paul continued. "Fred just told me the family got back from their camping trip this morning. He asked them to check their mileage. Sure enough, there were some thirty more miles on the car than there'd been and . . ."

"And?"

"And they'd given Edgar Allenton the keys when he offered to watch their campsite for them."

"Means and opportunity," Mark said. "Enough to get a search warrant."

"Yep."

"Did Fred check out Allenton?"

"No," Paul said. "The management there told him several of the campers went to Molly's funeral, and Allenton's SUV was gone."

"He's here." Involuntarily, Mark looked around. The man could literally be hiding in this crowd.

"Good."

"Mark!"

The two men faced Laura who approached and wore an acceptably subdued smile on her face.

"You've done a nice job, here Ms. Campbell," Paul said. "This is a nice gesture for the family and the community."

"Thanks."

"You're welcome. Now, I think I'll leave you two alone. I have some business to deal with."

"What business?" But Paul was gone, and Mark was alone with Laura. That familiar tug that had haunted him whenever he saw her—the same one that started near his belt and worked his way down—wasn't there. The warmth he'd always felt when he was around her had mysteriously disappeared.

Unlike this afternoon, there was no sharpness in her tone. She purred, "Hi Mark. It was a lovely funeral, wasn't it?"

"Yes. Nice turnout despite the weather."

Laura turned in the direction of Molly's family. "I'm glad they're holding together. Terrible tragedy."

Mark glanced over to Annie and contrasted them. Annie with her light blonde hair and blue eyes, her skin almost translucent, Laura with her black hair and skin almost olive from the time spent in the sun. Both beautiful women. Both exciting in bed. But one big difference. Annie was passionate and loving and needed to be loved in return. She gave. Laura was not passionate, not loving—didn't need to be loved. And Laura gave nothing.

Laura turned to gaze where Mark was looking. "So, I see you've hit it off with our Dr. O'Brien? Pretty girl."

Mark felt his jaws clench. He tried to smile through it. "She's lovely. Also, nice."

Laura's mouth tensed. "Yes, she seems nice enough. How well do you know her, Mark?"

He shrugged. "Well enough, I suppose, why?"

"Well then, I'm sure you know she's married."

He wanted—so badly, to be rid of this woman. "Annie's divorced, Laura. Not married."

"Mark, honey, I have it from good authority, she's still married."

"Good authority? Who?" He stared at this jezebel who was lowering her eyelashes and bringing them up again. Flirting. Mark took Laura by the arm, smiling, trying to be charming. "Come sit down with me. I'll buy you a drink. Then you can tell me all about how you know this."

They sat at a round table near the bar. But while the waiter took their order, she pushed her chair as close to him as she could, without being on top of him. She glanced in the direction of Annie. Mark wanted to knock off a smug expression of satisfaction.

Annie observed them. He'd have to explain. He also noticed the tall blond man who wore glasses and dressed in the dark suit, making his way into the lobby. As he did, Annie took her eyes off Mark and Laura, and her gaze followed him out of the lobby. Mark thought it time to quit stalling and get real information.

Laura tapped his arm for attention.

"Mark, now what is it you want to know?"

"So, Laura, Dr. O'Brien is divorced from someone named Duncan Byrne. What makes you think she's still married?"

"Because Mark. I happen to know there's a private investigator who's been hired to bring her back to New York. There's some issues with her mental stability and the fact she threw herself down the stairs when she was pregnant. She's wanted for the murder of her unborn child, Mark."

Mark took a stomach punch with that remark. He rubbed behind his ear and tilted his head side-ways. He patted Laura's hand with his fingers. "God, who's throwing this stuff out at you? I'd really like you to point out who wants to take Annie back to New York." He took those fingers and squeezed. Not too hard, but hard enough.

Laura jerked her hand away and nearly knocked over her drink. "Jeez, Mark. Let go. I'm only telling you this, so you don't get hurt." She gave him that look that said "again." *The bitch.*

"Darling," he said. "I'm not going to get hurt again. Ever. Now that we got that straight, I want a name. Who is this private investigator?" He could already guess.

"Uh . . . His name is Edgar Allenton. He's staying here at the Campbell Inn. He's a PI hired by her family to get her back."

"Annie doesn't have family, Laura."

Laura shook her head, pushed her hair back over her shoulder. "She doesn't? Are you *sure?*"

"Yes, I'm damned sure. Now, who the hell is he?"

"Well," Laura said. "He was just here. I think he went into the lobby."

"And?" "And what?"

Mark had about enough. He took Laura's hand. Smiled at the world and squeezed hard. "Now, not a peep or I'll break this little wrist of yours and damned the consequences. Got it?"

Laura paled. "Yes."

"Good. What did he look like?"

"Blond, a little taller than you and wore a dark suit. He just walked out. He'll be back, I'm sure of it."

"Laura, did you get Annie and me here so this PI could get to her?"

Laura's eyes darted away, then back and she held his gaze. "No, darling. I got you here, so I could get to *you!*"

Chapter 52

Annie was holding her own in a crowd of professionals deeply involved in a discussion about whether it was ethical for a doctor to give lethal injections in an execution. Cheerful topic, Annie thought. She had the corner of her eye held on Mark and Laura. They were almost joined at the hip. It hadn't taken Laura long to move in on him. Annie tried to hide the disbelief that Mark would dump her and go back to Laura, but that's exactly what seemed to be happening. She caught Julia's expression. Her eyes had turned to pin pricks. But Laura—Laura exchanged a polite yet mocking smile at her. Suggestive. I've-got-your-man type smile. And there-isn't-anything-you-can-do-about-it.

Oh yeah? If I were to squeeze that little pressure point just below your elbow a sharp squeeze, I'll bet it could wipe off that grin. Or better yet just sock you in the jaw.

But why should she agonize over it? Even Julia couldn't deter Annie's pre-ordained fate. She was destined to be alone. Mark wouldn't be part of a permanent, happily ever after. Not with her, anyway. It was just as well she'd find that out sooner than later. Laura was always what he'd wanted and now, it seemed, he could have her.

Simone tapped Annie on the shoulder. "Honey don't worry about Laura. It will never happen between them, believe me. She's a class A manipulator, but she'll never get that man. And even if she did, she wouldn't want him. The woman has Tiffany tastes."

Annie smiled at her newfound friend. She was right. What would play out between them would have to play out—but as far as Laura, Mark would never be able to suit Laura's tastes. In fact, it was too bad she hadn't gotten together with Duncan. Laura would have loved living in Sutton Place.

"Let's get out of here and powder our faces, shall we?" Simone said. "We can talk if you want. Or not, if you prefer. I'm packing in case we run into trouble."

Annie laughed knowing it was a strange reaction for a woman who could be losing the man of her dreams. But Simone had a way.

Mark was still sitting with Laura. He couldn't have been any closer. Julia was engrossed in conversation. Paul was on his cell phone in the corner of the room.

"Okay, the ladies' room it is."

"Hold on." Annie tapped Julia on the shoulder. "Simone and I are going to the ladies' room. We'll be right back."

Julia's eyes rested on Annie. She glanced back at Mark. "Hmmm." Then, she patted Annie on the arm. "Don't leave Simone, okay?"

"Right."

Annie and Simone were almost out the door when Molly's mother's voice came over the microphone. "And, I'd like us all to say a prayer for Molly and my unborn grandchild."

Several people came in from the lobby. Some held hands. The idea of Mark holding hands with Laura was too much to bear.

Not looking back, Annie followed Simone out the door.

Simone led Annie to the ladies' room, peeking around corners, like a CSI agent.

"So, what do you think I need to do? Put on gobs of mascara and eye shadow? Dark blood-red lipstick and wear see-through black tops with spangled jeans?" Annie took out the clip in her hair and brushed it out.

"You probably could pull it off, and it would be fun to watch. Laura would have a spasm."

Annie stopped playing with her lipstick and paid attention to Simone. "You don't seem to like Laura much."

"I—none of the girls in our class liked Laura much. She'd go after our boyfriends just 'cause she could. It wasn't until she started going with Mark, that we all felt safe.

But, trust me, even Mark isn't Laura's type. That millionaire in Virginia is what she wanted. He dumped her."

"Oh. Justice served."

"Yep. What goes around comes around."

"Mark cares for her though."

Simone shook her head. "No. Mark cares for you. He's interrogating *her*."

That brought her to attention. She hadn't thought about it in those terms. Now she felt guilty. Oh bother. "That's how he interrogates?"

"When he has to."

"You think Laura knows something about Duncan?"

"I . . ."

Simone didn't have a chance to answer. From the mirror, Annie saw one of the stalls open. Before she could spin and kick, Simone was down.

Annie's gut instinct was to hover over Simone, making sure she was all right. But her karate instructor had taught her differently. Subdue the perpetrator before attending to the victim.

By the time she remembered to put her strategy in place, a hand had covered her mouth—a hand with a cloth—a cloth with something sickly pungent. And Annie's lights went out.

Chapter 53

"**W**ell," Mark said, rising from the table. "I have a job to do. I'll see you later."

"Promise?" Laura asked.

Not if I can help it. "You've done an excellent job here, Laura, congratulations. But I do have to go."

He joined the hospital crowd. "Mark?" Julia turned away from her colleagues with a tilt of her head. "What's wrong?"

Mark acknowledged the medical director and others he'd known since he was a child. "Have you seen Annie?"

"Yes," Julia said. "She and Simone went out to the rest room.

They should be back soon. Did you need . . ."

But Mark had already made it for the double doors that led into the lobby. Annie and Simone weren't there. Ladies' room.

He stood outside and waited. No one came out.

He barged into a small group of hospital nurses who'd left the restaurant. They were mourning Molly and what a loss her death would be for Nager.

"Sorry, but did you see Dr. Annie O'Brien and Simone Glen come in here a few minutes ago?"

The group looked at each other and shook their heads. "No. Sorry."

"Wait," one of the women Mark knew by sight said. "I saw them go into the ladies' room."

"When did they come out?"

A tall African American man, who Mark remembered as Marvin said, "I saw her with a man."

"Simone must have left—because it was only the two of them."

"Where did they go?"

"Don't know."

"Thanks." He looked out toward the porch.

Marvin snapped his fingers and tapped Mark on the shoulder. "I remember. Dr. O'Brien was with this man. She looked like she'd had too much to drink because she was kind of staggering. They went outside onto the porch, I thought she needed to sober up. Your deputy wasn't with them."

Crap. Mark ran to the porch. Rain poured down and nobody was taking advantage of the situation.

One of the nurses opened the door and said, "Detective Driscoll. You have to come here—now." She was pointing toward the ladies' room. "I . . . She . . ."

"She's . . . who?"

"Lying on the floor."

Mark jerked around and ran after the woman into the ladies' room. Several women stood around the lying figure of Simone, who was trying to get up, but could only manage a groan.

Mark kneeled next to her. "Don't try to move. How bad is it?" "Hurts. Hit in the back of my head." She reached back and blood oozed over her hand. "Ohhh," she moaned. "That doesn't look too good."

"No," Mark said gently. "Simone, where's Annie?"

"Mark . . . she's gone." Simone tried to sit, but fell back into Mark's arms.

Julia raced in. "Oh my God! What the hell happened here?" Five people spoke, simultaneously.

"Okay. I'll get an ambulance and ride with Simone. Mark, I assume this means Annie's been kidnapped?"

"You assume right. I'm going to find her." As Mark left, Simone was holding onto the back of her head—blood trickling down her fingers.

"Jesus Christ. No!" Paul was standing in the lobby. "We put every precaution in place. How the hell did this happen?"

"The guy said he was a salesman from California. He's a guest I spoke to Laura a few minutes ago."

"What does Laura know about this?"

"Way too much. Someone needs to talk with her further to see if she instigated any of this. This is what she told me. Some private investigator is looking for Annie. Wants to bring her back to New York. Said there's a warrant for her arrest and the NYPD are looking for her."

"Bull shit. I just spoke with Rodriguez. He would have told me." "Either that's a hit man or it's Duncan in disguise. And Annie didn't recognize him. He looks nothing like his picture."

Paul was flipping up the phone. "What was the name of this guy. "Edgar Allen . . . holy shit."

"What?"

"Edgar Allenton taken from Edgar Allen Poe. What a warped sense of humor."

"So, you think it's Duncan Byrne?" Paul asked. "The guy looked nothing like him."

"Not only was the man a shrink, but he was also an actor."

A man, soaked to the skin, came through the lobby. "Stupid day for someone to be taking a boat across the lake."

Mark spun around. "What did you say?"

"Some jerk and his girlfriend are motoring across the lake."

Chapter 54

Lightning ripped across the sky. The worst place they could be in a thunderstorm—on a lake. But here she was. The rain was so heavy Annie couldn't see the shoreline. Just the mountains and valleys of waves that came straight at them. She huddled against the side of the boat, her hands tied behind her back. If she fell overboard, she'd flounder and drown.

The boat crashed head-on into the waves, and she bounced—hard—nearly catapulting over the side of the boat.

How the hell had she gotten into this position? She'd always known Duncan had stage training and did some off-Broadway productions while he attended college. But damn to be this proficient in the art of disguise was something she'd never known about him. He'd changed his appearance so completely, she hadn't recognized him. And she'd lived with him for years.

As soon as they'd gotten out onto the open water, the glasses came off and his demeanor changed. He wasn't the Duncan she'd once known, but he certainly wasn't a sales rep called Edgar Allenton.

"Duncan, slow down. You'll break the boat apart." She screamed over the racket of the rain.

Duncan shot her a malicious glance; she decided she'd better be quiet. For now. Meanwhile, she had to figure out how to get the ropes untied.

The boat ran into a wave that must have been at least three feet. And then she saw it. Duncan had thrown his hunting jacket over the seat next to her. The handle of a knife poked out of the jacket pocket. Thank you, Duncan, she thought.

Duncan's attention focused on the waves hammering at the bow, intensified by the wind and rain. Another bolt of lightning came from somewhere in the west. God help them if they got struck.

Annie leaned back and picked up the knife.

Duncan had gotten his prize, all tied up in one pretty, wet package. She'd soon learn what became of those who betrayed him.

Full force, he slammed into three-foot waves. He caught a glimpse of her banging her arm into the side of the boat.

Hell, maybe he wouldn't die alongside her. He could make his way up to Beaver Lake and his campsite and drive back home. He'd have to leave his nice, reliable SUV at the Campbell Inn, where they'd eventually discover, Edgar Allenton never existed. And all this time Duncan Byrne had been at a convention in New York City. Poor Dr. O'Brien. Murdered by person or persons unknown.

Mark hurried to the docks where the small fishing boats were crashing up and down against the piers. An old man with gray hair came running down the dock, his raingear flapping behind him.

"Hey, you can't take that out there, are you nuts? I won't have you people stealing my boat just because there's a storm and you don't think I can see you."

"Police." Mark flashed his badge at him. "I have to catch that boat." He pointed to where he thought Duncan's boat might be, but the rain was coming down so hard there was no way anyone could see anyhow.

"Okay, but I'm driving." The old man jumped into his boat, before Mark could say no way. The engine sputtered. "No problem, just a little water in the engine, s'all." He turned the key again. Another sputter. "Damn, frigging, stupid engine." The old man kicked it. This time when he turned the key, the engine started right up. "See? You just have to show 'em who's boss."

Oh great, a comedian. But he did need him. The guy was an expert at negotiating the waves, getting the most out of his little boat. "Okay, but when we get to our destination," Mark yelled, "don't play cop. You get the hell out. I'll have police cars waiting up the hill."

"Yeah, yeah." He sounded disappointed.

The rain let up a bit. The storm clouds moved eastward and although the thunder was still loud, the lighting seemed fainter and the distance between the cracks was getting farther apart. Maybe they wouldn't be electrocuted after all.

"One thing," the old man shouted above the screeching wind. "That fourteen-foot fishing boat the other guy stole?"

"Yeah?" Mark yelled back.

"It ain't got so much horsepower. We can overtake them in this baby."

"No shit."

Chapter 55

Duncan slowed the boat, easing into the pond at the end of the lake.

Annie had cut through the ropes and threw the knife overboard. There would be no knife in her ribs today, thank God. Somehow in all this, Duncan had not noticed what she'd been doing. Now he turned back to her—his upturned mouth more like a snarl than a grin.

"We're here," he said. "Home sweet home."

Maybe you are, sweetheart, Annie thought. *But this isn't my home. Not yet.*

They trolled into the middle of the pond and Duncan cut the motor. "Too bad the rain is slowing down. But you can't have everything, I suppose."

But just enough to push the bastard into the water and take off, Annie thought.

Duncan turned toward her, kneeling to grab his jacket. As he felt in the pocket where the knife had been, a grim black expression crossed his face.

He's realized the knife is gone. She didn't wait for him to digest the information. Annie sprung. With all her weight, she pushed Duncan. He slipped on the slick surface and catapulted over the side.

Annie heard him scream "Bitch," as she scooted to the front of the boat. She slipped and fell into the front seat.

Duncan had reached the side, grabbed her and pulled. She held on to the edge of the boat for dear life, but she was no match for him. The boat was so slick she had no traction. Somehow, he got hold of her arms and yanked. Annie went overboard. Her feet touched bottom. The water was over her head, but not by much. Frantically, she tried to swim her way up, but there were so many stems from the lily pads that it was hard to get a firm kick.

She was under and so was Duncan. His hands were going for her neck.

Annie held her breath and dodged away from him, coming up momentarily for air. He caught her and brought her down again, holding her under. Determined she would not die today, Annie grabbed his hands and kneed him in the ribs. He let go.

Annie was a strong swimmer from her high school days on Long Island beaches and school pools, and she'd kept it up. Duncan could swim, and he was fit, but he had no technique to speak of. Annie kicked off and headed for shore, Duncan right behind. But she out swam him and reached the shore first.

First thing she felt were rocks, jagged. She'd lost her sandals somewhere along the way and bare feet on rocks weren't exactly conducive to running fast. But, when she saw Duncan coming out of the pond, she ran like hell.

She ran up the service road, bare feet running in slow motion under the weight of the mud. She was no match for Duncan, and she knew it. She swung on a low slimy branch, slipped, jumped up again and caught it. She pulled herself up onto a hill, found a small path and ran. Duncan had continued along the service road. She was running parallel to him. He could climb up this hill in a matter of seconds.

"Annabelle, come down here. You're not a climber my dear and I am."

Annie hid in the underbrush, not daring to breathe.

"I'll find you."

He was about twenty feet directly below her. Another thirty feet up the slope was a naturally carved stone staircase. Slippery now, but if he did manage to climb up there, he would reach her trail and she'd be a dead woman.

The rain had almost stopped when she heard another crack of thunder. Oh no. Dear God, not again. The rain fell harder. The only good news in that was it would be more difficult for Duncan to reach her. The mud would cause him to lose traction.

"Annabelle."

Annie held her breath again.

"Ready or not here I come." The voice sounded like a kid playing hide-and-seek. Damn the guy was crazy.

"Oh Annabelle." Now sing-songy. "Anna . . . belle . . . Lee." The Lee was high pitched. "Come out, come out, wherever you are. You cannot hide from meee.

"Dearest Annabelle, you'll catch cold. Your mother wouldn't like that now would she?"

Her mother? Her mother had been dead for over ten years.

Duncan had never met her mother.

"She'll put you in a closet with other naughty little boys and girls. She'll make you stay there and not let you have any porridge."

Oh Duncan, did your mother do that to you? God, why didn't I know this about you?

Thunder rumbled.

"Fee fi fo fum, I smell the blood of a disloyal woman. But now she lives, next she'll be dead." Giggle. "My mother was a disloyal woman. She died. Now you are a disloyal woman. Now, you will die." Silence. "Oh, Anna . . . belle. I have a riddle for you. What's:

One for sorrow Two for joy Three for a girl Four for a boy Five for silver Six for gold Seven for a secret Never been told.

What's the secret Annabelle?"

Annie started to tremble. That was as close to a confession as she'd ever heard from him.

She could now see him calling from the service road. He looked in her direction, but looked back and forth, back and forth. He still wasn't sure of her exact location.

Then another sound. The low guttural sound of a boat. Then sirens from the top of the hill. They were coming after her. If they could find her. If she yelled, not only would they know her location, but so would Duncan. He might not have that knife, or even a gun, but he had the strength and agility of a trained athlete——a karate expert. He could walk up to her, snap her neck and keep going without missing a step.

Rustling behind her. Annie jumped. A hand over her mouth stopped her before she could cry out.

"Shh. It's only me. Stay here and don't move. I'm going down and get the bastard. Does he have a gun or knife on him?"

"I don't think so. He had a knife in his hunting jacket on the boat. I threw it overboard."

"Good girl."

"I don't know about a gun. I haven't seen one."

Mark started to turn away. Annie grabbed his arm. "Mark, Duncan is deadly in martial arts. His arms and legs are lethal. And he'll kill you as soon as look at you."

Mark grinned and stroked the rain from her cheeks. "Did I ever tell you about my black belt?"

Annie's eyes open wide, and she blinked. "No, somehow you left that part out."

"I need the practice. This should be fun."

With a peck on her check, he scrambled out the underbrush, ripping his jeans. "Damn." He was gone.

Thunder rumbled in the distance, but Annie didn't see the lightning. It must have moved farther off to the east. The rain started to slow. She concentrated on the two figures on the service road.

Mark jumped out onto the service road downhill from Duncan. He was by the tree she'd grabbed to climb up to her path.

Duncan jerked around. "Oh yeah, country boy. You'll have to shoot me to take me. I'm unarmed."

Mark's face showed no emotion. "So be it, Mr. Byrne."

"Dr. Byrne."

"Dr. Byrne. We can do this the easy way or the hard way. You surrender and I won't hurt you. You don't and I'll probably shoot you. I'm pretty accurate, so I might kill you."

Duncan stood, knees bent slightly, legs apart. "So, come get me country boy. Come get me. I can't do anything to you. And you're not going to be able to charge me with anything because I haven't done anything you can prove."

Mark moved toward him. "Don't be too sure of that. I can charge you with the murder in Brighton, kidnapping and attempted murder of Dr. O'Brien, the attempted murder of me, breaking and entering and vandalism. And that's only the good stuff. There's the little issue of an eight-month-old unborn baby who was never born because of you."

Duncan huffed his chest. "Oh, did the good Dr. O'Brien tell you that? You want to know the facts? Your girlfriend wasn't crazy with the idea of being tied down with a kid. The woman became imbalanced. She threw herself down those stairs."

Mark tensed. "I don't think it happened quite that way, Dr. Byrne. Nor does the NYPD. We've had quite a little chat about you and your so-called prestigious position in the New York academic community. They think you're a loose cannon. Do you know that? If you do happen to get out of these charges, which I doubt, you'll never be able to practice again." God that felt good.

Duncan's face grew black, his eyes narrowed in rage, but he didn't waiver. "You know you want to shoot me, so why don't you, country boy?" Duncan signaled him with his fingers to come on. A bully on the playground. Mark took a step forward.

Duncan held.

With his free hand, Mark pulled out the cuffs from his back belt. Duncan laughed. "You'll never get those on me. You have to get close enough."

"I intend to do just that Dr. Byrne."

Another siren wailed on top of the hill.

"Duncan you can't get away. I have police officers up on the highway. Let's just make this easy okay?" Mark walked toward him.

"Dr. Byrne, I'm arresting you for . . ."

He didn't get it out. Duncan's foot caught Mark in the arm, and the gun flew out of Mark's hand. Duncan caught Mark in the stomach.

Mark didn't think too long about how stupid he'd just been. He got himself into karate position and kicked back. When Duncan kicked out at his head, Mark ducked and tripped him.

More thunder. This time the rumbling was steady and getting closer. That's not thunder, Mark thought. As Duncan pulled himself to his feet and got ready for another attack, Mark grabbed the tree limb and pulled himself up the hill. He reached down to grab Duncan's hand. "Give me your hand."

"I'll not give you my hand, my lad. You will not take me today." "Duncan, flashflood coming down the hill. Come on!"

"Another one of your ruses, Mr. Detective? I'll not fall for that. I say again, you will not take me alive." "Duncan!"

Too late. A rush of water, mud and debris with the force of a load of cement surged down the service road taking everything in its path. Including Duncan. Within seconds he was gone.

Chapter 56

“Hi Mark.” Laura Campbell stood behind the register and broke into an open friendly, if not slightly flirtatious smile. “How can I help you? Hmm. Let me count the ways. Your place or mine?”

“This isn’t a social call.”

Her upturned mouth fell into neutral. “Oh? Then?”

“I need you to give me a statement as to your connection to Dr. Duncan Byrne.”

The neutral fell into grim.

“No, I’ve already told your officer. I did not know the man that well. I will not give the police a statement, Mark. I won’t sign anything.” She turned and booted up her computer.

Mark stared until her fingers slipped on the keys.

Laura turned back. “Let me see if I understand this. Edgar Allenton . . . was really Duncan Byrne, Dr. O’Brien’s ex-husband. He got swept away in the flash flood? Good riddance to bad garbage. You seem to know everything. Why do you need me?”

Mark leaned on the register counter of The Campbell Inn. His mouth turned up in a thin-lipped grin, his gaze didn’t leave Laura Campbell’s face. “Because darlin’, you knew all that before even I did.”

Laura fidgeted with some pens on the counter. “Not all of it. His identification as Edgar Allenton was good. He said he was a computer software salesman, and he was here to mix business with pleasure. That happens all the time. But then he changed his story. Said he was a private investigator working for Dr. O'Brien's parents in New York. Said she was mentally unstable, a danger to herself ever since she threw herself down the stairs and killed her baby. That's what he said."

Laura stopped and held his gaze, then continued. "He said he was hired to bring her home. I had no reason to doubt him."

"Didn't it ever occur to you to call Paul or me and let us know about this?" Mark controlled the bridled anger in his tone, considering he wanted to choke the woman.

Her eyes caught and held his. "No, Mark. You weren't talking to me. I'm sorry." She shifted her eyes. He held his and narrowed his eyebrows.

"Darlin'," he said. "That's too bad, because now I may have to arrest you."

"For what?" Her tone shrilled.

"Oh, being an accessory to kidnapping, attempted murder and assault on a police officer for starters."

She huffed and stamped her foot. "Oh no you don't. You're not pinning what Duncan did on me."

"Oh, but I can, Laura. You lured her . . . us over here so Dr. Byrne could get close enough to grab her. She very nearly got killed. And Simone is still in the hospital with a concussion."

Laura picked up the phone and pressed a button. "Daddy! Mark's down here and he wants to arrest me for . . ." She put her hand over the receiver. "What was the charge again?"

"All I want from you is a statement as to exactly what went on, okay? Nothing left out that makes you look bad. You might have to talk to the DA."

"Oh God."

Laura was no longer flirting when Mark left the Campbell Inn.

Mark stopped by at the police station. Paul was yelling and sounding as intimidating as Mark had ever heard him. "What the hell do you mean, you can't find the body? That's your job. Keep looking until you do. Dredge the damned lake. I don't care if it takes until doomsday." He slammed down the phone.

"It's been a week," Paul said. "They still haven't found the body.

How's Annie holding up?"

"Better. She looks more relaxed than I've ever seen her. She's going back to work on Monday."

"Good," Paul said. "So, when are you going to ask her to marry you?"

Mark felt the heat coming into his face. Claustrophobic almost. "Marriage, huh?" He went and sat at his desk, picking up files and putting them back down again. "What makes you think Annie wants to get married?"

He ignored Paul's raised eyebrow. "She needs to be her own person for a while. She wants to be alone."

"Oh, did she tell you that?"

"Well, no. I just figured after that relationship with that psychopath, Annie wouldn't want any commitments for a while."

"Ah," Paul said gently. "In other words, you don't want to get married."

Mark shrugged. "If the right . . ." He stopped. Paul's stare almost knocked him over.

"If you say, 'if the right girl comes along', I'm coming over there and personally deck you. When are you going to realize the right girl has come along?"

"Yeah," Mark said. "But detectives have no place in the domestic world. You know that. And Annie doesn't want to get married."

"Like hell she doesn't." Paul muttered, but Mark heard him anyway.

Two weeks later Annie was back at work, happier than she'd ever been. The strain of the past weeks started to subside. Only one thing bothered her. The still hadn't located Duncan's body.

She'd also found out Duncan had left his entire estate to her. It boggled her mind. His estate included his home in Sutton Place and an enormous amount invested in stocks, bonds and mutual funds. She had no idea he'd been so rich.

Another piece of good news, although she wasn't planning on taking them up on it, NYU had called her and offered her a position--a dream job of instructor and psychoanalyst. She'd said, she'd think about it.

She stood on the porch steps and looked out over the lake. She loved it here. She didn't want to go back and live in New York City again.

But there was still one issue she needed to resolve. Annie found Mark working on his boat.

He slid from under a cabin seat, wrench in hand, rubbed his hands and jumped onto the dock. "Annie," he said, a big smile crossing his face.

"Hey," she said. "Can we talk?"

His grin turned neutral. "Sure, honey. What's up?"

Annie took off her shoes, sat on the dock and dangled her feet in the water.

Mark sat next to her, not looking at her, but he'd tensed considerably.

"Mark," she said slowly, trying not to show her nervousness. "Where are we going?"

"Uh . . . What do you mean?"

She hadn't turned to look at him, but she felt his gaze land on her. "I mean our relationship. We have such a great friendship and . . . sex." She added.

"Yes, we do. What are you asking, Annie? If we have a future?"

She turned and gazed in his eyes. His expression looked troubled. He was blinking. Now frowning. Not a good sign for what she needed to know.

"Yes, I guess I do mean that. We can't stay at Julia's forever." She sighed and looked across the lake. "Although I wish we could."

Mark lay his hand on her arm. "I'd been thinking about going back to my apartment." He swallowed then went on. "You need a place. Why don't you come li . . . stay with me?" He looked away for a minute as though thinking. Then he said, "Until you find a place of your own. I'll help you look."

Annie caught the slip. He was going to ask her to live with him then changed his mind. Only stay with him, until she got a place of her own. They would not be moving forward. They would move backward. In time they would cease altogether.

"That will be quite an adjustment."

"Not necessarily. We can continue going on as we are. We'd be closer to work. Then, you can be free to live your own life. We can still be friends."

"Friends." That dreaded word to any relationship. Suddenly, she could no longer bear to look at him. The sting in her eyes forced her to look away. She wanted to cry. She should have known better.

He'd protected her. It had been his job. And he'd gone above and beyond the call of duty.

She braced herself on the dock and rose to her feet. "I see." Mark raised his hand, but Annie continued. "No, it's all right. I know your feelings about commitment—love that sort of thing. Look, I just want you to know, I got an offer from NYU a little while ago. I'm going to think seriously about taking it." She bent over to kiss him on the cheek.

He bolted up. "Just like that? You're going to quit your job here and go back to New York?"

She stared at him before replying. "Possibly. My decision rested on you. And, well, now maybe I will." She forced herself to breathe steadily—not to let him see the turmoil, the hurt that raged inside. "I want you to know, Mark, I'll never forget you." She looked down, avoiding his glare. "We've come a long way from our first meeting at the health center. You did your job of protecting me admirably. I enjoyed every minute." She laughed, just a little.

Mark didn't respond.

She turned. "I'm going back up to the house now." As she walked up the porch steps, she turned and saw him standing on the dock looking at her, running his fingers through his hair.

And that was it. She was sitting in the living room curled up on the sofa when he came in. Without a word he went upstairs and came back down, a duffle bag slung over his shoulder. She raised her head to gaze at him. He wore a tight-lipped grimace.

"If my mother wants to know where I am, tell her I've gone back to my apartment. If anyone wants me, I'll be at The Hole tonight. See you Annie. Have fun in New York."

And he walked out of her life. Just like that, they were no longer a couple.

Chapter 57

Mark slammed the porch door and hurried down the stairs. When he reached the driver's side of his car, he stopped and leaned against it. Damn, Annie was leaving him.

A bitter laugh forced its way up from deep within. What goes around comes around. How many women had he dated and then dumped when they'd become inconvenient? Well, suddenly, he'd become inconvenient.

Something gnawed inside his stomach. He wanted to grab it and force it to go away. The woman he'd been living with for the past month—living with? *No*, he decided. The woman with whom he'd been playing house. It had been temporary. He knew it. It had been something that had been hanging over both of them.

Annie needed her independence. She couldn't be confined in a relationship. He'd hoped maybe if she came to stay with him, she wouldn't want to leave—ever. She'd realize that not all men were like that murderous jerk she'd been married to. But she'd wanted her independence so badly, she'd decided to move back to New York. Back home.

He took a deep breath of the hot, muggy air, opened the car door and got in. The inside was as hot as his mood. He started the engine.

A new chapter. He was back in full swing. Watch out ladies. The old Mark Driscoll was back.

He picked up his cell phone as he peeled out of the driveway. Laura Campbell. She was no longer suspected as being an accomplice. She'd been duped like everyone else. Maybe he'd call her. Get together for a drink. Make him forget about the woman who was tearing his soul apart.

Annie closed her book. Mark had only offered to let her stay with him until she got a place to live. What then? No plans of long-term commitments—marriage. Was it because she couldn't have children, or because he was so afraid of committing to anyone? She hadn't planned on breaking up with him. That had been the farthest thing from her mind. Suddenly, Annie didn't feel so well. Once again, she was losing a key figure in her life—a person she loved.

Destiny—alone.

Suddenly, she felt lunch starting to lurch in her stomach and she raced for the bathroom. Annie felt sick, body and soul. Her head was hot and throbbing. Suddenly, everything in her stomach needed to get out of there. The bathroom seemed miles away.

Everything came up. All the anguish, the hurt, the tension and stress--everything. She couldn't stop. In between lurches, she sobbed. When she finally calmed down, she had to throw up again.

A shadow covered the floor next to her and she looked up. Julia was resting her arm against the door frame. Annie hadn't heard her come in.

"Does Mark know?" she asked.

Annie stared, not grasping what she was asking. Her throat burned. "Know what?" She had to whisper. It hurt to talk.

"That you're pregnant, of course," Julia said.

Annie's eyes grew wide. "I can't be."

Julia smiled and shrugged. "Why not? Because some doctor in New York said so?" She grabbed a washcloth, poured cold water over it and handed it to Annie.

When Annie had finished wiping off her face, she turned the faucet back on and cupped her hands for a sip of cold water.

Julia put her arm around Annie's shoulders and helped her to the living room. "Look Annie. I recognize the signs. I'm an obstetrician, remember? Maybe you've got the flu or something, but I doubt it. Take a pregnancy test."

Annie brooded while Julia went shopping for a pregnancy test kit. She didn't want to leave these people. Her friends—more like her family. She couldn't imagine not spending the night with Mark again. What if she was pregnant? What would be the repercussion on her body, and what the hell would Mark say? She shuddered to think of an expression of rejection. That would be unbearable. And she couldn't stay here. To see him going back to Laura Campbell or anyone else while she was raising his child. He wouldn't do that to her, would he? But she didn't want him to marry her out of obligation. That would be the worst thing in the world.

Julia came back.

The stick turned pink. Annie was pregnant.

Julia looked at the stick—a huge shit-eating grin growing wide across her face. "I'm going to be a grandmother. I never thought I'd live to see the day."

Annie was sitting at the table.

"I think tomorrow, we'd still better go in and have you checked out."

"So, you'll be my doctor then?" Annie asked. "Maybe you'll find all the reasons why they thought I couldn't get pregnant in the first place."

Julia sat and took her hand. "If you want. And, yes, I'll give you a thorough going over. I'm even going to call your doctor in New York and get some information. I'll need his—"

"Her," Annie said. She gave Julia the information.

Annie drove to town, thinking how she was going to break the news to Mark. He didn't want the responsibility of a child. Julia did. She relished playing the role of grandmother. But one grandmother and one mother seemed a little incomplete without the father.

Chapter 58

The Hole was crowded with the five o'clock regulars. Annie spotted Mark at a booth at the far end of the bar.

As she'd threaded through the groups of patrons and tables, she could only see a portion of him. He wasn't looking in her direction.

"Mark." The voice was low, throaty, sexy and familiar. Annie stopped—dead. Somebody stepped on her heel and excused themselves. But she barely recognized the intrusion.

"Mark, why don't we start all over again? I never should have left you in the first place."

"I'll say," Mark replied.

Annie remained frozen to the spot.

The voice belonging to Laura Campbell purred. "Well, it didn't turn out so badly did it? After all, it made me realize where my priorities lie. Right here. And it made you appreciate me all the more. Right?"

No answer.

"In any case, I have more money than I know what to do with. We can have a house full of kids running around—I know you want kids."

Mark wanted kids. He'd never mentioned that. "Look, Laura, let's slow down here."

"Okay," her voice purred low. Seductive. The woman was a master, Annie thought. She could never compete with that.

"Why don't we go over to your place for a nightcap?" Laura suggested.

"Excuse me miss," someone said, as he bumped into Annie pushing her against Mark and Laura's table. And there Annie stood. By his booth. Mark holding hands with Laura Campbell.

"Oh!" Stunned, an inexplicable wave of panic crept over her. The instincts of a mother. A family she didn't even have yet was in jeopardy.

The startled and guilty look that crept across Mark's face said it all. His head jerked around, and he pulled his hands away. The same way he'd done when he'd pulled his hands away from hers the night Laura had walked by their table. So long ago—

It didn't matter who'd broken up with whom and that he had every right to see anybody he wanted. Heat rose to her face in embarrassment.

"Hi, Laura," she said. "I'm so sorry. I didn't mean to intrude. I, well, I'll see you later, Mark."

Mark grabbed Annie by the hand. "Hi Annie." He slurred the hi, so it took twice as long to formulate the word. "Thought you might like to stay for a drink." He grinned. If she hadn't been so hurt, she'd have thought it was funny. Mark was sloshed.

Annie backed away a step.

Laura said, "No, don't go. I heard you're going back to New York. I'm sorry it didn't work out for you here. But glad you've gotten yourself such a prestigious position at NYU."

Annie looked at Mark. He was looking down at his drink. "Well, it seems word has gotten out, hasn't it?"

Mark gave Annie a grudging nod. "Yes, it has. So, let's drink to great jobs and relationships." He waved to the bartender. "A farewell drink. Annie, what are you having?"

Annie jerked out of his grasp and backed up another step. "I can't Mark. Thank you. I'm sorry to—I didn't know you had a date." She looked for a clear track to the exit.

"No Annie. Come sit by me," Laura said, moving and patting the empty side of the bench. She took Annie's arm and pulled her down into the seat.

Laura's attention focused back on Mark. "We're celebrating more than just your job, aren't we sweetie?" She lowered her eyelids one time and the corner of her mouth turned upward. "You know, Mark and I were engaged several years back."

Oh God. Annie's stomach started to churn. Burning bile rose up in her throat. *Please don't have committed to marry this woman Mark. Please.*

"Well, Mark and I." Laura reached over and grabbed Mark's hands.

Mark pulled his hands away but wouldn't look at either one. "Mark and I are getting back together again. We were just discussing living together." Laura made her comment and sat back in her seat, her gaze moving up and down Annie's face.

She wants a reaction from me, Annie thought. Well, she's not going to get one.

The waiter brought Annie a mug of beer. Stunned she looked at the beer and then at Mark. "I can't drink at the moment," Annie said, hoping the hint might shake him awake.

"Oh? Can't drink and fly?" he asked.

Crap. *No, can't drink and be pregnant, she thought.*

Something she would dearly love to say but wouldn't in front of Laura.

Annie rose. "I'll talk to you at another time." She turned to Laura. "Congratulations, Laura. I hope the two of you . . ." *Don't break Annie.* "Will be very happy." What could she have said, "*Hello Laura. Congratulations. We have something in common? You'll be living with the father of my child?*" She nearly tripped getting up, and heard the faint sound of "Annie," over the roar of conversation.

Hot and muggy hit her as she left the bar. She put her hands on her knees and wanted to throw up again. But this time from so much more. From all the losses in her life. Her parents, her aunt, her child, her husband and now the only man she'd ever really loved. Too much loss. She'd believed in the family unit—the support of loved ones. She'd believed in God. Why was He turning on her once again?

She punched open her car door with the resounding click, and with a heavy heart and her happiness level down to a new low, she drove home to pack her things and make a plane reservation to New York.

Chapter 59

The house was quiet with only the TV blaring.

"On the top of the hour, in national news, the gang who shot the border guards on the Mexican-United States border has been rounded up. Only one member is still at large. Adriano Menendez was last seen . . ." Annie turned off the TV.

"Julia?"

Nothing. Maybe Julia wasn't home? Her car was there. Maybe Paul had taken her somewhere? That sent a warm fuzzy through her. Julia and Paul. She'd like to see them together.

She looked up the stairs. She didn't have many clothes to pack. Shouldn't take long. But her gun was still in the basement. She and Julia had been target practicing again, just for the fun of it.

She opened the basement door and heard a whine. Like from a dog. "Lady?"

Those little prickles she got when danger was near, seemed to poke at her again. Stupid. Ridiculous. Duncan was gone. He couldn't have survived the flashflood. Caution had taught her not to go blasting her way into unknown situations, so Annie tiptoed down the basement stairs. Her gun was laying on the pool table along with the clips. She loaded the thing and put it in her blazer pocket.

Whine again. This time from behind her. Annie jerked the gun from her pocket.

The basement had been divided into two rooms. One for fun—or target practice, if you considered that fun, the other for laundry and utilities. Annie crept up to the door and sprung.

Lady wore a muzzle and was confined to a chain tied to a basement post. She saw Annie, shot up and started to paw, circle, whine.

"Shh," Annie whispered. She placed the gun into the deep pockets of the blazer and released the muzzle and the chain. "Shh. What's being going on here, girl? Where's Julia?"

Lady bounded for the stairs. Annie caught her just in time, grabbed her by the collar and quietly walked her up the stairs.

"Where is she?"

"She's in here." The harsh masculine voice caught Annie off guard, and she let go of Lady's collar. She wheeled around and almost hyperventilated from the surprise of an intruder standing there. But the muzzle of the semi-automatic gave her the greater shock.

"Holy hell—who are you? You shocked the hell out of me."

The man grinned with his mouth as his eyes remained pointed.

"As you can see, I'm not exactly a friend." The gun pointed down at Lady who was barking at him. "Leash this dog, please, and I won't shoot her."

Annie blinked several times then realized what she was supposed to do. "Lady. Here."

The dog looked at her and barked again. "No. Come here. Now!"

The man threw her a leash draped over the kitchen door. "Leash her."

"Yes, okay. Now what do you want me to do with her? Bring her back down to the basement?"

"Oh no. Tie her up there in the corner." He indicated the piano leg.

Annie kept an eye on him. "Come on Lady. Over here."

She wrapped the leash around the piano leg as loose as she thought she could get away with. Then came back.

"Okay, now." He threw the wireless phone at her. "Call Mark Driscoll."

"Mark? You want me to call Mark?"

"I don't think I can make it any clearer than that." The man cocked the gun at her. "Unless of course, you want me to get Julia to do it. Of course, that would mean you'd be dead."

"Holy . . . Yes. What do you want me to say?"

"That a girl. Cooperation is good. Very good. You tell him to get home, por favor."

"Supposing he doesn't want to come home?"

"You make it . . ." He raised an eyebrow and looked her up and down, "enticing for him, yes? A beautiful girl like you should have no problems."

"But . . ."

"Do it."

"Yes, sir."

Annie dialed Mark's cell phone. What would she say to him?

Hi Mark, I'm pregnant. Come home?

She looked at the phone. "Wait a minute. Who are you, anyway?"

"My name is not important. Let's just say I have a score to settle. And I never forget my scores."

Annie stared hard at him. "And if I knew who you were, you'd have to kill me."

The man remained deadpan. "Point taken."

Annie dialed Mark's number.

"'Lo."

"Mark."

"Annie. You in New York yet?"

Oh bother. This was not the time for him to be playing around. "No. I'm at your mother's. Um . . . we need you to come home right away."

"Oh, you do, do you? Just like that? I'm not taking you to the airport if that's . . ."

"No. Please just listen and don't talk, okay? Your mother needs you to take her to her karate lesson."

"Her what? My mother doesn't take karate and if she did, she has a car that can transport her."

Annie coughed. This wasn't going well. The man was staring steel nails at her. Damn. "Mark, her car wouldn't start."

Silence.

"Besides, I'm pregnant, and I need to talk to you. Please come home."

"Uh—what did you say?"

"I said, I'm pregnant."

"Annie, you . . ."

"Oh, for God's sake, come home now." She clicked off.

Now what was the problem?

Annie pregnant. Hah. If she really could get pregnant, she might have wanted to stay and marry him. Maybe that had been the whole damned problem.

"What is it Mark?" Laura took both hands in hers and rubbed his knuckle with her thumb.

"I have to go home."

"Home? I thought we were going back to your apartment." Now she looked miffed.

"Laura," Mark said. "We weren't going back to my apartment. That was never in my plans. I just wanted to have a drink. That's all."

"But I thought."

"You thought you could get any man you wanted, even if you'd stepped all over him and broken his heart. You need some help. I can't give it to you, Honey. Stop the games. It's not becoming. You're getting too old for them. I have to go. There's another woman in my life who I happen to love. Bye."

"Damn you Mark."

He could hear her swearing at him all the way out to the parking lot.

Chapter 60

Paul was driving into the lot as Mark pulled out. He signaled, and Paul stopped.

"Just got a weird phone call," Mark said. "Annie. Her tone was higher pitched than normal, and she said I had to come home to take Julia to her karate lesson."

"Julia doesn't take karate."

"Right. And, Annie said, besides, she was pregnant."

Paul grinned. "Really? She said that. I doubt she'd say it . . ."

"No," Mark said. "They wanted me to come home. Something's up, and Annie couldn't tell me."

"I got a heads up that Adriano Menendez escaped the patrols and he's headed this way. The Milwaukee police reported a security guard at the airport saw him—didn't recognize him until he saw his photo on CNN. You know that Menendez is—"

"Manny Menendez' brother. Yes. The boy came from a powerful drug family. Look, I'm going home. You want to follow me?"

"Yeah. I'll call for back up. We'll get this guy if he's here." Mark sighed. He hoped that this was something simple—like Annie being pregnant. But if Menendez had forced her to make this call, there'd be trouble. He would probably be holding them until he got there, where he'd exact revenge for his brother, on Mark's family. It would be up to them to capture Menendez and save Annie and his mother.

The little prickles had started poking out on his arm. He had a bad feeling about this.

He'd much rather find out he was going to be a father.

"You're Adriano Menendez, aren't you?" Annie asked, quietly. "Your picture has been plastered all over the news reports. You killed those border guards."

Menendez' expression was one of a stony mask. No emotion.

A warning cloud finally settled on his features. "I suggest, if you want to live, you keep very quiet. You already know too much."

Annie said, "I don't think it would make a difference whether I knew who you were or not."

He gave her a cold-eyed smile. "You're probably right."

"You aren't going to let us live, are you?"

"Probably not."

"Even if you knew I was carrying a child?"

"Ah." Menendez' voice got softer. "I am all for the family. I am a family man myself. My brother, who was as loved as a brother could be, was recently killed. I'm here for justice for the family."

"Oh. That boy that was killed . . ."

"Yes."

Annie didn't have a clue where she could go with this. An obstinate, cold-blood killer. A cartel member. And he was here for "an-eye-for-an-eye". But he was here because he loved his brother. Maybe . . . just maybe.

"Did you know your brother shot at one of our loved ones? Our police chief? Detective Driscoll had to shoot back, or our friend would have died," Annie said. "Our friend's wife died in a vengeance killing. Don't you think there's too much killing?"

Menendez shrugged.

"It's a life that never will be lived, never to be loved or to love. The children that will never be born and grow up to change the world somehow."

"Signora."

"You didn't kill Lady. You could have. It would have been easier than taking her to the basement. That shows you have compassion."

"For the animals, yes. I have much love for them."

"Signor Menendez, you haven't killed Julia, have you? She's my best friend."

He shook his head. "Not yet. She is safe." And he shut his mouth and refused to say more. And he avoided looking at her.

Not yet. What did that mean?

Being pregnant was a pain in many ways. The nausea came at the most inopportune times. Like now.

"May I use the bathroom?" she asked.

"Huh?" Menendez' eyes narrowed. "You stay—"

"Have you ever been pregnant?" Annie asked, her voice rising in alarm. "Um, do you have . . ." She started to lurch forward and ran. Damn the consequences.

"Keep that door—" Menendez yelled as Annie slammed the door and wretched.

This was the first time she'd ever been glad to throw up. It also gave her a chance to think. She had a gun in her pocket.

But he was more experienced. She started to hyperventilate again and now her side ached. Oh Lord was there no end to this?

Maybe if she got some air. Window. Open. Screen—easy to open.

Annie flushed again and ran the water. She undid the screen screws, stepped onto the bathtub and sprang to the window. She managed to crawl out with inches to spare, and she was on the ground. Annie crept around the house to Julia's window. Julia was tied to her bed.

She tried to open Julia's bedroom window. Damn, window locked. No! She tried again. The darn thing wouldn't budge. Finally, she found a stick and wedged it under the frame. Stuck with paint. But this time she was able to open it. She crawled in and raced to Julia. She pulled her gag off her mouth. "Julia, are you all right?"

"Thank God you're here. Be careful. The man is a maniac." She wiggled her hands, but the ropes cut into her wrist. "Hurts," she whispered. "Can you untie these ropes?"

"Julia, did he hurt you?"

Julia shook her head. "No. But I think he has something planned for all three of us."

"I'm sure he does. Hang on."

Annie checked the ropes. Tight, but not impossible. She drilled her pointer finger into the middle of the knot whole and it gave way. Annie untied Julia in a matter of seconds.

But there wasn't any time to rub wrists or make plans. "Shit." Footsteps running across the living room. Lady barked.

"Shut up," Menéndez growled. Lady whined. A door opened that Annie assumed must be the bathroom.

"My God, he's going to find out I'm not there," Annie said. She heard an "oomph" and someone jumping from the bathroom window.

"Quickly," Julia said. "Quickly. He's coming around the back. Let's get out the front."

Annie untied Lady as they rushed out of the living room and onto the porch where they bumped straight into—Menendez.

"Going somewhere, ladies?" He turned to Annie. "That was a really stupid thing to do. We will go back inside now and wait for this Detective Driscoll."

Oh bother. Annie had to throw up again. "I—"

"No more of that, Signora. I will not bite a second time."

But Annie couldn't hold it down and she barfed on Menendez' shoe.

"Crap!" The man jumped back, just as Lady decided to get involved. She jumped on him. Annie got out her pistol, and Julia kicked the gun from his hand.

"Damn!" he screamed, holding his wounded hand and trying to shake Lady off his leg. "Let go, you damned dog. I should have killed you when I had the chance."

"Probably should have," Annie said, pointing the gun at him. "But, lucky for her, you didn't."

Then, Menendez' mouth dropped open. "A pistol. You know how to work one of those, eh?"

"Oh yeah," Annie said. She motioned toward Julia with her head. "She taught me."

"Us girls stick together," Julia said, a triumphant look on her face. "Now, shall we tie him up?" She ran to the porch and came out with a pair of handcuffs. "Mark leaves his things all over the place."

Menendez said, "Ladies, I'm going to give you one last chance. You're not getting those things on me and frankly, I can overpower you."

Oh, you think so, do you? Annie was ready.

But when Menendez slid for his gun, Julia was the one that kicked it out of reach. Way out of reach. Like onto the porch roof.

"Signor Menendez," Annie said, holding onto her gun tighter. "As we said, you are no match for three fighting-mad females. Por favor, put your hands behind your back, or I'll shoot you in the head."

He did.

Annie cuffed him. "Police. Freeze."

Annie was never sure whether it was her great work, or that Mark stood by the side of the house and pointed his gun directly between Menendez' eyes. Paul stood behind him and Simone came around the other side of the house. Simone grinned at the sight of Annie, Julia and Lady—triumph written over their faces. She shrugged and put away her gun. "I'm always too late for the good stuff."

"Looks like you win this round," Menendez said.

Mark grinned. "Looks like it. Lucky, we came along. I wouldn't want these ladies mad at me. Nope."

The last Annie saw of Adriano Menendez, he was surrounded by the Lake Nager Police Department on his way to a squad car. Mark stayed behind, looking at the females in his immediate and extended family and scratching his head.

When he finally was able to get her alone, he asked, "This pregnancy thing. Did you just use that to get me here?"

An amused glint hit Annie's eyes.

"Or" Mark continued. "Am I really going to be a father?"

Chapter 61

Annie dangled her legs in the water. She wore white shorts and a blue tank top and was waiting for Mark to take her out on the boat.

He was already late, but it was giving her a chance to think about everything that had happened in such a short period.

Duncan was dead. His body finally drifted up from under the flashflood debris. He'd been flown back to New York to be buried next to his mother. God knows why he'd wanted his mother on one side of him and Annie on the other. Thinking about it gave her goose bumps. Well, part of his wish came true. She'd heard some of the faculty had attended his funeral. She hadn't.

Mark had been in interrogation meetings with Adriano Menendez. Then other meetings with the DA. Mark tried to call her several times—wanted to talk, but somehow, their schedules got messed up. But she'd gotten the reaction she wanted.

She took a deep breath and took in the August air.

And there he was, strutting down the porch steps. Handsome as the devil. He wore khaki's and a maroon polo shirt. Lady followed him and jumped into the boat.

"Hi," Annie said. She was almost tongue tied. She didn't know why. Nervous maybe?

His eyes never left her face. He lifted her chin and kissed her. He tasted like good wine. Always a good sign.

Mark jumped in the boat and gave Annie a hand. "Come," he said, as he escorted her to her captain's chair. "We're taking a quick trip to town."

"Oh, we are?"

"Yes. You promise you won't throw up?"

"If I do, there's plenty of water to . . ."

Mark grinned. "I got the picture."

He motored out onto the lake then let the boat idle.

"I thought we were going to town?" Annie looked at him questioningly.

"We are. But I needed to stop here first." He reached into his pocket and pulled out a small box.

Annie's heart went into overdrive.

"Annie, when you said you were pregnant, I couldn't believe that it might be true. I thought it was a ruse to get me to the house."

"It was."

"I know, but I couldn't believe the love I had in my heart when you told me it was true."

Annie felt the blood rushing to her head. "Um . . ."

"I wanted to make sure you and I were—well, that you weren't planning on moving back to New York."

"I want to stay," Annie said. "I love it here."

"There's one other thing I want you to love." "Oh? What could that be?"

"Uh . . . me?"

"Mark, I love you with all my heart. But do you want a commitment with me? I mean a real marriage?"

Mark smiled at her and opened the box. Inside was the most beautiful diamond she'd ever seen. "Oh, my God, Mark. That's—"

"The setting was from my grandmother's engagement ring. I really hope you like it Annie."

"I love it Mark." Annie bent over and kissed him. "And I love you."

Mark had a shit-eating grin across his face. "Well, I guess it's time to party. Paul and my mother are throwing us a picnic on the Green. My mother and Simone are dying to see what the jewelers did with the ring."

Lady scrambled up and sat directly between them before her head slid down onto Annie's lap.

About Patricia A. Guthrie

"Every experience is potential fodder for a novel.," says Patricia A. Guthrie. Guthrie is an accomplished musician: opera singer, church soloist, and music teacher. After leaving the opera, she became a music therapist in a school for special needs children and taught music in the Chicago Public School system. She is the author of romantic suspense novels, mysteries, and short stories. Her novels include *Legacy of Danger, In the Arms of the Enemy, Eerie Charms of the Short Story,* and *Waterlilies Over My Grave.*

Her short stories appear in online literary magazines L'Affaire du Coaeur and Skyline Magazine. Her non-fiction article appear in Collie Cassette and Nature Journal. A member of Fresh Ink Group, you can find her at FreshInkGroup.com and on her own website, PaGuthrie.wordpress.com.

Patricia kindly asks that, if you enjoyed these stories, please leave a review on Amazon, GoodReads, Barnes and Noble, or any of the other retailers. Reviews are what keep authors alive.

Fresh Ink Group

Independent Multi-media Publisher

Fresh Ink Group / Push Pull Press
Voice of Indie / GeezWriter

Hardcovers
Softcovers
All Ebook Formats
Audiobooks
Podcasts
Worldwide Distribution

Indie Author Services
Book Development, Editing, Proofing
Graphic/Cover Design
Video/Trailer Production
Website Creation
Social Media Marketing
Writing Contests
Writers' Blogs

Authors
Editors
Artists
Experts
Professionals

FreshInkGroup.com
info@FreshInkGroup.com
Twitter: @FreshInkGroup
Facebook.com/FreshInkGroup
LinkedIn: Fresh Ink Group

Elena Dkany inherits her family's castle in Romania, a land dipped in myths, folklore, and the legendary walking dead. The local proverb serves as warning: "Do not speak badly of the Devil, because you cannot know to whom you will belong." When she's attacked by an international assassin, only her deceased husband and her ex-boyfriend's live presence can protect her on her journey to the mountainous region of Transylvania.

But that's not the only problem troubling Elena. Who is that boy invading her dreams? And what really happened to a priceless gem-crusted silver cross buried by an earthquake in the fifteenth century? Who's stalking Elena? Who wants her dead and why?

Hardcover, Softcover, Ebooks

Fresh Ink Group
FreshInkGroup.com

Lucifer loses his day job, so he starts his own gig. A little girl's tantrum destroys her toys, but will they lash out in revenge? Can a miserable housewife find a new life for herself in a tear-stained old painting? Stories include a snake deciding the fate of the world, a slot machine choosing life's winners and losers, a malevolent fairy dancing men to their deaths, a couple desperate to escape a train station, the dog-show judge facing death, and more. Patricia A. Guthrie offers a cauldron of eerie delights that will please, delight, and yet terrify you!